THE RIVIERA HOUSE SWAP

GILLIAN HARVEY

Boldwood

First published in Great Britain in 2024 by Boldwood Books Ltd.

Cover Design by Alice Moore Design

Cover Photography: Shutterstock

A CIP catalogue record for this book is available from the British Library.

Paperback ISBN 978-1-80549-958-9

Large Print ISBN 978-1-80549-959-6

Hardback ISBN 978-1-80549-957-2

Ebook ISBN 978-1-80549-961-9

Kindle ISBN 978-1-80549-960-2

Audio CD ISBN 978-1-80549-952-7

MP3 CD ISBN 978-1-80549-953-4

Digital audio download ISBN 978-1-80549-954-1

Boldwood Books Ltd
23 Bowerdean Street
London SW6 3TN
www.boldwoodbooks.com

For Clare.

Two roads diverged in a yellow wood,
And sorry I could not travel both
And be one traveler

— ROBERT FROST

1

Nina poured herself another cup of coffee from the expensive percolator and sighed as the rich aroma of her new favourite blend hit her nostrils. She reached for her fresh, oven-warmed croissant and took an enormous bite, feeling the pastry yield softly between her teeth; tasting its buttery deliciousness on her tongue.

See? It was all about making the best of things. And when life deals you lemons, you make, well, maybe not lemonade, but you buy yourself the best of everything, treat yourself to some seriously decadent breakfast fodder and practice some good old-fashioned self-care.

So, what if it was her fortieth birthday? Lots of people still achieved tons in their forties, and these days it wasn't even considered particularly old. She wasn't going to let herself crumble under the pressure of a simple date on the calendar and wasn't going to beat herself up about the fact that she'd pretty much achieved nothing on her bucket list during her four decades on the planet. She was going to celebrate that she was here, that she was worth it; she was going to make the most of her day and see this as the start of something wonderful.

They say life begins at forty, don't they? Well, bring it on, she thought, taking a sip from her cup and letting out an audible 'mmm.'

Rory had been a freeze-dried granules man, baulking at the price of freshy ground, so buying herself a coffee pot and an overpriced selection of beans from a specialist store had been a kind of revenge. And he'd always hated the idea of croissants for breakfast, preferring to munch the same grey cereal from a generic packet for the last decade and a bit.

At least now every time she sipped her coffee, she'd know that she might be single, might be going through a divorce, might be hurtling towards middle-age, but at least she was enjoying a better breakfast than he was. Revenge was hers. And in this case, it was a dish better served slightly warmed in the oven and glazed with fresh strawberry jam.

(Sure, so it wasn't the finger-twiddling, evil-laugh-inducing revenge of a Bond villain, or the crafty, confidence-sapping payback of an ex set to gaslight their former lover into a state of madness. But Rory hadn't done anything wrong other than fall out of love with her. Their divorce had been as lacklustre as their marriage had become. They'd sort of drifted apart, and finally he'd taken it upon himself to make things official by hiring a lawyer. She hadn't the impetus or energy to key his car, or crank call his work, or report him to the police for something, let alone sabotage his future relationships. Anyway, they say the best revenge is living well – so that's what she was going to do. From now on.)

There was a gratifying thud as the post hit the doormat and she smiled to herself. Cards. Was it babyish to be excited about them? Probably. But she'd always loved receiving proper birthday cards – not because they'd sometimes used to contain money (although that had always been very welcome) but because they meant that someone had taken the time to choose a card, send her wishes, buy a stamp and pop it in the post to brighten her day.

She got up, slid her feet back into the 'Naughty Forty' slippers her best friend Bess had given her and padded to the doormat. Six white, card-like envelopes and one large, manilla one, with the tell-tale *do not bend* (probably a giant card from Bess), plus a couple of takeaway leaflets. Not a bad turn out.

'Happy birthday to me,' she said quietly as she made her way back to the kitchen table and its scattered crumbs.

She cleared a space in the rubble and put down her stack, starting with the smallest card first. Saving the best till last, she thought, looking at the manilla envelope. First card was from Mum and Dad, predictably with a picture of an impressionist oil painting on the front and garnished with a row of kisses in her mum's swooping handwriting. Then one from Carl, her cousin, no doubt written by his wife Kelly – Carl had never been the most organised of people but since meeting Kel, his birthday and Christmas card output had gone up 200 per cent.

The other cards were from her aunt, an old work colleague and a couple of friends from uni. None of them had much more than a scribbled *happy birthday* or the usual half-arsed *must meet up soon* but it was the thought that counted. And now, the pièce de résistance, she thought, running her finger under the flap of the large, cardboard envelope. What had Bess gone and done now? A montage of funny pictures from across the years? A personalised message? Maybe a voucher for a best buddies' spa day?

She jumped as the thick paper sliced into her finger and pulled her hand back, before sucking at the tiny, stinging wound. Then more carefully, she pulled the rest of the gummed paper open and gently slid out the interior, careful not to bleed all over the thick paper. Death by paper cut, she thought, how glamorous.

For a moment, when she turned the paper over, she felt her head spin and a prickle ran over her skin as her brain tried to marry up her expectations vs the reality.

The thick, card-like paper read *Decree Absolute*. The final paper in her divorce proceedings.

No happy birthday. No best wishes. No quips about her age. No cartoon women drinking from wine bottles.

Instead, a legal document. The rubber stamp on her single status. She was officially unattached.

* * *

'Hang on, hang on, stop crying!' Bess said, her voice crackling slightly over the phone. 'Aren't you meant to be happy about this?'

'I know...' she sobbed, feeling a runnel of snot descend from her nostril. 'It's... it's... just. It hit me.'

'What hit you?'

'Bess! I'm forty!' she said, her voice a strangled cry. 'I'm middle-aged and now I'm divorced.'

'I love you, honey. But none of this should be a surprise to you.'

'I just... I wasn't... ready.'

'You've been waiting three months for this piece of paper – and your solicitor warned you it was on its way,' Bess said calmly. 'And you've had the whole year to get used to the idea of the big 4-0.'

'I know but it didn't seem real. And now... Now it's really real!'

They were both silent for a moment, probably trying to extract meaning from the odd sentence.

'Are you sure all this is just about the decree absolute?' Bess asked, more gently.

Nina wiped her nose, trying to gather herself. 'It's just,' she said, 'it came today of all days. I mean, do you think Rory planned it?'

'Nina,' Bess said. 'Rory doesn't have the...'

'Oh, I know. He's a nice guy. He wouldn't be vindictive...'

'Actually I was going to say, there's no way Rory would be organised enough to arrange for a legal document to get to you on a set day. I mean, didn't he forget your anniversary every year?'

'Well, yes, but...'

'And remember the time he forgot to post the Christmas cards till January?'

'Well, yeah, but...'

'And I'm pretty sure it's the court that decides when it gets posted, not your ex-husband.'

'I know,' Nina sniffed. 'It just feels so personal somehow. Like, what are the chances?'

'I still think we can rule out deliberate birthday sabotage,' Bess said firmly.

'I suppose,' she admitted sulkily, scuffing her foot slightly against the kitchen tiles. 'But it doesn't change the facts.'

'Which are...?'

'Bess, I'm forty!'

'Yes. Me too. Look, you get used to it... you...'

'But you're married, you've got the 2.4 kids...'

'Just two – unless you're fat-shaming them?'

'And your career. You love your job, right?'

'Love is a very strong word.' Bess worked as a head midwife at the local hospital. 'But yeah, I suppose it's fulfilling in its own way.'

'See! See! That's why you can cope with being this age. Because you have things to show for it,' said Nina miserably. 'What do I have? A decree absolute, a house that's being sold from under me – and even then, barely has any equity. And a job that was meant to just be a stop gap but that I've stuck at for fifteen years.'

Bess was silent. 'You've got a cat,' she said at last.

'Even he doesn't spend any time at home if he can help it.'

'Well, to be fair, he is a cat.'

'Or I'm such a loser even my cat doesn't want to spend time with me.' Nina joked, feeling herself calm slightly.

'Hey. No one,' Bess said firmly, 'calls my best friend a loser.'

Nina felt herself smile a little. 'Look, I know I was meant to be sticking two fingers up to ageing and embracing a new decade and being single and... well all the things,' she said. 'It's just thinking it was a big birthday card and finding... *that* instead. It just rocked me off my axis a bit.'

'Look, do you want me to buy an enormous birthday card? Is that what this is about?'

Nina laughed. 'Not particularly.'

'Do you want Rory to burst through the door, rose between his teeth, rip up the divorce papers and make mad, passionate love to you on the kitchen table?'

Nina gave an involuntary shudder. 'Definitely not,' she said. 'And thanks for putting me off my croissants.'

'Do you want the solicitor to ring and tell you there's been another delay with the paperwork?'

'Obviously not!'

'Well then. In so many ways, you've got exactly what you wanted for your birthday. Freedom!' The last word was bellowed out, to the tune of an old George Michael song.

Nina sighed, grateful for her friend's efforts to cheer her up. 'I know you're right, really. I suppose I've got everything I could hope for in my situation. It's just... when I look back to my teens and think of all the hopes I had for... I don't know, things I'd experience: romance, travel, a job I loved, kids... well, I didn't imagine my forties would begin like this.'

'Nina, when we were seventeen, we thought we were going to form a band and take the world by storm.'

'Well, yeah.'

'Except neither of us could hold a note...'

'True.'

'Or play an instrument.'

'Details, details,' Nina grinned.

'We liked crimping our hair and tying it in bunches.'

'There's no accounting for taste.'

'We thought we were going to marry Justin and Chris from NSYNC.'

'They'd have been lucky to have us.'

Bess laughed. 'You're right. But the point is Nina, we didn't know what the feck we were on about back then. We didn't know about mortgages and boring jobs and partners and bills and washing and smear tests and... well, the stuff of life. We didn't have a clue. So don't listen to that voice in your head. You're doing fine.'

'I guess you're right,' Nina said, sinking back into her chair and playing with the remaining corner of her croissant. 'I'm being stupid.'

'Plus, trust me – being a mum isn't all it's cracked up to be.'

'But you love being a mum!'

'Yes. Sometimes. But you know what? Not *all* the time. Not *every single little minute* of the time,' Bess admitted.

'You're just trying to make me feel better.'

'Anyway, didn't you always say you weren't really the maternal type?'

'That's not the point, though. The point is the choice being taken away by Mother Nature! It's a bereavement.'

Bess sighed affectionately. 'Nina, it's not being taken away. You can be a mum at any age these days. I just read that a woman in her seventies...'

'Not the optimum time for procreation. Face it. I'm forty, menopause is calling.'

'Not necessarily. Plus there are other routes: adoption, surrogacy. Meeting a hot, single dad. The point is, Mother Nature doesn't have as much clout as you think she has.'

'OK,' Nina said. 'You make a fair point.' She was already feeling better; it was impossible not to smile when talking to Bess.

'I get it, though,' Bess said. 'It was spectacularly bad timing for the divorce thing. But look, let's turn it on its head. Celebrate it. Double celebration tonight. I'm buying.'

'You're buying? It really must be a once-in-a-lifetime occasion,' teased Nina. They'd planned to meet in their favourite pub tonight for a few drinks, and she'd been looking forward to it. Hopefully by tonight, she'd have her mojo back and be able to enjoy herself.

'Ha. Well, let's make the most of it then,' said her friend, kindly. 'And Sal can make it after all – did I tell you? We'll have a laugh and put the world to rights.'

'Oh brilliant.'

'Until then, my shift starts in an hour so I'd better hop in the bathroom while it's free,' Bess said. 'As long as you're alright?'

'Much better, thanks,' Nina smiled. 'Ready to seize the day, or at least face it... I think.'

'Got anything planned?' Bess wheedled.

'Popping in to see Mum and Dad. Haircut. Nails,' said Nina.

'Good. Well, it'll keep you occupied. No more miserable introspection, OK? I forbid it.'

'Yes sir!' Nina grinned.

Once she'd hung the phone up, she pushed the envelope, complete with its life-altering certificate, into a drawer and shut it determinedly. Enough for one day. She wanted to be able to embrace her former mood. To shake the cobwebs off her glad rags and really see in the new decade with a smile on her face.

But as she walked upstairs into the bathroom and caught a glimpse of herself in the mirror, she felt her determination slip slightly. There was no denying the date on the calendar, the lines on her face. Her hair, a grown-out short cut that needed a good tidy and some seriously bright highlights to lift the dull brown, wasn't helping things. She was truly, absolutely, middle-aged. Was this a moment she could use to pivot her into a brand-new life? Or had she simply missed the bucket-list boat?

2

JUNE – THEN

'Just think,' said Bess, as they looked out over the choppy Channel waters. 'This is what freedom must feel like.'

Nina looked at the huddle of teachers out on the deck, two of them engrossed in conversation, the others chatting or looking out to sea. 'You think?' she said.

'Oh, don't worry about *them*,' said Bess. 'Imagine, you and me a few years' time, setting off for an adventure. Once we're eighteen, we can go *anywhere*.'

'If we have the money,' Nina said.

'Well, yeah. But think about it. Complete freedom, no parents, seeing the world.' Bess sighed. 'And this trip, it's just the start, isn't it. We're practically out of school. A-levels and then boom!'

'Boom?'

'Freedom!' Bess laughed. She scrunched her hand in her hair to make sure her curls hadn't fallen out on the coach journey, then reached in her pocket for a cherry lip-gloss.

'What about uni?' Nina asked.

'Gap year,' Bess said, firmly. 'Everyone expects it these days.'

Nina smiled. It did sound tempting. 'You really think we could do it, just us?'

'First France, then everywhere,' Bess said, dramatically. 'The world is our *escargot!*'

'Isn't it meant to be an oyster?'

'Nina, we're on the way to France. It's *escar-GO big or escar-GO home*!'

Nina couldn't help but laugh.

3

NOW

DIVORCE

Pros:
Whole bed to myself
No more arguments
No joint account – can buy shoes without having to explain
New start!

Cons:
Lonely?
No conversation – house too quiet
Have to sell the house
Not sure I have the energy to start again

The bar was heaving with life, despite the fact it was only Tuesday. Flicking her newly highlighted hair, Nina stepped in, waving at Sal and Bess at their corner table. Her new nails glittered in the light from the quirky, metal light fittings and as the music flooded her senses, she began to get that particular prickle of excitement she always had when anticipating a night out.

Her day hadn't been the relax-fest she'd hoped. When she'd booked a day off work, she'd imagined herself popping into her parents for the obligatory cup of coffee, before sauntering to the salon for a massage and facial, followed by treating herself to a new 'do' and sparkling nails. She'd contemplated a couple of 'tweakments' too but had baulked at the price – perhaps when they finally sold their house, she'd feel a little more flush. But right now, she'd decided she'd have to make do with the kind of lift that came from bright colours rather than muscle-freezing chemicals.

But, when she'd popped into her mum and dad's that morning, she'd found her seventy-five-year-old father up a ladder, being 'supported' by the rather shaky hold of her mum as he tried to clear leaves out of the guttering. The ladder, which itself had seen better days, had been thin, spindly and looked as if it might give way at any minute. Her mum, in her desire to keep her husband from falling, was gripping the bottom of it so tightly that any slight movement from her made the whole ladder inch a little from the edge of the roof.

'Oh, hello love!' her mum had said delightedly, taking one hand off the ladder to give an enthusiastic but unnecessary wave. Her father, at the top of the ladder, now veering wildly like a flag in the hand of an excited toddler, had taken one reckless hand off too and given her a similar greeting.

So instead of relaxing back on a massage bench, she'd spent most of the morning coaxing an elderly man from atop a ladder and convincing him to take a trip to B&Q with her to buy a ladder that was less likely to lead to a premature demise. Then, donning a pair of borrowed slacks from her mum, she'd taken her life in her hands to fish leaves out of plastic guttering that had seen better days. All while pretending that it wasn't any hassle and honestly, she didn't have anything better to do on her day off, on her birthday, on the day when her single status and prospective homelessness (or at least the necessity to move back to their place) had been confirmed.

To top it all, when she'd called the hairdresser and spa to cancel everything but the hair appointment, she'd been informed that, as she hadn't given the obligatory twenty-four hours' notice, she would be charged, so she was out of pocket yet still had knots in her shoulders when she finally staggered into 'Belle's Beauty' with leaf mulch in her hair and every one of her forty years and more engraved into lines on her face a few hours later.

Sitting in front of the mirror, her head covered in tinfoil twists, had done nothing for her self-esteem either – even though the resulting short, highlighted bob admittedly looked pretty sleek – and it had been all she could do to pull on a pair of tight navy jeans and a black, V-neck top when she got home, rather than crawl under the duvet and simply give up.

In short, she needed a drink.

Before continuing her walk, she paused to take a deep breath and reset herself. Right. She wasn't going to give in to the misery that had been bubbling beneath the surface since this morning. She was going to be loud, proud, happy and healthy, seeing in this new year with her friends. A brand new, positive her.

* * *

'And another thing,' she slurred, four hours later and several glasses of wine down, 'is knowing that I'm probably halfway through my life and have nothing to show for it.' The table was scattered with the remnants of wrapping paper – and she was sporting a new pair of earrings (Bess) and a new bracelet (Sal).

'That was the *first* thing,' Bess said, giving Sal a sideways glance.

'What?'

'You said that one first, you said, "the worst thing was not having anything to show for it."'

'That was about an hour ago,' Sal added helpfully. 'Before you told us about Rory's bad foot hygiene.'

'Oh,' said Nina, slightly put off her stride.

'And then you said what's the point of having a bucket list when you never bother to do anything on it,' Sal reminded her.

'Then that you blame Rory for stealing your childbearing years and convincing you that you didn't want children...' Bess added.

'Even though you've mentioned in the past that babies seem more trouble than they're worth,' Sal pointed out.

Had she said that? Probably.

'Well, maybe,' she admitted. 'But then they grow into lovely young kids like yours,' she said. 'And I know I get to babysit and spend time with Casey and the boys but—'

'And hand them back when you've had enough,' Bess reminded her darkly.

'Yes. True. But you know what, I do get broody sometimes. Not when I see babies so much. But I know your kids now. They're people. You can talk to them. It must be nice to have kids like that.'

'You are aware that you can't gestate a foetus until it's ten years old though, right?' Bess said.

'God, how dilated would you have to be for that labour?' Sal shuddered.

'Imagine the kicks!' Bess exclaimed.

'And the cringeworthy embarrassment when they realised what the tunnel they'd just travelled through was!' Sal added, grimacing.

'Yep, you'd definitely have to go through the baby bit too.'

'Very funny.' Nina said, smiling and shaking her head.

'Then you were saying how you might as well book into an old people's home now,' said Bess, 'because surely if the next forty years were the same as the previous, there really wasn't anything to stick around for.'

Nina nodded. 'Yes. Yes. Well,' she said. 'That's the *other* other thing. What makes me think that I'm going to get anything right in the next forty years, I—'

She was interrupted by a tap on her shoulder. She tutted loudly – what was it now?

'Do you mind?' she said, with the haughty pride that comes with several red wines and two hours of ranting. 'I was just in the middle of something.'

'Nina!' Bess warned.

Turning, she was faced with a young man dressed in a black shirt. In his hands, he carried a cake, pink and formed into the number '40'. Red faced, he put it down on the table between them and lit the candles (there were only ten, Nina noticed) with a lighter. Then two other bar staff came and stood by his side. None of them smiled.

'I...' began Nina, as Bess looked at her with a smile-grimace combination.

'Happy birthday to you, happy birthday to youuuuu. Happy birthday to youuuuuu! Happy birthday to you!' the staff sung dutifully, with Bess and Sal joining in rather more quietly. Then, they disappeared without a glance, leaving the rather soggy-looking cake melting slightly on the table.

'Oh,' said Nina.

'Sorry,' Bess said. 'It seemed like a good idea at the time.'

'No. Oh don't apologise!' Nina said. 'It's a lovely thing. I've ruined it with my... well, you know.'

'It's not ruined! It still looks delicious!' Sal said, with a fixed grin.

'Yummy!' Bess said.

'No,' Nina said, sadly. 'I've ruined it. Like I ruin everything.'

'Still, you should probably blow the candles out,' Sal said, nodding towards the practical inferno between them on the table.

'Make a wish!' Bess said brightly as Nina obliged, puffing out the candles in three goes.

They sat for a moment, all contemplating the slightly smoking, icing-covered lump in front of them, before Nina looked up, her eyes swimming with tears.

She had transitioned to the next stage of drunkenness. Tearful sentimentality.

'I'm lucky to have you,' she said. 'I suppose,' she wiped her eye, 'at least I've got the friendship bit right.'

'That's the spirit,' said Bess, pulling part of the *4* off the cake and popping it into her mouth.

They were silent for a minute.

'Another wine?' Sal asked, brightly, brandishing the bottle they'd bought to share.

'Oh God, why not,' said Nina. 'I mean, what's the worst that could happen?' Then, paused, thinking about the evening so far. Even in her drunken state, she could see that alcohol hadn't exactly helped her to have a happy night. 'Maybe not, actually,' she said, covering the glass with her hand, too late for Sal to react. Sal tipped the bottle to pour a generous glass and the wine flowed freely over Nina's hand, across the slightly sticky surface of the wooden table and wetly onto the floor, covering Nina's shoes. Her new shoes.

'Oh, Nina. I'm sorry!'

'It's my fault,' Nina said, looking at the shoes mournfully. 'It's just, I changed my mind about the wine. I suddenly thought maybe I should live life more – what do they say? – mindfully. Cautiously. I gave it all up for love. I took a risk and married Rory.

And look where it got me.' She shook her head darkly as she cleaned up the wine with her sleeve. 'No. New me. New resolution. I'm not taking any chances. From now on, everything I do will be carefully planned and executed. No more giving into fate. No more throwing caution to the wind. And no... well, *less* wine.'

Bess and Sal looked at one another.

'What?' Nina said.

'Well,' Bess said, nodding slightly at Sal, 'it's just... you're not exactly a risk-taker, Nina.'

'What do you mean?'

'For starters, when you married Rory, you drew up that spreadsheet, do you remember? The pros and cons.'

'That was a joke, mostly.'

'And you took that office manager job, didn't you, in Hamish and Co., because it offered healthcare and a longer-term contract.'

'And training,' added Sal.

'Yes,' said Bess. 'The *training*. You didn't take that job you really wanted. What was it? As a runner in the TV company – because you wouldn't be working towards a qualification, and it was a one-month contract, on a temporary basis. Too risky.'

'Yes, but don't forget that Hamish and Co. let me do those business exams. Plus they were going to open that French office – I thought I might end up in Paris!' she protested.

'True. But then it's been twelve years since that project bit the dust...'

'God, that seems like a long time ago,' said Nina, remembering how torn she'd been at the time. She'd done months of French classes to tune up her language skills – all for nothing. Bitterly disappointed, she'd thought about leaving the firm to pursue another avenue when they'd told her that Paris was a no-go. But her friends were right – she'd played it safe and simply stayed.

'And what about when you were going to come interrailing

with me, but you chickened out at the last minute?' Bess said. 'We were just about to book the tickets and everything.'

'But you still got to go!' Nina pointed out. 'You had a great time.'

'Exactly. But what did you do?'

'I just wanted to save up. Get ready for uni...' Nina trailed off.

'All we're saying is, maybe you're already pretty cautious?' suggested Bess gently.

'Plus, you never have given into "fate". You don't believe in fate, right? You never have,' Sal added.

'Face it, Nina, the only way you could take fewer risks in life is if you decided to move from your ordinary house into a padded cell.'

'No sharp edges,' said Sal.

'No spicy food.'

'Eating only purée.'

'Doctor on standby.'

As Nina watched them giggling, she suddenly didn't feel like joining in. Because they were right, weren't they? She was forty years old and had played it safe all her life. She hadn't risked it all with Rory; she'd made a sensible choice to settle with a sensible man (who'd sensibly divorced her when he realised she didn't fully love him the way he deserved). What if fate did exist? What if it had been trying to get her attention all these years and she'd simply ignored it?

'You're right,' she said, rubbing her eyes with her damp sleeve and smelling an odd mixture of wine and fabric conditioner. She felt her eyes re-fill.

'Oh, don't cry,' Bess said, touching her arm. 'We were only joking!'

'Maybe it's just my fate to be boring, single and miserable.'

'So now you *do* believe in fate?'

'Seriously, it's the drink talking,' Sal said. 'I mean, look at us! Me and Bess, I mean. We're hardly daredevils.'

'But you've done things,' Nina said. 'And you've both got... I don't know. Good jobs. Good lives.'

Sal wrinkled her nose. 'Hate to rain on your parade,' she said. 'But I'm a single mum. That's hardly winning the life lottery. At least on paper. And I work two jobs.'

'Two jobs?' Nina knew that Sal worked part-time as a teaching assistant, but had thought that was it.

'Didn't I tell you? You are looking at the latest St Albans Roman Theatre guide. It's only once a week, but I have to dress up in full Roman garb.'

'Which is?'

Sal shook her head. 'Nina, how long have you lived in St Albans? There are pictures of Romans all over the place.'

Nina grimaced. 'Yes, but they're mostly men,' she said. 'All the armour and red, feathery things.'

Sal laughed. 'Well, my costume is more of a large bedsheet,' she said. 'It's meant to be a tunic, but honestly I wonder whether I should just wrap my duvet around me and be done with it.'

They laughed.

'It's great, though,' Sal said. 'One more step on my journey to being a proper history teacher.'

Since taking the assistant job at her daughter's school three years ago, Sal had been debating whether it was time to go back to education, to qualify as a teacher. So far, money had been too tight for her to give up work to train, even with a potential bursary. But there was a chance she might be accepted into job-based training next year, and this would hopefully be a great addition to her CV.

'Ah, you'll get there,' Bess said. 'And until that, at least you get to look hot!'

'Hot? I'll be wearing a duvet. I'll be bloody boiling!'

'Anyway, you're happy, right? And you have your gorgeous girl to keep you company?' Nina said, getting back on track with her misery-induced life comparison.

'True,' said Sal, raising her glass. 'But I'm only happy because I have a glass half-empty philosophy.'

'Don't you mean glass half-full?'

'No, I mean whenever I feel lonely, I drink some wine,' said Sal, grinning and draining the last few inches from her glass and laughing.

Nina reached out a hand. 'Oh Sal...'

'Ah, I'm fine,' said Sal. 'I mean, I wouldn't say no if a handsome man came along, someone take on half the chores and be a father figure to Rosie, and shower me with love and gifts and sex...'

'Can you actually shower someone with sex?' Bess mused.

Nina grimaced. 'Probably, but not sure it's something I'd enjoy...'

Sal laughed. 'Anyway, what I'm saying is life is OK. Good even. Yes. I'm happy, I suppose. But nothing's perfect – it can just look that way sometimes from the outside, especially if you're feeling a bit wobbly.'

'Plus kids, schmidz – not all it's cracked up to be. Trust me,' said Bess, taking a large sip of wine. 'Do you know what Casey called me yesterday?'

'What?'

'An opp.'

They were silent for a minute.

'Which means?'

Bess shook her head. 'I have no idea. But it was definitely a bad thing.'

'OK, I get that kids can be hard work. But you guys have lived, you've had adventures.' Nina said.

'And so have you. You... you went on that last-minute trip to

Brighton a few years ago – do you remember? Called in sick at work. And there was that time you... you... you...' said Bess, her face registering panic as she realised she'd run out of anecdotes.

'That's it!' said Nina, tapping her glass against the table. The stem came off the glass and clattered to the floor. She stood up, still holding the rest of the glass, knocking the stool behind her backwards slightly. 'That's it, everyone!' she said to the disinterested bar, flinging her arms wide and sending a shower of red wine over the woman next to them. 'From now on, I am going to say *yes*. I am going to *take* risks! I am going to live my life to the fullest! And what is more, I am going to listen to fate! I'm going to let the stars dictate my future!' she cried, stumbling, clutching at the table but falling nevertheless, face first into the pink iced cake at the centre of the table.

'That sounds fabulous, lovely,' said Bess, taking her by the arm as she stood up, her nose pink with icing. 'But maybe we should get you home and start the risk-taking tomorrow morning.'

4

The next morning, Nina's alarm shocked her awake at 6.30 a.m. and she groaned. It was the first hangover she'd had in around a decade and now she remembered why she'd resolved not to drink to excess Ever Again. Her head throbbed, she felt stale and sweaty, and her mouth tasted like the inside of a dog's bottom. Not that she had a frame of reference for that. But she was pretty sure it was an accurate description.

And now she had to go to work. Because she'd booked yesterday off for her birthday to *pamper* herself. She'd imagined getting up this morning, after a lovely but sedate night out, newly coiffed and tweaked and strutting into work as a brand-new version of herself.

Well, she thought, looking in the mirror. She would at least look different from usual. Only, having a slight green tinge to her complexion wasn't the difference she'd been hoping for. Still, there was nothing for it, she thought, turning the shower down a few degrees in the hope of waking herself up.

Ten minutes later, she was sitting at the kitchen table eating a stale croissant and drinking instant coffee – a kind of low-budget version of yesterday's extravagance – and scrolling through her mobile phone at the latest headlines. All of which were thoroughly depressing. Worse, too, some sort of algorithm spying technique had flagged to someone in cyber land that she was now forty and therefore her feed ought to be peppered with references to anti-ageing treatments, pension plans and lists of things she should achieve in the next decade. Thanks Google.

She thought back to last night – the bits that she could remember – and tried to smile. It had been nice putting the world to rights with Sal and Bess. Nice to vent a little bit. But she hadn't meant to make it into a pity-fest. She blushed thinking about the cake destruction and the noisy proclamation she'd made in the bar. Hopefully, the loud music and the fact that most of the other punters were several drinks down meant that her spectacle hadn't made an impression on anyone other than her friends.

She thought back to the things she'd lamented. It was true that she'd chosen safe options more often than not over the years. There was that time she'd signed up for adult dance classes but chickened out at the last minute, the job she'd been offered in TV that she'd turned down due to its unpredictability; she'd shunned a gap year back in the day because she'd wanted to save for uni – and worked in a bank instead. And of course there was Pierre. The one who got away. Or, to be more precise, the one she could have gone to but had decided not to, instead, settling for Rory a few years later as a 'safe bet.'

It had been over twenty years since she'd met Pierre, and at least a decade since she'd thought about him. The seventeen-year-old student she'd met on French exchange who'd proclaimed his love to her and suggested they elope. She'd agreed, until the school coach had arrived back on British soil and the idea of trekking back with her life savings and backpack, leaving a note for her parents, as she'd planned, had started to seem faintly ridiculous.

Instead, she'd married steadfast Rory, whom she'd met in her first year at uni. And she'd had a nice life. A good enough marriage. Until it wasn't.

Just... looking back, she wondered where she might have been if her choices had been just a little more adventurous. Perhaps she'd be wandering the Champs-Élysées right now, or tap dancing her way around theatres of the world. Maybe she'd have found the perfect location on her travels and settled there, basking in the sunshine. Or perhaps Pierre would have given everything she'd lacked with Rory: passion, adventure and possibly even children.

'Stop it,' she said to herself as she realised tears had formed in her eyes. She couldn't go to work tear-stained as well as hungover. It was the nostalgia talking. Yes, maybe she should have had more adventures, but she couldn't change the past, couldn't chastise some younger version of herself for being cautious. You live, you learn. She'd be more adventurous going forward. If the opportunity arose.

She couldn't exactly book a trip away right now though, and although she kind of liked the idea of kids, she wasn't about to jump on the next virile-looking bloke who passed by her front door. As for dancing, she was barely fit enough to do the chicken dance, let alone a pirouette. And Pierre would have well and truly got away by now. He was no doubt happily married to some impossibly glamorous, French supermodel. She needed new goals. Forty-friendly goals. Softer. Realistic. With elasticated waist-bands and forgiving, longer sleeves.

Whatever fate had had in store for her down those roads untravelled, each one was now firmly closed. She ought to be sensible and get to work and try to think about her future and what kind of life she wanted to build going forward.

She pulled on her work clothes – black trousers and a sensible blouse – quickly blow dried her short bob and snatched up her keys and handbag.

'Right,' she said to herself, walking into the hallway and grabbing her coat from the hook. This was the first day of the rest of her life. And she was going to make it count – hangover or no hangover. She was going to see what fate had in store for her.

Seconds later, as if in answer to her thoughts, a leaflet dropped through the door. A small, photocopied, low-resolution rectangle advertising *Mandy's Movers*. She picked it up. 'A dance class for over 30s, guaranteed to de-stress and get things moving!', Nina read aloud. The first session was tonight, at 6.30 p.m., in the local church hall.

She shook her head. Yes, she was thinking about dance classes, but this didn't sound quite right. She'd been thinking of going into the local dance school or somewhere a bit more upmarket. She already did a local yoga class once a week, so her desire for dance wasn't purely about exercise. She wanted to get some serious training, see if she could harness some of her old flexibility.

She popped the leaflet on the hall table and was about to unlock the door when she stopped. Wasn't this exactly what she was complaining about last night? The opportunities she'd wasted? The experiences she'd turned her back on over the years? Surely if fate did exist, the leaflet dropping in her hallway just now when she was thinking about it all was exactly the sort of thing she ought to force herself to try?

What harm could it do, after all?

Before she had time to think, she copied the mobile number into her phone and sent a quick message.

> Just got your leaflet! Is there space for me to try tonight?

There promptly came an enthusiastic reply.

Of course! Wear something with plenty of give.

She fired back a quick OK, feeling slightly less certain. Plenty of 'give' sounded ominous. Why not 'something comfortable' or 'sportswear?' 'Give' sounded... mildly dangerous.

Still, it was done. She ran quickly up the stairs and shoved a pair of leggings, some trainers and a T-shirt into a carrier bag – she could go to the class on the way home.

She opened the door and walked out into the autumn morning. It was still warm, despite the fact it was October, and the air smelled fresh. She walked quickly to her car and climbed in, turning the key in the ignition and pulling out carefully into the road. The familiar journey to work passed in a flash and she was soon pulling up in the usual car park and making sure her pass was displayed in the window.

She sighed as she exited the car. Her stomach still felt uneasy, but her headache was lifting. It wasn't the hangover causing her low mood, nor the prospect of a dance class this evening involving untested levels of flexibility. It was the sameness of it all. Fifteen years in the same job – a job she liked well enough but didn't love, wasn't passionate about. Would she be still locking up her car and making her way to the office in fifteen more years' time, aged fifty-five? Then, ten years on from that, retiring to some beige bungalow down an unnamed road and fading into the background of everyone's lives?

'Come on,' she said to herself aloud, causing a woman walking her dog near the car park entrance to look up, confused. *Pull yourself together, Nina*, she added, keeping her voice inside her head this time.

The woman walked on, her pace quickening. The little dog tugged on the lead, pleased at the increase in pace, and the woman half-tripped. 'Pierre!' she admonished the small chihuahua. 'Steady!'

Pierre. That name again. Could it be another sign from the universe? Nina mused. Some small signal from some vague entity out there that Pierre could still be part of her life? But then, surely the universe, if it had time to send signs to forty-something admin workers on a Tuesday morning, would choose something more impressive than a chihuahua with a significant name.

Get a grip. Pushing back her shoulders, straightening her stance and trying out a half-hearted smile, Nina stepped into work mode and started to make her way towards the familiar building with its familiar desk in the familiar office that had been her daily destination for far too many years. And in doing so, stepped in a tiny present that dog-Pierre had left on the pavement, its soft form yielding against her court shoe.

'Pierre!' shouted the dog's owner, noticing what had happened. 'I am so sorry, love,' she said, looking at the brown garnish on Nina's black leather.

'That's OK,' Nina lied, inwardly seething. Had the woman not heard of picking up after her dog?

Pierre regarded her, his head on the side. 'Still, it's meant to be good luck, isn't it?' the woman said, her head taking on a similar angle to her dog's, a wistful look crossing her face.

'I'm sorry, what?'

'You know. Stepping in doggy-do. That's meant to be good luck, I think.' The woman sounded slightly less sure of herself.

'That's bird poo,' Nina said, scraping her shoe against the edge of a drain. 'Not dog poo.'

'Oh,' said the woman. 'Are you sure?'

'Very.'

'Oh, well,' she said, 'I bet any kind of poo will do. I bet you're going to have a lucky day.'

'I suppose.' Nina was beginning to feel she'd stepped into some strange alternative reality where people discussed different sorts of excrement in the street and their various significances. *Rabbit poo? That means you'll make a new friend. Cat? Ooh, better buy a lottery ticket, you'll be coming into some money.*

She shook her head. Reading tea leaves was something, but she wasn't sure this type of brown clairvoyance would ever catch on.

'Well, good luck anyway!' The woman smiled. She seemed quite buoyed by the whole episode and gave Nina a cheery wave as she walked away. 'Come on Pierre,' she said. 'And no more presents for nice ladies, young man!'

'Bye,' said Nina, not really knowing why. As the woman disappeared around the corner, Nina realised that the woman had disappeared without cleaning what was left of dog-Pierre's good-luck charm from the concrete. She found a few leaves to throw over the flattened remnants, in an attempt to spare anyone else the same fate (or good luck – depending on how you viewed it).

Her shoe as clean as it was going to get, she turned and continued her walk towards the glass sliding doors into the building that would swallow up another day of her life. Just in time for a large, white present from a friendly bird in the sky to slap onto her hair in the strongest message from fate she'd had yet.

Maybe, she thought, the poo gods *were* smiling on her. Maybe fate *was* on her side.

She just wished they'd find another way to let her know.

5

The office was practically empty. Ever since their boss had decided to give people the opportunity to work from home three days a week, it had lost its heart – or whatever heart it'd had previously – and because the days spent at home were flexible, you were never quite sure who you were going to get or what the atmosphere was going to be like when you ventured in.

Today, it turned out, just two of the other staff were there – Terry from accounts and George, the trainee who spent most of the time surreptitiously texting his girlfriend. In times gone by, Nina had welcomed a half-empty office, but these days, with Rory gone and only her oft-absent cat, Rupert, to keep her company, she'd have welcomed a little more social interaction than the brief grunt she received from George and the couple of remarks about the weather she received from Terry.

She hated the loneliness of a deserted office, but at least today it meant she had the ladies' loos to herself when she first got in. It gave her a chance to de-poo herself as best she could. She ran a little water over the relevant section of her hair and attempted to dry it under the hand dryer. Then she slipped off her shoe and held her breath as she let the hot tap run over its sole. After drying it with a paper-towel, she straightened her clothing and made her way to her desk.

Sitting in the near silence, entering data into a spreadsheet and updating the staff files, Nina felt as if time was almost standing still. Eventually, home time came around and she tidied her desk and stood up. She'd go home, she decided, treat herself to a take-away, then just collapse in front of the TV. The hangover had lifted by midday, but she had a kind of post night-out fatigue – it would be great to finally kick back and relax.

Then she remembered.

The dance class.

Damn. She checked her phone to see if 'Mandy' had by some wonderful chance cancelled the whole thing. But no. No messages.

Of course, she thought, as she zipped up her coat at 5 p.m., she could just leave it. Start next week. Find a different class entirely. Problem was, she had a sneaking suspicion that it was now or never. If she went home tonight, fifteen more years would somehow slip by and she'd have nothing to show for them once again.

Sighing at her own annoying self-resolve, she said goodbye to George, who – as far as she could tell – had stuffed a few envelopes today and spent the rest of the time on social media, and left the building. She grabbed a sandwich from the small supermarket near the car park and ate it in the car. Then, brushing the crumbs from her trousers, she started the car and made her way to the church hall close to her house, still having to force herself to keep going in the face of her almost all-consuming reluctance.

The hall was gently lit from the inside, throwing a yellow glow into the shadowed half-light of early evening. Nina watched as a few other women walked into the hall, laughing and joking together. None of them looked offputtingly fit or bendy, and most of them looked around her age and relatively friendly. It was A Good Sign.

She parked close to the wall in the corner of the small car parking area and shuffled into the back with her carrier bag. It would be better to change here – everyone else seemed to have arrived in their kit and she didn't want to be the odd one out, having to change in the toilet and probably dropping her trousers in a puddle in the process.

It had been a while since she'd wriggled out of a pair of trousers in the back of a car – and she'd forgotten both how undignified and how difficult it could be. She'd just managed to remove her smart work trousers and was trying to work out whether the leggings were inside out or not when there was a knock on the window. She froze like a rabbit in headlights, startled into stiffness in her rather grey, oversized knickers. A woman who looked to be in her late sixties, her silver hair tied into a bun like a ballerina, grinned at her on the other side of the glass, then raised a hand and motioned that she wind down the window.

Reluctantly, she acquiesced.

'Hello love,' said the woman, who seemed completely unfazed at the sight of Nina's half-nakedness. 'Do you know if this is the right place for the dance class?' She smiled, sending a wave of wrinkles across her face.

Nina, unsuccessfully trying to cover at least some of her modesty with the leggings, forced a smile. 'Yes, I think so,' she said. 'Just getting changed.'

'Thank you,' the woman said, seemingly in no desire to rush off. She stayed at the window. 'This your first time too?'

'Yes,' said Nina, feeling goosebumps begin to appear on her legs. 'Came straight from work,' she said, nodding towards the crumpled trousers to ensure the woman realised the reason for her state of undress. 'Just quickly getting ready.'

'Gosh, it's nerve-wracking, isn't it!' said the woman, fingering a gold necklace at her collar. 'I haven't tried anything new for a while, but when the leaflet came through, I thought – well, why not! I used to do a bit of dance back in the day – and there's life in the old legs yet.'

'Right! Same!' said Nina, nodding. 'Well, I guess I'll see you in there?'

'Actually,' said the woman, her head now virtually through the gap in the window. 'Do you mind if I wait for you? I feel a little bit nervous – so unlike me! – and it'd be nice to have someone to go in there with.'

'Sure, of course.' Nina said, nodding again towards her clothing. 'I'll just...'

'Oh! Of course!' the woman said as if just realising Nina was half-reclined on the back seat wearing her underwear. 'I'll wait.'

'Thanks.' Nina raised the leggings and gave them a flap as if to indicate it was time to look away. But the woman's head remained in situ. In the end, Nina had no choice but to wriggle herself into the leggings, which to her annoyance were her oldest, tightest pair and likely had no 'give' whatsoever, with the woman chattering way as if the whole situation was completely normal.

'I'm Marjory, by the way,' she said. 'Live just over by the doctor's surgery. Useful at my age... Never had a bunion in my life till I was seventy, now they seem to sprout out on a monthly basis, and don't get me started on piles...'

By the time Nina staggered out of the car, in half-twisted leggings, she was already regretting her decision to come. But she shouldn't write it off, she told herself. Just because Marjory had no sense of personal space didn't mean the class wouldn't be just what she needed. She could always find a spot away from her new 'friend' and give it a proper chance.

Inside the room, eight other women stood, barefoot, in readiness for the class to begin. Nina followed their lead and took off her trainers, stuffing her socks inside and piling them in the corner, together with her handbag. Then she took a space on the floor, at the back of the room, and tried to stretch her legs a little, leaning forward to touch her toes.

Moments later, the door to the hall creaked open, screeching as it swung back into place, and a hush fell over the room. Nina straightened to see a woman, probably mid-sixties, with curled hair piled high on her head. She was wearing a pair of below-the-knee leggings, after which her legs were bare of everything except a jungle of coarse, black hair. Her feet, also bare, were enormous, and each toe sported a ring. She clacked across the floor, carrying an old-fashioned CD player in one hand, and (ominously) a tambourine in the other.

'Welcome one and all. I'm Mandy!' she said, delighted with herself. She set the CD player on the floor and beamed at the women in the class. 'Lovely to see some new faces!' she said in a breathy, earnest voice. 'Let's hope the healing power of movement will bring us all together this evening!'

Mandy bent down, the material of her leggings stretching to reveal the pinkness of her skin beneath, and pressed play on the ancient machine. The sound of panpipes, drums and chanting began to fill the room. Mandy turned, her eyes sparkling with enthusiasm, and raised her hands in the air. 'Let the music fill your soul!' she said. 'Move, give in to the rhythm!' She closed her eyes and began to move, trance-like, bucking and swishing her body in time to the uneven drumbeat.

Nina felt a sense of rising panic. She'd been expecting more instruction, more standard dance moves, rather than, than... whatever this was. She glanced up at the other participants, hoping to see some of them looking equally baffled, but everyone else seemed to have fallen under Mandy's spell. They were moving, jerking, and even spinning, their eyes firmly closed, their faces rapturous. Even Marjory looked gripped.

'Feel free to open your lips and give in to the call of the wild!' cried Mandy above the din. She let out a strange, animal cry – a little like the sound Rupert had made once when Nina had accidentally trod on his tail.

A cacophony of similar sounds began emanating from the lips of all the ordinary-looking women in the class with Nina. A whooping, chucking, clucking, calling, bird-like, beast-like, jungle of noise.

And it was too much.

Nina was just weaving and half-dancing her way to the back towards the door with the hope of sneaking off when she heard a voice.

'You!'

She took a few more steps, but sensed the class had turned to look. She raised her eyes.

'You! Yes!' said Mandy, as she locked eyes with Nina. 'I *love* what you're doing! The speed! The movement! What would you call it?'

'Um, I just…' Nina began to stammer.

To her horror, Mandy dropped her shoulders to a stoop and began to step, on tip toes across the front of the room. She moved her head back and forth to the music as she did so, giving herself the appearance of a drunk pigeon. 'I love it!' she cried. 'Let's name it the "Snazzy Walk"! Now ladies, let's all give this a go. And a one, two three four…' The entire class turned and began to tiptoe walk to the opposite wall, arms and heads rocking to the beat. 'Yes!' said Mandy. 'Oh, wonderful!'

No longer caring, Nina bolted through the women and raced to the back of the room, grabbing her shoes and bag and running barefoot into the cold car park. Reaching her car, she looked up to see Mandy, still in full trance, rocking by the floodlit window.

She started the engine and accelerated out of the car park as if chased.

This. This was why she played it safe more often than not, she told herself. This was why she didn't try new things. Because new was not always good. Stepping out of your comfort zone was not always good. And fate? Fate could do one.

The roads were clear on the way home and once she was sure she wasn't being followed, she began to relax. She pictured Mandy's Movers still replicating her dance moves and her attempted escape. It was hard not to smile.

It hadn't been what she was looking for. But it had been an experience. And what harm had it done her? She'd pushed her boundaries, even if she'd pushed them in an unexpected direction.

By the time she locked the car and walked the few steps to her front door, she was laughing softly to herself.

She had survived. And now she knew. She didn't have to wonder whether she should have done it.

You don't regret what you do, you regret what you don't, she thought to herself as she unlocked the door.

6

THEN

Nina was one of the last to be claimed by her host family. Brigitte arrived, looking a little taller than when they'd last met, but otherwise unchanged. She was OK. A little quiet, a little serious. But OK. When she'd come to stay with Nina the previous February, she'd spent a lot of her time with her head in a book, or writing earnestly in her diary in beautiful, cursive script. Bess's pen pal had been a little more fun – wanting to explore St Albans, go to London, sneaking cigarettes into Bess's room for a crafty puff out of the window.

This time, Bridgette was flanked by her parents – who smiled at Nina and apologised for their lateness. 'Bridgette had her piano recital,' her mother explained.

Nina smiled and said it was fine. All the same, she couldn't help but wonder whether the week was going to be a little dull. Still, she supposed it was about learning French more than anything else.

7

NOW

'When should I come and pick the last of my stuff up?' Rory's voice was matter of fact on the phone the following morning.

'Well, hello Nina, how are you doing?' she said, petulantly.

'Sorry,' he said. 'It's just... you know. I probably should start to get rid of a few things. You know. Move them out. Before...'

'I know,' she said.

'Sorry.'

'It's OK. Just one of those things.' She tried to remind herself that Rory was an OK guy. A good guy even. And he'd ended their relationship for all the right reasons. She'd probably have drifted relatively happily to the death do us part bit, but he wanted more and that was fine.

'How about tomorrow?' she said. 'I'll be at work but, you know...'

'OK,' he said.

It was both awkward and endless, this finalising of things after their split. In her past relationships – not that there had been many – the breakup aftermath had been relatively easy. A last call or text, an afternoon spent listening to sad songs.

Maybe the odd binge on ice cream if it had hit particularly hard.

But this, the forensic picking over shared possessions, shared memories. The paperwork. The solicitors. It made the whole thing into more of a bereavement. Something that had already stretched over a few months and would continue – even though they'd got their final decree absolute – until the house was sold and Rory picked up the stuff that he'd negotiated with her to keep.

It was a work-from-home day today and perhaps she ought to have told him to come over this morning. It wasn't like they were at each other's throats. But it was draining, seeing him. And she could do without it. She opened up her laptop on the kitchen table, where she tended to work these days, and logged in but found she couldn't focus after his call. There was a meeting at 10 a.m., but nothing much to tie her to the screen for the hour beforehand.

Perhaps she ought to be sorting things out too. She could always catch up with work later, and she felt too restless to settle to the boring admin tasks she had flagged for today.

With a sigh, she got up and went to their once-shared bedroom – she now slept in the guest room with its impersonal bedding and lack of memories – and opened the door. The room was neat, clean: not scattered with physical signs of their cohabitation. But somehow, she found being in there overwhelming. The years they'd spent in there. The laughing, the cuddling, the sex, the companionship, the getting up with a groan on workdays or the snuggling till late on weekends. Rory had been a good husband, and a good friend. It was hard to have to let go of both of those things at once. Weird somehow, how you could never really be friends with someone you were that close to. All or nothing.

She'd already cleared most of the wardrobe on her side, apart from a few boxes of shoes she'd likely never wear again but couldn't bear to part with. Long, narrow-heeled shoes she could probably no longer walk in but held memories of dancing and laughing and tripping along pavements after nights out. Boots that stretched to the knee that she'd used to wear in the winter teamed with skinny jeans. Her most tottering heels that she'd worn almost constantly until about five years ago when a particularly comfortable pair of flats had spoiled her for all other shoes.

She piled the boxes to one side and discovered a belt she'd thought she'd lost, a pile of paperwork she'd meant to file, a few odds and ends of clothing that she'd flung in when doing a quick tidy and forgotten all about.

And a single, more battered shoe box, the logo *Clarks* crossed out, adorned with the words:

Nina's Stuff KEEP OUT

She smiled when she drew it towards her, knowing already it would contain the printed photos from her uni days, ticket stubs from concerts that had seemed too important to throw out, notes from friends passed in lectures and classes. Valentine's cards from long-forgotten crushes. A necklace – a heart pierced with a silver arrow – something Pierre had given to her. Plus his letters.

She reached in and pulled one of them out. It was light, written on airmail paper, and had discoloured slightly in the twenty years plus it had been consigned to the box of memories. Seeing the slightly curled, yellowed edges made her feel about a thousand years old. But she read the missive anyway, her mouth turned up slightly as she remembered details she'd long forgotten: how they'd met one heady week aged seventeen on the French exchange; how he'd grabbed her hand during a dance arranged by the teachers and run with her until they were breathless and finally alone. And how he'd taken her in his arms and kissed her; how everything from then had become a blur of passion and romance and something both brand new and timeless.

She touched her lips lightly. It had been her first real kiss. Not an amateur, wet-lipped slobber from an at-school boyfriend, but something real and adult and filled with passion. No wonder she'd fallen into his arms and let him undress her.

No wonder, after that, she'd been desperate not to leave him – to leave the place where she'd given someone both her heart and her virginity.

She'd cried on the coach on the way home, clutching his address in her hand and hoping against hope he'd write. And he had.

She looked at the letter in her hand – one of the last he'd sent.

My love,

I have not received a reply to my two last letters. And I am so worried! But perhaps they get lost in the post.

I have spoken to my mother and she says you are welcome to come and stay any time – so you must speak to your parents again. Tell them how serious we are about each other! And then they will understand. Or perhaps my mother can call your parents and reassure her that I am a good guy.

I can't wait until the summer when you come back. When we can start the rest of our lives!

Please do reply to my letter. I am longing to hear from you and I hope that everything is truly OK.

Until then, je t'adore.

Pierre x

She almost laughed at the childish ardour of it. It was so sweet, how deeply he had fallen for her – and her for him. He had seemed so more in touch with his emotions, so much more intense than the British boys she'd been used to. Of course she'd been swept off her feet.

For the first month after she'd returned, she'd written similar letters back. Then she'd gradually come to realise, with help from Bess, that returning to France to get married at seventeen probably wasn't a good idea. Eventually, as the memory of Pierre had faded and her exams had started to loom, she had come to believe that there was a better, greater future love out there for her one day. She'd considered running away to France – just once, after an argument with her mum. But her sensible chip had kicked in and she'd simply let him go.

Without thinking, she raised the thin paper to her mouth and gave the letter a little kiss. Then laughed at herself – she was getting far too nostalgic. The work meeting would soon bring her back to reality. She placed the letter back in the box and was just gathering her things to take into the spare room – clearing the way for Rory's entrance tomorrow – when a photograph slipped out form between the messy piles of souvenirs.

She picked it up. There she was, hair long, dotted with butterfly clips, sitting on a bench with Pierre. His eyes were fixed on the camera, his hair flopping slightly forward. They were both smiling – laughing, perhaps – at something. Her eyes were closed – they always seemed to automatically click shut in pictures, and in this time before digital cameras, she'd only find out when collecting her envelope of printed pics from Snappy Snaps.

He had been even better looking than she'd remembered. His dark hair and eyes, the light tan of his skin. His baggy jeans and tee looking dated, yet somehow so cute. She thought about the way she had changed since – some ways for the better, others probably not so much – and wondered how he'd look nowadays if she could find him.

Her phone beeped to signal the start of the meeting and she

quickly made her way down to the kitchen to find her boss, Jemima, already large on the screen. 'Sorry I'm late,' said, before realising that Jemima could neither see nor hear her, and was simply seeing a black screen with a name across it in white text – one that had popped up automatically when the meeting started.

What a relief! She slipped into the chair and clicked the volume with her mouse. 'I think everyone's here...' Jemima was saying. 'Terry, Adrian, Amanda, Clara, Steph, Sh—' she stopped and her brow furrowed. 'Oh dear,' she said, humourlessly, 'I think someone might need to change their name entry.'

Nina looked down at the tiny screen to check Jemima wasn't referring to her. Then froze as she realised that she was. The name *Shithead* was written in white letters across the black of her screen.

'Oh,' she said, colouring. 'Sorry.' She quickly deleted the name and wrote her own in its place then started her webcam. Jemima remained frozen for a moment – possibly a computer glitch, possibly not. Then pushed her glasses back up her face and began the meeting.

Shithead. How could this have happened? Nobody had been in the house, nobody had her password, nobody could have accessed her laptop to put the offensive name. And even if they had, who did she know that would sabotage her like that?

Scrolling, whilst trying to pay attention to Jemima – who was ostensibly reading out something that could easily have been included in an email rather than take an hour of each of their time – she noticed the name at the top of the screen. Rory. The once-shared laptop had auto signed into her ex-husband's account and what she'd experienced was a bit of his office humour gone wrong.

At least she wasn't going mad and nobody was out to get her, she thought, making a couple of notes on a pad next to her laptop.

'And the next item,' Jemima was saying, 'is the office kitchen.

Could we all make sure that we wash our mugs thoroughly when we...'

Confident that she could safely tune out a further five minutes or so of Jemima's complaining, Nina pulled up another internet page and began to scroll through today's headlines. Then, for fun, she popped the name *Pierre Dupont* into Google. There were over forty-two million results.

But she persevered, adding his school, the year he'd have taken his exams, the town in which he'd lived as a child, each time the numbers dropping. Once she had all the information she knew in the search, there were still thousands of results, but she clicked on images just for fun. Just to see if she could recognise the seventeen-year-old boy in any of the pictures of fully grown men that appeared on her screen.

Jemima was just waffling on about the need for everyone who spent time in the office to contribute to the teabag fund when Nina gasped. Because, four rows down, she'd suddenly found herself looking into the eyes of what she was sure was a middle-aged version of her teenage crush. Despite the shorter hair, stubble, suit and tie, she could see the younger man shining out of him. What were the chances? Was it fate? she wondered briefly before realising she'd literally narrowed the search down and scrolled through hundreds of results to find him.

More written in the stalker's handbook than written in the stars.

Well, he had certainly kept his looks, she thought. And it was hard not to compare this rather gorgeous specimen with the one she'd just divorced. It wasn't fair, of course – but looking at the prize she could have won if she'd just taken more of a risk, she couldn't help but wonder whether ghosting Pierre had been the worst mistake of her life.

She clicked on the picture and was taken through to the site of a chain of patisseries, of which Pierre was the manager/owner. So... rich too, she thought. And with a limitless supply of pastries. It put Rory, with his steady but modestly paid job and his dislike of desserts, to shame.

'...which will be moved to the last working day of every month, as opposed to the last Thursday of every month,' droned Jemima.

Nina found a couple of bios of Pierre's through another link, but nothing referred to any sort of love or family life. All strictly business. Did this mean he was single? Available? Or just private?

Then she laughed inwardly and closed the page. What was she suggesting? That she'd track down a crush twenty-three years too late and see if he was still interested? Even Tinder seemed a more viable and less desperate solution to her love-life woes.

She settled to listen to the rest of the unnecessary meeting before closing the laptop and making her way back upstairs. Once there, she tucked the shoebox into the spare room wardrobe and closed the door.

Noticing, when she did, Pierre's letter still on the bed, she slipped it into a beside drawer out of sight, turned out the light and returned to her kitchen office.

8

'So,' said Bess in a rather too-loud voice, head between her legs and gazing at Nina from an unflattering angle at their weekly yoga class that evening. 'You've actually tracked down the one who got away?'

'Shh,' someone at the front of the class hissed.

'And now, descend into child's pose, then stretch forward, turn your toes and bring yourself into downward dog,' the teacher continued in her soft, hypnotic tones.

'Yes,' croaked Nina as softly as possible, feeling her thighs roar with protest at the stretch. 'He still lives in Cagnes-sur-Mer, as far as I can tell. Or nearby.'

'Near Nice?'

'Yeah, you know, same place we went to on French exchange.'

Bess had been a witness to Nina's first crush, but at the time had been too concerned with her own pen pal and all the fun she was having to realise what an impact Pierre had had on her friend – plus she'd been none-too-happy that Nina had dropped her in his favour during the week they'd spent in France. But now, happily married and old enough to be nostalgic about past misdemeanours, she grinned – her face red in her upside-down position.

'So he hasn't moved far from home then?'

'And step or jump forward into forward-fold.'

With a grunt, Nina managed to bring her reluctant legs forward and, doubled-over, looked at her friend. 'Seems not,' she said, hoarsely.

'That's amazing,' said Bess. 'God, I hope nobody from that era is stalking me on the internet!'

'And slowly, carefully roll yourself up into standing...'

'Bess, it is *not* stalking. I was just curious. I mean, he meant something to me back then.'

'Arms over your heads and down into prayer pose...'

'Nina,' said Bess out of the corner of her mouth. 'Robbie Williams meant something to you back then.'

'Well yes, but...'

'Plus, you were fantasy-cheating on him with Brad Pitt,' she said, raising an eyebrow.

'Shh!' this time a woman to their left frowned at them.

'Sorry,' Bess whispered, then turned back to Nina with an unrepentant grin. 'I'm not saying it wasn't cute. Apart from the fact it meant I was on my tod for half of the trips out.'

'You were not! You and your pen pal were tight as anything! It was me who was practically left to her own devices,' she countered.

'Oh, I forgive you. I think twenty years plus is time to put these things aside, don't you?' Bess said.

'Sounds about right.' She grinned.

'And up again into downward dog, making sure you keep your back flat, stretch out those hamstrings...'

'I couldn't help thinking, looking at him, you know. What if?' Nina said. 'I mean, you were telling me,' she jumped forward as instructed into forward fold, 'you were saying I never take risks, that I don't believe in fate. But this could have been my fate, Bess! What if I'd been braver, taken a chance back then? I could be happily married. Be living on the French Riviera, for God's sake. Maybe even have a kid or two.'

Bess shook her head – quite a feat from her upside-down position. 'Don't be daft,' she said. 'That's not the sort of risk we meant. You had a good thing with Rory. People split up. It doesn't mean the whole of your marriage was a mistake.'

Nina felt the blood rush to her head as she stood up too fast. She stumbled slightly before regaining her composure and putting her hands together, as instructed. 'But what if it was doomed from the start?' she whispered. 'What if the fact that I was still carrying a torch for – maybe was even in love with – another man, meant that Rory and I never stood a chance?'

'Oh Nina. You weren't in love. Lust, maybe. Come on, you barely knew the bloke really,' said Bess. 'It was just a week, a shag behind a disco. A few letters... It's natural to wonder, of course. But seriously. You'd have gone over, had a brief fling, realised you were too young, or incompatible, or that it was just about sex or whatever, and come back.'

'Maybe.'

'The risk thing – the things we said. It was more about now. More about trying to help you – encourage you – to open yourself up. About what you do next, not what you didn't do twenty-three years ago. I mean, I know we're forty, but come on, I still feel young,' Bess said, groaning as they were once again asked to move into downward dog. 'Relatively young,' she added in a more choked voice, her head once again upside down.

Nina laughed as she turned her face towards her friend. 'Speak for yourself,' she said quietly. 'I think my days of being bendy and fit might be seriously limited.'

They gratefully retreated into child's pose, kneeling down, their arms tucked around, heads on the mat.

'It wasn't really what you said,' Nina explained. 'That's what started me thinking, maybe. But I suppose it was me. I started to think of all the times I've turned my back on adventure.'

Bess nodded, her head wobbling on the mat. 'I get that,' she said. 'We all feel like that sometimes, no matter how good things are in real life. It's normal. But you have to look forward. I'll—'

'Yes, but the more I thought about it. The more I read his letters,' said Nina. 'The more I remembered how he made me feel. The more I wondered whether not going to him when I could have might have been the mistake that sort of set my life on this course.'

'Oh Nina...'

'I know it sounds crazy. I get it. But looking at how he is now – oh God, Bess, he still has those eyes... I could imagine myself being with him. What if I let my chance of happiness go? What if we're soulmates?'

'You don't believe in soulmates,' said Bess, clambering up and swinging her legs forward before lying down for the relaxation part of the session.

'Well, what if that was a mistake too?' Nina said. 'What if there are soulmates fated to be together and Pierre is mine, and I've turned my back on him all these years? I mean, finding his picture so... well, relatively easily online. Finding so much about his life now. Surely it has to mean something.'

'It means,' hissed Bess out of the corner of her mouth, eyes now closed, 'that you were very bored in that work meeting and spent an inordinate amount of time sifting through Pierres to find your one true love.'

'Not that much time.'

'Nina,' Bess opened one eye, its eyebrow arched. 'Seriously, don't beat yourself up about it. It was a long time ago. And maybe you would have been happy. Who knows? But I reckon there are some brilliant things in your future. Really, I do.'

'You could be right,' Nina said, turning her head towards her friend's as the teacher walked around the room asking them to imagine floating above their bodies, feeling weightless. She noticed the woman in front glare at her and made an apologetic grimace. But somehow she couldn't let this go, couldn't wait until after the class. 'Because I'm going to go and find him.'

Bess's eyes snapped open. 'What the actual *fuck?*' she said, loudly enough for all the heads to turn towards them. 'Sorry,' she said holding up her palms. Everyone seemed to be glowering at them both. 'It's just that she...' She looked at Nina, who was shaking her head. 'Sorry. Look, we'll go, we'll go.' She stood up and grabbed her water bottle. 'Coming?'

Her face on fire, Nina followed her friend, still feeling the eyes of the room – judging and annoyed – on them both. Outside, they descended into the type of giggles they'd used to have when they'd got in trouble with a teacher at school. 'Oh God,' Bess said. 'We're going to have to find a new class, aren't we?'

'*You* are,' said Nina. 'I might have talked a bit, but at least I didn't yell out the f-word during meditation.' She smiled and linked her arm through her friend's. 'Come on, let's go and get coffee or something.'

They left the gym and exited onto the cold street, each pulling her hoody more closely as the air hit them. 'Christ, I should have brought a coat,' Bess said.

'Do you want mine? It's in my bag. I'm still quite warm.'

'No let's just get inside,' said Bess, diving into their familiar coffee shop. It was just after lunch and the place was filled with the debris of the meal before, and the chatter of customers. It was a relief to be able to talk properly at last. 'You didn't mean it, right?' she said, when they were queueing to order their post-yoga lattes.

'Why not?' Nina said. 'I've got the money, I can get some time off work, I reckon. Why not have a trip to France?'

'Yes, that bit sounds relatively... sane,' her friend said. 'But tracking down your French exchange crush? Seriously? That is the stuff of madness.'

'Or great, classic love stories.'

'What?'

'Well, you know. Estranged lovers reunited after years... second-chance romance. Listening to fate at last. All of that.'

'You know you sound completely insane, right?'

'Yes,' said Nina. 'I do! But don't you think it's about time?'

'What? About time you went insane?'

'About time,' Nina said, leaning on the counter as the man in front of them in the queue was served, 'I did something crazy for love.'

'Oh Nina. Don't you think you ought to... Two lattes please, and a chocolate muffin,' said Bess as the server looked at her expectantly. 'I think it's great you want to have an adventure. But why pick the past? Why not look to the future? Go on holiday, have a great time. France, even, if you want. But tracking down this poor, middle-aged and probably balding...'

'Actually, he has a fine head of hair. And it wouldn't matter if he didn't!' said Nina, loyally.

'...OK, glossy haired, probably married or messed up, or gay or... a thousand other things. This poor, unsuspecting bloke! Face it, you're adorable, but you're probably going to be rejected. It's been so long and it's kind of... well, odd. And then how are you going to feel?'

'Well, stupid,' said Nina, taking the tray and walking to the nearest table. 'But I've realised, there are worse things than feeling stupid. I shouldn't be so afraid of it. I mean, I told you about the dance class, right?'

'Trying out a dance class and trying on a whole new life are completely different things, hon,' said Bess softly, taking a sip of her latte.

'Maybe.'

'I just don't want you to get hurt.'

'I won't. Or if I do... at least I'll know. At least I won't have to wonder any more.' Nina said, pulling a chunk off the muffin with her fingers.

'You're seriously serious?' Bess plucked a chocolate chip out of the muffin as it began to crumble.

'I'm seriously serious. No more regrets. No more roads untravelled. I'm going to France, I'm going to find Pierre and I'm just going to see.'

'What walk up to him and say, "Sorry I'm twenty-three years late"?'

'Maybe not. Maybe just see if we can bump into each other naturally?'

'And by naturally, you mean by design?'

'Well, obviously. But he doesn't need to know that!'

Bess shook her head. 'Nina,' she said. 'I mean, hats off to you for the risk taking. But...'

'I know. It's crazy. But I sort of... what with all the divorce and my crappy job and not really knowing what I want to do with the rest of my life. I just... it feels like it's the perfect time. A now-or-never moment.'

'You're really serious?' said Bess, her face furrowing with new concern.

'I really, really am.' She smiled. 'Oh look, I realise it's probably going to be a complete dead end. I just... I have this urge to do something, you know? And besides, I'm curious. What's the worst that can happen?'

'Do you seriously want me to answer that?' Bess said, arching an eyebrow.

Nina grinned. 'Oh, I know. But put it this way: I'm going to have a fabulous holiday. I'm going to try all the French things I've missed. I'm going to have a break from my life and work out what I want. Pierre, if it works out, would just be – well, the icing on the cake. But the cake's pretty good on its own too... And if fate does exist, I'm just giving it a helping hand.'

'Ah, now that makes more sense. A girls' holiday I can really get on board with!' Bess said. 'Do you want me to come with? I can probably... I reckon I can get a week off in a month or so's time.'

Nina shook her head. 'Not because I don't love you,' she said. 'I just... it feels like something I should do alone. Because, well. I'm single now. Maybe I've got to get a bit more used to my own company.'

'Oh Nina.'

'No, it's good. It's fine. I haven't been alone for years. And I think I've been afraid of it. But maybe it's time I faced up to it. Maybe even enjoyed it.'

Bess raised her latte to her lips. 'Well, as long as you're realistic. Or realistic-ish about the Pierre thing.'

'You know me!'

'And as long as you call me every single night and whenever you have a crisis or whatever.'

'You know I will.'

'Then, my crazy, lovelorn and seriously risk-taking friend, I suppose I have to give you my blessing.'

'Thank you,' Nina smiled. 'I'll be OK, you know. It's the adventure, the experience I'm after. The thing with Pierre... I just want to see. Close the chapter properly.'

Bess nodded. 'Well, you're a brave woman,' she said, lifting her latte and clinking it with Nina's. 'But I salute you. To bravery!'

'To love,' Nina said clinking back.

'Yes. Let's raise a toast to love.'

9

THEN

The coach was practically new and had air conditioning – a league above the usual standard of school bus they were accustomed to. The whole year group from the Lycée were coming in addition to the exchange pupils. Bess had already told her she'd noticed some seriously buff boys in the other coach, and spent most of the journey tending to her fringe in a tiny mirror to make sure it was 'just so.'

Nina wasn't especially interested in boys. Her experiences so far hadn't made her feel particularly disposed to seeking out romance. A random snog at a fairground with a boy from Year 12, a date to the cinema to watch a movie that had given her nightmares for weeks, a couple of trips to Pizza Express. So far almost completely cons and not a pro in sight. But she smiled along and tried to catch Bess's enthusiasm nonetheless. 'Give us that,' she said, taking the mirror and pouting into it. 'Ooh, I'm Bess, I'm *soo* beautiful!' she said.

'Hey!' Bess objected, wrenching it back. Then they both dissolved into giggles.

10

NOW

QUITTING JOB

Pros:
Get away from depressing office
Find something I enjoy doing!
Go to France and find Pierre!
I can take a year off, if I use my 'savings'

Cons:
What if nobody employs me EVER again?
What if I don't find anything I want to do?
Pierre is probably off the market or will think I'm mad.
Have to face the wrath of Jemima

The next morning, she felt a little less brave. A little less like throwing caution to the wind.

She'd written her resignation letter, then redrafted it and printed it out four times before feeling it fully expressed what she wanted to say. That she appreciated her time at the firm and the opportunities they'd given her (and the money, she didn't add), but that it was time for something new. Still, when she knocked on Jemima's office door the following morning, she was a bundle of nerves.

Hopefully, she could hand the letter to her boss, leave her office, wait a bit and then go back in for a chat, once Jemima had ingested all her words, all her reasoning. It wasn't as if she was a big financial player in the firm, or irreplaceable. Just an office manager, keeping the admin flowing, managing a few staff issues, holiday leave, that kind of thing. Something a virtual PA could probably do – saving the company a fortune in the process. In many ways, she told herself, she was doing them all a favour.

'Come in,' said the lofty voice and Nina pushed open the door and walked into the small, glass-fronted space with its ultra-clean desk and small, white monitor. Jemima looked up, her skin high-lighted by the light from her screen. A flicker of annoyance seemed to pass across her face before she broke into an artificial-looking smile. 'Nina,' she said, in what some might describe as a warm tone, but which Nina – having been familiar with it over the years – knew was only skating on the surface of a sneer. 'What can I do for you?'

'I just wanted to give you this,' Nina said, holding out the white envelope for Jemima to take. Her boss didn't stretch out a receiving hand so instead, she put it on the white surface of her desk where it sat, menacingly, between them.

'You're leaving?' Jemima said, having not even touched the envelope.

At first, Nina was nonplussed – was Jemima psychic? – but she came to realise that – of course – nobody wrote letters within an office any more. There would be few other reasons she'd hand a white envelope to her boss. In fact, when she thought about it, all of this could have been put into an email, removing the need for face-to-face at all. Damn her old-fashioned, face-up-to-things method. So 1990s.

'Well, yes,' she said. 'It's all in the letter... I...'

'Take a seat,' said Jemima, still not making a move to touch the envelope.

'Well, OK,' she said, sliding into the white and chrome chair facing the desk. 'But if you read...'

'So, why are you leaving us?' Jemima said, fixing a cool, blue gaze in her direction. 'Because if you've had a better offer, I'm sure we could come up with some sort of deal.'

This was a surprise. She'd felt sure that Jemima would have grabbed her resignation letter with glee. Been unable to disguise her delight.

'Oh, no. It's not... I'm just going to. I'm sort of having a bit of time out. To travel,' she said. 'So I'm not going anywhere else.'

'Oh?' Jemima's lip curled.

'Yes,' Nina said, trying to smile.

'Do excuse me,' her boss said, leaning forward slightly. 'But could you not simply take a bit of annual leave? You still have three weeks...'

Nina shook her head. 'It's more than that,' she said. 'I'm looking to... well, change things a bit. My life, I suppose. You know. Make a new start.'

'You're moving?'

'No, just going away for a bit.'

'What? Safari? Thailand? A retreat?'

'Well, just to France. For starters, that is,' Nina added hastily.

Jemima leaned back, her hands now clasped together across her torso like a villain in a movie, or a doctor, delivering bad news. 'It's just that it's not the most convenient of times. You do realise this?'

'Um...' Nina struggled to think how to respond to this. Was she meant to take this sort of thing into account when making large life decisions? The effect on 'the firm'? It wasn't as if she was a brain surgeon or a teacher or someone who would be actually missed.

'Yes. I mean, I realise your contract only obligates you to give a week's notice – it's something I need to review, on reflection – but it'll take us at least a month to recruit someone new. Then there's the training... and we'd need to really familiarise any replacement with our systems. In effect, we'd need you in role, overseeing any replacement.'

'Well, yes but...' Nina wanted to say, *How is this* my *problem?* but stopped herself.

Jemima was silent for a moment. A moment in which Nina could feel her heart thundering. Why was she still made nervous by this woman? She'd literally just quit – all Jemima's power over her was redundant. She wanted to tell her boss to OPEN THE LETTER in which she'd spelled everything out.

'OK, here's where I'm at,' Jemima said, smiling a smile that didn't quite reach her eyes. 'You've worked here for what, fifteen years?'

'Yes.'

Jemima nodded as if this confirmed something specific. 'Perhaps we could have done more in that time to make you feel valued,' she said, as if this had only just occurred to her. 'Because you know, Nina, you are the backbone of this firm.'

'I am?'

'Well, one of several backbones.'

How many backbones could one entity have?

'Oh.'

'But,' Jemima said, leaning forward, a little lipstick on her bright white teeth, 'my main concern in this is for you, Nina.'

'For me?' Nina put a hand to her chest as if confirming this was who she was.

'Yes. Oh, I know we don't know each other that well, personally. But believe me, I understand what it's like to be a woman in business.' She nodded conspiratorially at Nina and tilted her head to one side. 'It's not easy, is it?'

'Well, no,' said Nina, although to be fair, she'd never really considered herself to be in business at all.

'And I understand that... well, we have to cope with a little more than our male counterparts at times,' Jemima continued, clearly getting into her flow. 'If you know what I mean.'

'Uh huh,' Nina said, nodding. Although she wasn't 100 per cent sure. Did she mean periods? Glass ceilings? Sexual harassment? Common or garden misogyny?

'And,' Jemima now leaned a little closer, her face now less than a metre from Nina's, 'I hope you don't mind me saying, woman to woman, that I think I know what's going on here.'

'You do?' Did Jemima somehow know about Pierre? Did she know about Nina's ridiculous plan? Had she been at the yoga class, eavesdropping during her savasana?

Jemima nodded, a sympathetic look on her face. 'Obviously I know about the divorce,' she said. 'But I was thinking more of your life stage. You,' she lowered her voice 'have passed a pretty big milestone recently, I believe?'

'You mean, I've turned forty?' Nina said, her voice with its normal volume sounding shout-loud in contrast.

'Yes,' said Jemima, clearly alarmed by Nina's not wanting to keep this information hush-hush. 'Yes. And we all know what comes next for women, don't we?'

'We do?'

Jemima nodded sadly. 'It can be a tumultuous time,' she said.

'It can?'

'Yes, hormonally. I don't mind telling you that I've had the odd… eh… hormonal incident myself.'

'Oh.' Nina was aching to know what that meant. A hot flash in a meeting? Shouting at a colleague? Making advances on the security guy?

'Yes. You'll be surprised, no doubt, to learn I'm actually approaching my mid-forties!' she announced.

Nina was quick to mould her features into an expression of shock. 'Well,' she lied. 'You don't look it!'

Jemima nodded sagely, 'Botox,' she whispered, as if trying to keep secret that she'd had a little work done despite the evidence being written all over her face.

'Wow,' Nina said, again feigning surprise.

Jemima forced her lips into a smile. 'Look, Nina. I'm going to level with you. I think that this need to travel, or whatever,' she waved her hand dismissively, 'might be some sort of crisis, or temporary need,' she said. 'I would hate for you to find that you were acting… impulsively.'

Nina sat up straighter. 'It's not at all!' she said. 'I really want to make a change… I…'

The hand waved again. 'What I'm saying is,' Jemima said, 'and you'll have to keep this on the down low because it's not something I can offer to others. But what if we could give you a month off? A little respite after your… hard year and your many years of loyal service. Two weeks paid, two weeks unpaid. You can go to France or wherever, get the experience out of your system and come back refreshed!' she said. She sat back triumphantly as if she'd made an offer no one in their right mind could refuse. 'It's a risk-free way of having your cake and eating it too. Although, when it comes to hormones, diet is important of course. So perhaps that isn't quite the right expression for ladies in our stage of life!' she grinned, delighted with herself.

'Oh,' said Nina. 'Thank you. Um...' She searched for the right words. 'That's incredibly generous of you, but I really think I need to make a proper break... I...'

'Nina, Nina,' Jemima said, now once again leaning forward and shaking her head sadly. 'I'm not sure you realise how *difficult* the job market is, especially for someone in... middle age. I just don't want to see you getting... well, out of your depth.'

'I don't think...'

'Wouldn't it be better to go with the knowledge that you have a financial safety net, a career safety net, to come back to? To have the security of income, the ability to pay your mortgage, to return to let's say "normal life" after your... your adventures?' Jemima, now in the role of 'helpful friend', suggested. She looked at Nina meaningfully.

'Well,' Nina said, then trailed off. Jasmine was being both sexist, insulting and borderline annoying. But maybe, despite this, she was making a sound point.

Yes, Nina had been determined to take risks.

But the idea of needing an emergency backup sent a cold shiver through her. Despite her patronising tone, was Jemima on to something? Perhaps it was unwise to throw everything away to go on this mad escapade. Wouldn't it be nice to know that things were waiting for her if she decided to take up the reins again on her return? She could always quit later – by email.

'Well?' Jemima prompted, sensing she had snared her prey.

'Well, well yes. I suppose that would be... a solution,' said Nina, carefully, already feeling a sense of disappointment in her chest.

This was meant to be her moment of severance. Of handing her letter in and walking away lighter, a clean break. Forcing herself out of her comfort zone. And what had she achieved instead? Two weeks' additional unpaid leave?

'Wonderful,' Jemima said, standing up abruptly and making

Nina feel obliged to do the same. She stuck out a hand for Nina to shake. 'I'll get legal to draft something. But looks like you've bagged yourself a pretty enviable rest!'

'Thank you.'

'No problem,' Jemima smiled graciously, having won the battle. 'And we'll see you fresh and bright and back in the office afterwards, ready to fully commit to the company once more.'

Nina nodded, unable to say anything.

Then she went back to her desk and sat there for a stunned moment. Was she really so weak? Was she so easily swayed? Or had she been sensible?

MONTH'S LEAVE

Pros:
Get to go to France for a month!
Can still hand notice in afterwards, if I want
Less stressful – job to come back to
Will be paid for at least half the holiday
Nothing wrong with being 'safe'

Cons:
Have to return to THE FIRM
Jemima may have an ulterior motive
I wanted to be IMPULSIVE, but this is PLAYING it SAFE

On paper, it seemed like the ideal solution.

Only deep inside, she felt a dragging sense of disappointment.

Her phone beeped in her bag and she lifted it out. It was Rory. His message read:

We've had an offer on the house!

She sent him a thumbs up – which she knew he would find annoying. It looked like, whatever she wanted, things were going to change significantly.

She sighed and booted her computer into life. She could think about the Jemima stuff later. Maybe email her from France and renege on the deal. For now, she'd at least bought the time she needed to make a start.

She typed in, *month-long let in Cagnes-sur-Mer* and began to scroll through the various sites. She'd get something booked as soon as possible before her sensible chip disrupted any more of her plans.

11

It took two days to thrash out the details on the house sale with Rory and their buyers. They had accepted the offer, which was for the full asking price. But Nina had pushed for a provisional moving date no sooner than in two months' time ('but surely we don't want them to change their minds!' Rory had protested. She'd pointed out that he already had somewhere else to live, and said she wanted the stability of knowing where she'd be living in next two months' time – conveniently failing to mention her parents had said she could stay as long as she wanted).

She had an ulterior motive for wanting to push the move date back as far as possible, although she hadn't shared that with Rory. The last two evenings had been spent online searching for accommodation in France and she'd found the perfect place. Only it wasn't a rental as much as the opportunity for a house swap – a guy right in the centre of Cagnes-sur-Mer had listed his home on a holiday swap site and it looked adorable. His write-up explained that he wanted to improve his English and was particularly interested in exploring places with a rich history. With the Roman ruins practically a stone's throw from her house, it couldn't be more perfect.

She'd quickly emailed him, explaining her circumstances (at least, some of them) and that she wanted to travel as soon as possible and had been thrilled to receive an almost immediate response. He owned his own garage and said he could leave his staff in charge and come whenever she wanted. He seemed almost too excited at the prospect of spending a month in a three-bed terrace in St Albans, and she hoped her photos of the house hadn't proven too well angled, that he hadn't got the impression she lived in a modern, well-finished property rather than the slightly shabby-interior-that-could-do-with-a-lick-of-paint Victorian cottage she'd shared with her errant husband for a decade.

Still, she hadn't lied. And there were probably a few cobwebs and scruffy corners in his house too, she reasoned. It was the location that was important in this instance, for both of them. He'd confided that although his day job was as a mechanic, his real passion was history; he'd enrolled in a degree course online. Staying in St Albans with its Roman history and its proximity to London would be ideal.

She and Rory had thought about going on a site like this before to nab a cheap holiday, but it had always felt a little too personal – letting a stranger stay in your home when you weren't there. What if they went through your knicker drawer, or logged in to your PC and discovered all your dark secrets? (Even though the darkest secret they'd shared was the amount of diet coke they ordered weekly from Tesco, against their better judgement)

But now, with Rory's stuff gone, the house had started to feel more generic, less personal. And it didn't seem to matter any more whether she kept her privacy. She would get her boxing up done early, would lock various things in her closet, including her underwear, more from embarrassment at the ragged state of it than anything else, and she was taking the shoebox with her. Anything else, her guest was welcome to.

She emailed Jemima to check that it was OK to schedule her trip in for next week and having received a reluctant *of course* (how Jemima managed to get her emails to be so passive-aggressive, she'd never know), Nina went on and confirmed everything with her soon-to-be host. Then, once she'd completed her set hours, she picked up the phone, thought better of it, and instead hopped in her car to head around Bess's.

Bess answered the door in a dressing gown, her hair in disarray.

'God, is everything alright?' Nina asked, wondering if she should have called ahead.

'Do I look that bad?' her friend replied. 'Nah, I'm on night shift is all. Just got up.'

Nina looked at her watch. It was 7 p.m. 'Oh, do you have time for...?'

'Always. Not in till ten and like to make sure I'm fully caffeinated. There's plenty of coffee in the pot. Plus, Sal's here already putting the world to rights.'

'Where are the kids?'

As if in answer to the question, there was a thunder of footsteps on the stairs and two eleven-year-old boys burst into view. They stopped when they saw Nina, then raced forward and gave her a hug that almost knocked her off her feet. 'Hello Auntie Nina!' said Thomas, the more outgoing of the pair. 'Dad took us to McDonald's for tea!'

'Well! Aren't you lucky!' she said, tousling his hair.

'And he got us McFlurries!' added James, grinning up at her.

'Well, I'm jealous!' Nina said, smiling.

'Come on you two, let Auntie Nina come and have a coffee,' said Bess affectionately. 'And weren't you meant to be doing homework soon?'

Laughing, the pair raced back up the stairs. 'Can't HEAR you!' Thomas said cheekily over his shoulder. A door slammed and silence reigned once more.

'Sorry about that,' Bess said. 'Death by cuddles.'

'Don't be silly,' Nina smiled. She always loved the way the boys greeted her when she popped in. It felt a bit like being a celebrity, only with very sticky fans.

'Anyway, come through,' Bess said, turning towards the kitchen.

'Nice of Steve to take the boys out,' Nina said.

'Was it?' Bess arched an eyebrow. 'Or is he earning all the brownie points from the kids, who don't actually appreciate the vegetables I spend ages peeling for all their other meals on a daily basis? Easy win if you ask me.' But she was smiling.

'Good point. Although they do have veggies at McDonald's now, so I'm told. Where is Steve anyway?'

'He's having a relaxing bath to "recover",' Bess said, grinning. 'He says it was exhausting, but I'm willing to bet he's just overindulged on Big Macs and wants a bit of space to himself.'

Smiling, Nina followed Bess into the kitchen where Sal was sitting sipping from a mug with a picture of a Teletubby on it. 'Hi,' she said, leaning down to give her friend a kiss on the cheek.

'Hi yourself.' Sal grinned.

Nina slid out a chair and sat down as Bess poured her a coffee into an enormous mug emblazoned with the words *World's Best Dad*. She then swept a few magazines from the cluttered kitchen table, plonked the mug down in front of Nina and indicated the milk and sugar, already present among the melange of crumb-covered plates, sticky jam knives and half-drunk glasses of milk and orange juice.

'Help yourself to any delicious delicacies that catch your eye,' Bess joked. 'I know you're partial to a bit of stale bread crust and jam. It's Steve's turn to clear up breakfast and I'm holding out for a miracle.'

'Thanks,' Nina said, adding a large slug of milk to the very strong concoction she'd been given. 'I think I'll resist!' She took a sip and grimaced. Unlike Bess, she was heading for bed in a few hours, so she should probably go easy on the pick-me-ups.

'So, what's up?' Bess said, picking up a piece of half-eaten toast and biting into the corner. 'Everything OK?'

'Why does something have to be up?' Nina said. 'Can't a woman just drop in on her bestie in the evening without causing suspicion?'

'A woman can. Sal can. You can't. You're a bona-fide planner, my dear. Three weeks' notice is your average, if my maths is correct.'

Nina laughed. 'Well, maybe this is the new, risk-taking version of me. Spontaneous, rash?' she suggested.

Bess looked at her pointedly. 'Nina...' she coaxed. 'Unless you're here to tell us that you do, indeed, have a spontaneous rash (which I sincerely hope you don't) then you have to let me know what's up.'

'Yes, come on!' Sal said. 'I need some gossip to distract me after another nightmare day at work.'

Nina laughed. Sal worked as a teaching assistant – a job she adored, but found exhausting at times. 'A nightmare? What happened?' she asked.

'One of the other assistants was absent, so instead of being in English classes, I was moved to maths.'

The other two made appropriate faces. Sal's aversion to maths was legendary.

'Anyway, I spent most of the day trying to explain long division and fractions and bloody isosceles triangles – I needed about a pint of coffee just to keep going!'

'Come on, you love it though,' Nina joked.

'I love the job. Not so keen on the maths. Anyway, don't let my impending caffeine overdose distract Nina from spilling the beans. Come on, let's have it!'

'Alright,' Nina said, flushing. 'I do have something on my mind.'

'Rory? House woes?' Bess suggested.

'Surprisingly not,' Nina said. '*Surprisingly*, I have a good thing on my mind.'

Bess took another enormous bite. 'Now I *am* intrigued,' she said, spraying a few crumbs onto the table. 'God, sorry,' she said, wiping them with her sleeve. 'Can't take me anywhere.'

Sal laughed, pretending to wipe a crumb from her face. 'Can't beat a bit of toast-crumb exfoliation.'

They all laughed, then the two of them looked at Nina expectantly.

'I've taken the plunge,' she announced. 'I'm off to France next week!'

'What? I thought that it was just...'

'Just what?' Nina asked.

'Just... well, a Nina thing,' Bess said.

'A Nina thing?'

'Yes. We thought it wouldn't stand up to the scrutiny of one of your lists!' Sal added, grinning.

Nina felt herself get hot. She didn't want to mention that she had actually made a list. After all this was meant to be a New Her. 'But...' she said.

'Yes?'

'This isn't about lists.'

'Bloody hell.' Bess feigned chest pain and looked at her, eyes wide. 'Are you sure you don't want me to take your temperature?'

Nina smiled stiffly. 'Come on,' she said. 'I'm not that bad.'

Sal put a hand on her arm. 'We're only kidding,' she said. 'Anyway, it's good to be careful, sensible.' She smiled, her blonde hair almost golden in the cosy kitchen light.

'Thank you,' Nina said. 'But anyway, it's not about lists. It's about living. I'm off to France. For a month, maybe more.' She explained the situation to them, the resignation that wasn't a resignation ('cheeky bitch!'), the month off ('well that sounds good') and finally the fact that she was swapping houses with someone called Jean-Luc whom she'd never met.

'Right,' Bess said, taking a thoughtful sip.

'So, what do you think?' Nina asked.

'Does it matter what I think?' Bess said. 'Is that the risk-taking Nina talking, or the sensible one worrying?'

'Bit of both probably.'

'And you're OK with letting some stranger live in your house?' Sal said, surprised. 'Do you know anything about him?'

'For starters, it's not my house for much longer so it doesn't really matter,' replied Nina. 'And Jean-Luc, well, he sounds really nice. I've checked him out, as much as I can. He has great feedback on the site. He's a mechanic, but wants to study history – hence wanting to explore St Albans and London. He sounds really interesting, actually.'

'History?' Sal said, her interest piqued.

'Yes, particularly the Romans, apparently. So he's very excited about coming here.'

'Maybe you should stay here?' Bess suggested. 'Sounds like he could be quite a catch.'

Nina gave her a look. 'There's only one French man I'm interested in,' she said, grinning. 'You know that.'

'Aw chick,' Bess touched her hand on Nina's briefly. 'I think it sounds like it could be a lot of fun. But I'm worried you might get your hopes up too much about Pierre.'

'You mean the potential love of my life? The man the stars are suggesting I'm meant to marry and have hundreds of babies with, so long as my biological clock hasn't gone into a downward spiral?' joked Nina. 'Yes, I know. I mean, I realise the whole thing sounds barking mad. And it sort of is. But it'll be the chance for a break, a holiday. To immerse myself in French culture. And yes, I am going to try to meet him to see if there's any... well, spark. If he's single. If maybe there is something out there organising our fate.'

Bess smiled, 'But you know that—'

'Wait, hang on,' Nina said. 'I'm not completely deluded. It's not all about Pierre. It's more about... me. I suppose it's my way of saying this is a new chapter in my life. A chapter in which I have adventures. And if love comes into it, all the better.' She smiled, triumphant at her own rehearsed speech. She didn't mention the daydream she'd had earlier in which Pierre whisked her up into his arms, cue romantic music, curtain falls, happy ever after. Because however crazy it seemed, she was allowed to dream.

Bess was silent for a moment. 'OK,' she said. 'Well that sounds like fun. I wish. I mean, you know I'd have come with you – for some of it, at least.'

'I know. I just feel as if I need to seize the day. Before I get bogged down in house moves and work and I don't know, meet some average guy at a work do, and make another sensible choice,' said Nina.

'You could always join Tinder?' Sal suggested.

'Hang on, you said when you tried it last time, the only matches you seemed to get were balding, elderly men wanting one-night stands!'

Sal shrugged, grinning. 'Well, trust me. After a few years of being single, you take what you can get.'

'Think I'll take my chances in France, if it's OK with you?' Nina said, smiling.

'Fine. But if you do meet up with the gorgeous Pierre, ask him if he's got a friend?'

'It's a deal!'

'Anyway, for what it's worth...' Bess said, scraping back her chair and taking another piece of bread from a sliced packet on the side then waving it at Nina and Sal. 'Want some?' Both shook their heads. 'For what it's worth,' Bess repeated, putting the bread into the toaster and pushing down the lever, 'it sounds quite... fun and, well...'

'And what.'

'Well, quite sensible – for the most part,' she finished. 'Although that's probably not what you want to hear. But, taking time out, with your work waiting for you. Who wouldn't want that? Getting away after everything you've been through. It's just what you need. As long as you aren't going to start rugby-tackling unsuspecting forty-year-old men and forcing them down the aisle, I think it sounds like an ideal trip.'

Nina laughed. 'Thank you. I'll try to restrain myself!'

'So you have my blessing,' Bess grinned.

'Or your Bess-ing?' Nina suggested. 'Sorry that was awful.'

Sal grinned. 'Don't worry, you've said worse. And for what it's worth, I think it sounds like fun.'

'Thank you.' Nina smiled. It felt better having told them – more real. She was really going to do this!

'Actually, I need to ask you a favour as well. Can you kind of look out for this guy, Jean-Luc when he's here? He'll need to collect a key off one of you, and I guess – although he seems great on paper – can you just check he's not too weird? Or, like, that he doesn't turn up with a thousand friends determined to wreck the place? I've told Rory a friend is staying, and he's not too happy about that. I don't think he'd agree at all if he knew he was actually a complete stranger.'

Sal looked at her. 'You're asking me if I'll keep an eye on your interesting, historically curious, possibly single, French house-guest for you?'

'Well, yes.'

'And you said he has a penchant for Romans?'

'Not a penchant exactly...'

Sal laughed, her eyes twinkling with mischief. 'Oh, that'll be no problem. Especially if he's hot!'

'Sal!' Nina laughed.

'Seriously though, you said he was interested in history?' Sal said. 'I could definitely give him a tour of the Roman theatre.'

'Don't worry. I'll keep an eye on Jean-Luc AND Sal,' Bess said, winking. 'I'll keep them both on a tight rein.'

'Spoil sport,' Sal quipped.

'And you think it's OK?' Nina said, suddenly doubtful. 'With the Rory thing, I mean? It's still his house too, after all.'

Bess snorted. 'Did Rory set any ground rules before he left? No, he did not. He relinquished his rights to say what goes on there when he moved into that flat. It's your house as far as I'm concerned and you should be able to do what you like.'

'Other than start a crack den.'

'Oh, crack dens are over. So 1990s. You'd make more money converting it into a meth lab,' Sal suggested.

Nina laughed. 'I'll bear that in mind.'

'We're always on hand for more sound financial advice, should you need it.' Bess said, popping up her toast and beginning to butter it.

They were quiet for a moment, the sound of a knife scraping over the rough surface the only noise in the room.

'Thank you, by the way,' Nina said.

'No worries. It's not like your house is a thousand miles away.'

'Plus, we haven't really done anything yet,' Sal said.

'No, not just for that. For everything, you know. You're good friends.'

'Right back at you,' Sal said, touching her hand gently.

Bess was silent for a moment. 'Don't be silly,' she said, but her voice sounded slightly choked.

'Well,' said Nina, 'you are. And I don't know what I'd do without you guys to prop me up.'

'Well, same,' said Bess, turning, her eyes slightly glistening.

'Are you OK?' Sal asked, looking at Bess with concern.

'Ignore me,' Bess said. 'It's just nice to hear somebody say that. The boys – I know they love me, and I know they appreciate everything I do, or they will one day – posthumously, knowing my luck – and I know Steve does too. It's just you get into this role and then... well, you work bloody hard. And it sometimes seems as if nobody notices you at all.' She roughly flicked a tear from her eye. 'And as you can see, night shifts wreak havoc on my emotions.'

She walked to the table and plonked herself down.

Sal stood up and wrapped an arm around her back. 'Well, we should say it more then,' she said. 'Because you're brilliant.'

'Seconded,' said Nina, reaching out a hand briefly. 'And you are appreciated. You really are. By all of them, I'm sure. And definitely by us.'

Bess nodded. 'Well, likewise,' she croaked. 'Now, can we talk about something else before I end up going to work looking like a puffy-faced old hag?'

Nina smiled. 'Of course,' she said. 'Enough sentimental claptrap. Let's talk about how I'm going to accost my crush of twenty-three years ago and convince him to take me back, despite the fact that I abandoned him over two decades ago.'

'Now that,' said Sal, 'sounds like a completely run-of-the-mill task.'

As they laughed and drank coffee, Nina felt a dip of misgiving in her stomach thinking of what she'd just said. They were her own words; it had been her own joke. But somehow, describing her forthcoming adventure in that way had put a dampener on her mood. Was she completely and utterly mad to be doing what she was doing? And would it all end in tears?

12

THEN

'You are Brigitte's pen pal, oui?' said a voice in her ear as she stood against the wall and tried to complete a worksheet on a clipboard that seemed determined to fly away in the light breeze.

'Yes,' she said, not looking up. 'I mean, oui.'

The boy laughed. 'It is OK, I understand the word "yes",' he said, in perfect English.

Blushing, Nina lifted her head to look at him. The first thing she noticed was his smile – his neat, even teeth, dimples, full lips. Then his hair – dark, shiny with frosted tips messily gelled.

'I'm Pierre,' he said.

'Nina,' she replied.

He took her hand for what she thought was going to be a small shake, but in fact, he put his lips to it and gave it a kiss. Her face felt hot. 'Enchanté,' he said before disappearing across the courtyard into a crowd of boys, with a teacher at its helm.

'You alright?' Bess said moments later, exiting the chateau's gift shop.

'Yeah,' she said. 'Yeah, I'm fine.'

She never did manage to complete the worksheet.

13

NOW

Dear Jean-Luc,

Welcome to my humble abode. I hope that you enjoy your time living in St Albans. My two friends, Sal and Bess (contact details attached), are on hand make sure you're OK. Or you can always drop me an email if you'd prefer.

I've left some takeaway leaflets on the kitchen counter and a map of the area, showing the Roman ruins and with a few nice restaurants marked. The cathedral is well worth a visit too – as is the gorgeous lake. Train timetable is there, but you can always check online for more up-to-date info. Usually, there's one to London about every half hour.

Many thanks for trusting me with your house in France!

Best wishes,

Nina

Nina checked the letter one more time. Then looked in her handbag and checked her passport, tickets, itinerary, phone, charger, adapter and all other journey essentials. This was the worst part of travelling for her – the moment when she had to trust that she'd got everything she needed and that she wasn't going to fall at the first hurdle. These were not the moves of a risk-taker, she realised, but a paranoid, infrequent traveller. Still, it was better to check one more time before the taxi came. The letters were in her suitcase with her clothes, but she slipped Pierre's necklace into her pocket – not wanting it to get lost en route.

The trip to the airport was half an hour long, and as she slid into the back of the taxi, she felt a sense of dread at the prospect of potentially having to make small talk about her travels with the driver. Usually, she didn't mind the benign queries about her destination and her plans – but usually, she'd be heading to a package holiday with her husband, with the sole intention of laying by a pool like most other normal people. This time, her plans were a little more left field.

It started almost immediately.

'Going somewhere nice?'

'Yes. France. Near to Nice.'

'Oh, lovely.' The driver signalled and turned out of her estate. 'On your own, or meeting friends?'

'Just me,' she replied.

'Ah,' he said admiringly, 'I'd love to do that one day – just head out somewhere on me own. Three kids though.' He indicated a slightly tattered picture of three little children sellotaped to his dashboard.

'Oh, lovely,' she said. 'I expect they keep you busy.'

He snorted. 'Just a bit,' he said affectionately. 'Ah, but it's worth it, right?'

She wanted to tell him that she wouldn't know, that she didn't – might never – have kids and that it was none of his business in any case. But he meant well; he just hadn't thought.

She allowed silence to descend around them and hoped this was the end of things. A braver person would be chatting away now, sharing snippets from their plans, enjoying the company. Or would be brave enough to say, *Do you mind if we don't talk?* or something equally fine and polite. But she wasn't brave. And had a strange fear of upsetting anyone at all, which meant she often had to enter into conversation even though it was the last thing she wanted to do.

Last night, she'd saved all the details she knew about Pierre into a document on her phone. It had looked quite impressive all in all, and she'd fancied herself as quite the young Miss Marple – albeit with the help of technology, plus a few lucky breaks when it came to Pierre's privacy settings. She knew where he worked – not in a patisserie, but in a managerial office for the chain, housed in a building not far from where she was staying. She knew what he looked like. She hadn't been able to discover where he lived, but seeing as his work was close to Cagnes-sur-Mer it was likely that he'd live nearby. There were no details of kids or a partner, and while that didn't rule them out, it made it less likely. Surely most proud parents would post a pic of their kids online, and there were usually wedding photos or pictures from days out to help work out a person's marital status?

She felt a shiver of excitement at the prospect of potentially finding him, as well as spending a whole month in France – taking in the scenery, dining in style, practising her language and simply getting away from the humdrum rhythm of her normal life. Yes, the Pierre part felt a little crazy. But what if this was the thing she was meant to do? What if somehow, she was kickstarting a whole happy chapter of her life? What if, just for once, things worked out, Pierre remembered her, still had some feelings for her? They reconnected and she ended up in the place she should have always been?

'You look happy, love,' the driver commented.

'What?'

'You're smiling. Still, can't say I blame you. Better weather over there, right?' He stopped to let a cyclist turn out of a driveway. 'Can't stand all this rain.'

She laughed. 'It's a bit better. Not hot, though. Not this time of year.'

'So why you going then?' he asked. 'Work stuff?'

'Oh no. Just... just a break,' she said.

'Meeting up with some friends out there?'

'Maybe an old friend,' she said, feeling herself get hot. *Why all the questions?* she wanted to ask. But she knew, really, he was just being polite, passing the time.

'Ah, got ya,' he said, tapping his nose as if she'd just revealed a huge secret. 'Say no more.'

She managed to deflect further interrogation by aiming her own carefully crafted questions at him (aha, how the tables turned!) so that by the time they arrived at Luton airport, he was probably quite ready to get away from her. He'd told her about his wife, kids, job, even a little about his childhood. He was probably exhausted. She tapped into the app once he'd driven off and gave him five stars for putting up with her.

Then, before she knew it, she was settling into her place on the plane, drinking weak tea and watching the sky outside turn from grey to white to a light, hopeful blue.

After what seemed like a lightning-fast flight, she exited and made her way across the tarmac to the terminal. Nice airport was busy, and it took a while to get her luggage, but once she located her wheeled suitcase, she made it through passport control in record time and was finally standing outside the glass-fronted building in the deliciously warm air. The outside area was large and neatly paved, with enormous palm trees, so sturdy and strong that she wondered whether they'd preceded the airport. It was twenty degrees – a good ten warmer than it had been in London –

and she'd already removed her cardigan and tied it around her waist. It wasn't the dramatic whoosh of heat she'd experienced before when travelling to sunnier climes, but the air felt fresh and warm, and she felt the kind of lift she often experienced when the first sun of spring grazed her arms.

Breathing deeply, she gave herself a moment to appreciate where she was, what she was doing. She thought of the others in her office, still beavering away. Of Rory, probably typing something boring on his laptop or giving yet another presentation. Of Bess, working away to deliver babies, and Sal in her teaching-assistant role. Everything from her ordinary life felt a million miles away.

She snapped back to attention when a small child rammed into her from behind and promptly fell over. 'I'm so sorry,' she said, as the mother leant over and picked the small boy up. Nina realised she'd been standing in front of the exit and had been so caught up in her own thoughts that people had had to stream around her.

Apologising again, she made her way to the pick-up point and managed to locate another taxi driver. Luckily, Cagnes-sur-Mer was only a twenty-minute drive from the airport and, luckily, this driver barely said a word. She settled into her seat, feeling quite nervous, and watched the city morph into motorway, then smaller roads as she approached her destination, remembering that seemingly endless coach ride twenty-three years ago, staring out of the window at the red-roofed houses dotted between greenery, their peach or white painted walls looking somehow more Spanish than French.

It was a weekday afternoon and people were strolling on the pavements in the centre, or sitting in cafés enjoying the last of the welcome sun. Everyone looked relaxed and cheerful; most were well dressed in light-coloured clothes – a world away from St Albans where even now, people were beginning to dig out their winter scarves and hats. She scrutinised the faces, trying to see some resemblance to some of the teenagers she'd met long ago – perhaps Brigitte or even Pierre. Although she realised this was bordering on ridiculous, it was hard not to be on the lookout.

Seeing some of the younger women, clustering in giggling groups or walking with shopping bags, she couldn't help but wonder how she'd look in comparison. She was forty, but – and she might be kidding herself – she didn't feel she looked anything like forty years old. People liked to believe that ages became 'younger' over the years – always saying sixty was the new forty, forty was the new thirty – all sorts of strange and wonderful maths, and she'd always thought they were just trying to make themselves feel better.

Could she pass for younger? And, if so, were her insides also erring on the side of youthful? Could she still possibly have a baby one day? She'd read articles in which women in their fifties had given birth, so surely she wasn't completely out of time if that turned out to be something she wanted to do.

Rory had never wanted children. But that had seemed OK all those years ago when they'd had the talk. She hadn't been sure about them herself at that point – and everyone she'd spoken to had been so confident that they'd both change their tune in future years. Besides, kids had seemed like a hurdle they'd have to clear in the future – and time had seemed to stretch on almost endlessly when they were in their late twenties.

But now here she was, in the back of a taxi, divorced and in her fifth decade, searching for a romance that had escaped her twenty-three years before – and it felt as if those years had passed lightning-fast.

She shook her head. This wasn't helping anyone. Instead, she began to study the houses as they moved closer to the one owned by Jean-Luc. She'd seen so many pictures of it, she felt she'd know it anywhere: a gorgeous, neat, whitewashed building set in lush vegetation, with a first-floor balcony and terracotta roof. There was a pool, too, built above-ground in wood, and a decked area for summer barbecues. Probably only for the brave at this time of year, though.

'Voila,' said the driver suddenly, pulling up next to a white-washed wall, topped with a little red 'roof' of tiles. Wisteria climbed over from inside the garden – some of it in bloom still from the tail end of summer. There was an audible buzz from the insect life, as if by travelling the 600 miles between St Albans and Nice, she'd also wound back the clock: time-travelled to a season that wasn't yet completely over, which still had life, warmth and the ghost of summer in the air.

'This is it?' she said.

'Yes,' he replied, stepping out of the taxi to retrieve her case.

And suddenly, she was alone, looking up at the neat, beautiful building, suitcase on wheels at her feet, feeling warm and excited and terrified and stupid and wonderful all at once.

14

'You are Nina?' said a voice.

A young man with light-brown hair, wearing a checked, short-sleeved shirt with shorts and trainers, appeared at her side, a few moments after she'd called the number Jean-Luc had given her.

'Antoine?' she said.

'Yes, that's me,' he said in rapid French, brandishing a key on a red ribbon. 'Jean-Luc, my brother, said I should give you the key and check if you have any questions.'

'Thank you,' she said, only catching every second word with her rusty A-level French, but getting the gist.

He smiled, his brown eyes shining, as he handed her the key and said something else she didn't quite catch.

'I'm sorry, could you speak a little slower, *monsieur*?' she asked.

'Ah, of course,' he said. 'I can speak English, too, if you like?'

'No, I'd like to practice,' she said, thinking about the sweet nothings she could whisper with Pierre in the language of love should her plan come to fruition.

He nodded, leaning past her and unlocking the door. He smelled of the outdoors: fresh, and clean with a hint of woods and the sea. Having turned the key and gently pushed the door open, he stepped back and gestured for her to go through.

The interior was beautiful – wooden beams ran the length of the ceiling, and the floors were polished parquet. There was a small living area with two cream-coloured sofas propped at angles, a wood-burner in the corner, bookshelves and a tiny TV. The other half of the room was given over to a worn, oak table with a bench either side, a few decorative ceramic balls in a gold-coloured dish at its centre.

'The kitchen is to the right,' said Antoine, indicating with his hand. 'And you will find three rooms upstairs. The biggest bedroom is Jean-Luc's, which he says you must use. There is a smaller room and an office – but I think you are here for pleasure, not work?'

'Definitely pleasure,' she said, smiling. Then blushing when he fixed his blue eyes on her. 'A holiday,' she added hastily.

He nodded, a small smile on his lips. 'Well, call me if you need any help with the house, or advice about the village,' he said. 'You have come here before?'

'Yes, but not for...' Nina looked at Antoine's face. He didn't look any older than thirty-five and she was embarrassed suddenly by the twenty-three years she had been about to say, and its implication about her age. 'Gosh, it must be more than fifteen years,' she said, thinking of how Bess would snort when she heard this. 'I was seventeen,' she added.

He nodded. 'Well, perhaps not so much has changed,' he smiled. 'I have lived here just three years, since I start work at Jean-Luc's garage, so I don't remember those times. But it is a nice place.' He shrugged. 'And I think you will find there is plenty to entertain you, even in this cold weather.'

'Cold weather? I came from England, remember,' she quipped. 'This is like a summer's day for me!'

He laughed. 'Then do not forget your sun cream,' he said. 'You do not want to get burnt.'

She was smiling when she closed the door a few moments later. Antoine had refused her offer of a drink, which was probably a good thing as she hadn't made it as far as the supermarket yet, but left with a cheery '*au revoir*' and a repetition of his request that she contact him should the need arise.

Once he was gone, she checked out the rest of the property, running up the stairs to peek in the spare room, the office, and Jean-Luc's room, which was enormous, with a huge, king-size bed decked out with fresh, clean linen. She stopped a moment to wonder what someone with such a beautiful, perfect living space had made of her Victorian terrace but decided to put the thoughts to the back of her mind. He would simply think it was 'quirky' and 'olde worlde' rather than in need of a lick of paint. Probably.

Instead, once she'd managed to locate the coffee and make herself a steaming mugful, she opened her laptop on the oak table and signed into Jean-Luc's Wi-Fi. There, she pulled up the picture of Pierre again, as if to remind herself why she was here.

'Bonjour, *mon coeur*,' she said as his gorgeous visage appeared on her screen.

Now there was nothing between her and her plan to track down this middle-aged version of her former crush, she felt her nerves begin to set in. Was she being completely insane?

The determination that had driven her to almost quit her job and swap her house with a French mechanic began to wane and, as she sipped, she reminded herself she wasn't solely here for him. She was here for the experience, the culture. If she wanted, she could abandon the Pierre plan altogether.

QUEST FOR PIERRE

Pros:
He's gorgeous and successful
I'll always wonder if I don't try
Maybe we were fated to be together(?)

Cons:
It's crazy
He might not remember me or be unavailable
I might not even find him

Then she remembered opening the decree absolute. The feeling that had flooded through her – of having failed, of being forty and having nothing brilliant to look back on. What she was contemplating doing was a bit unusual perhaps, but it was something she'd look back on with pleasure no matter how it went. Either with Pierre, as their meet-cute story, or on her own, laughing at whatever faux-pas might occur.

I'm doing it!

She'd lived long enough to realise that every disaster becomes an anecdote or a great story with a bit of time. The disastrous dance class had already had Bess roaring with laughter when she'd recounted it; the pleasure she felt at sharing the story outweighed any embarrassment she'd felt at the time – even the awkwardness she'd felt when the woman's head had lingered in her car window as she'd struggled into her leggings.

This would be no different, she decided shutting down the search page.

She pulled up her email and sent a quick, obligatory note to her parents.

Hi guys!

Here safe!

Speak soon, Nina xx

Five minutes later, she received a reply.

Dear Nina,

Glad to hear you're there safe! Very brave of you to go on holiday alone. Although you know your father and I would always happily come with you. It could be like old times!

Rupert's making himself at home – little scamp. He's curled up on my lap right now, purring away. Dad's not a fan, sadly – he accidentally sat on poor Rupert yesterday and ended up with quite the scratch! I've attached a picture – sorry about the resolution.

I told him he'll have to get used to it, because you're moving home for a bit and Rupert has definitely got his feet under the table. He's not convinced.

Enjoy your holidays!

Kisses,

MUM

Once she'd recovered from opening an attachment she could never unsee, she tried to get her mind off it by WhatsApping the girls to say she was here and safe. Scratched bottoms aside, it was nice, really, that so many people cared whether she'd made it or not.

She would spend this afternoon getting herself organised, explore the area a little, make herself at home. Then she'd find Pierre's office tomorrow and see if she could spot him in the flesh. After that, well, who knew? She didn't have to race over to him instantly – she could take her time, see where he went at lunchtime and after work and then pounce. Or perhaps something a bit more subtle.

She made her way to the bathroom and did the best job she could with her hair – a quick brush through and a little water to flatten it where it had started to frizz would do. She'd put a treatment on it later and make sure that she was looking her best for her potential meet-cute tomorrow. Whilst there, she splashed a little water on her face and dried it on one of Jean-Luc's white towels, leaving a print of her make-up on its perfect surface. Whoops. She'd better make sure she picked up some hardcore washing detergent.

Then she walked downstairs and found her purse, slipped the house key into her pocket, put her coffee cup by the sink and stepped out again into the warm, afternoon air.

She wasn't exactly sure where the town centre was, but had got the impression from the taxi ride of roughly where she needed to go. It would be nice to wander a little in any case and discover how much of the small town she remembered from her decades-ago trip.

Outside Jean-Luc's house, the pavement was quiet, save for a small, white cat sitting on a wall and watching her intently. She moved as if to stroke it, but it instantly vanished from view into the garden below.

As she wandered down the next street, she began to see more and more people. A woman walking a tiny dog who smiled as she passed. A couple, arms-linked, walking in the opposite direction. She turned again and the houses began to be replaced by larger, apartment buildings in bright white. She discovered a small grocery store at the base of one of these buildings and, grabbing a basket, stocked up on essentials then exited back onto the street, a carrier bag in each hand.

She had originally intended to make her way down to the seafront, perhaps wander past the school, but her ill-thought-out timing and penchant for Nutella (the heavy jar she'd bought weighed 1 kg on its own) meant that she was forced to retrace her steps to the house to deposit her groceries before doing anything else.

It was almost five o'clock by the time she made it back – shoulders screaming – so rather than cook some of the food she'd just invested in, she decided stash it in the cupboards and fridge, then splash out on a taxi to the front and to treat herself to a pre-Pierre dinner for one. After all, she was on holiday.

The air was cooler by the time the taxi drew up on the seafront at 7 p.m. and she was glad that she'd grabbed her cardigan. The sea stretched to the horizon and the sun, just beginning its autumnal descent, had stained the water orange and pink at its edges.

It was busy: cars trundled up and down the front, taking locals home from work; couples wandered hand-in-hand towards restaurants. A group of children – seemingly unfazed by the slight nip in the air – were playing softball on a grassy area overlooking the beach, screaming and yelling in delight.

Did she remember this place? Perhaps. She remembered visiting the beach with a group of exchange students, splashing at the ocean's edge. But was it this beach, or one further along the coast? She remembered buying strawberry ice cream from a beach-front kiosk, but not exactly where that had happened. Everything seemed familiar yet brand new at once. Her memory was of key moments on the trip – time spent with Pierre, the day they'd had to go to a French school and she hadn't understood a word, an awful meal they'd had in a restaurant, and the time when she'd had to stand in front of the rest of the class and read something out in French – but her memory softened as she tried to pin down specific days, locations, even faces, other than Pierre's.

Even if she did find Pierre, and he was single, and they fell in love all over again, could there really be a happy ever after? She couldn't imagine Pierre in St Albans. He belonged here, somehow. In the land where the summer stretched just a little bit further.

Could she live here? Move away from the people and places she knew and loved? Possibly. Could she imagine herself strolling along this promenade with Pierre, arm-in-arm as so many couples seemed to be? Definitely.

Drawing her cardigan more closely around her shoulders, she straightened up and looked at the row of restaurants, in the end selecting a modest-looking pizza place with a red awning and a warm glow from its interior.

She settled into her table for one and ordered a pasta dish and a glass of red wine, then looked through the glass at the town outside. Until recent months, her future had always seemed fairly fixed. She and Rory had had no plans to move or make any changes to their shared life. She had been relatively happy in her job and hadn't seen a reason to shake things up.

Now everything had changed and her future lay before her, completely uncertain. Not just in a romantic sense but in every sense of the word. The house was being sold, she might not go back to her job, Rory was long gone and suddenly – having put down roots so many years ago – she found herself in freefall. It was terrifying not to be able to see her future properly as she always had, but she tried to remind herself it was quite exciting too. If someone had told her even a month ago she'd be here, about to do what she was about to do, she wouldn't have believed them.

Yet here she was.

She swirled the red wine in her glass and made a silent toast to the future. Whatever happened next, she was determined to make some more happy memories.

15

THEN

The school looked much like any other she'd been to. Not so far removed from the secondary comp she attended in St Albans. Although, perhaps a little cleaner, a little more orderly, she thought. The children passing in the corridor were dressed in casual clothes – she envied the fact that they weren't forced into an ugly uniform every day until sixth form. She'd have loved to wear her own stuff to school when she was younger. Occasionally, one would meet her eye and greet her; the rest passed with their eyes down, serious and on their way to class.

The Year 12s, or *deuxième* year in Lycée, were gathered together in a parquet-floored hall, where they sat in groups on red, plastic chairs. Bess sat on one side of her, chatting a little with Lili, her French partner. Brigitte was on the other – tight-lipped and facing forwards, her hands in her lap. Nina found Brigitte quite an uncomfortable person to be around. She was nice enough, she supposed. But her parents were strict and she had no siblings, and it had made her a little dull, a little straightlaced, perhaps. She didn't meet up with the others in the evening even when they were allowed to – and Nina felt she was missing out on the 'real' French experience, whatever that was.

A teacher came to the front and began talking in rapid French. Nina strained to listen, trying to understand what was being said. They were going to shadow their partners today through lessons, then join them for lunch before going out on a trip to the beach later – to gather fossils rather than actually enjoy themselves. It was difficult to keep up and after a while, Nina dropped the thread entirely. She saw Brigitte taking copious notes; she'd check back with her later.

She looked around the auditorium and studied the various faces – French and English – that surrounded her. A boy from her maths class, a French boy who looked much older than the rest, a few teachers and... oh. It was him. Pierre looked up just at the moment her eyes rested on him and their gazes locked. 'Hi,' he mouthed.

She was tempted to look away, but somehow, she couldn't. 'Hi,' she mouthed back.

16

NOW

Nina's alarm rang at 7.30 a.m. and for a moment she had no idea where she was. Then she remembered, and sat up abruptly in bed. Last night, she'd double-checked the location of Pierre's office – it was just a fifteen-minute walk from Jean-Luc's house – and when she'd looked it up it on Google Earth, she'd noted there was a café opposite: perfect for her mission. Assuming he might come in sometime between 8.30 a.m. and 9.30 a.m. (and even that was a shot in the dark really), if she sat innocently in the café, sipping a black coffee and reading a book, she ought to be able to spot him on his way in. It was Part One of her 'Meet-Cute Plan.'

She wasn't about to accost him as he passed on the pavement, though. This was simply a spying mission. To verify that yes, Pierre did manage his business from these offices, to see how she felt when she saw him in the flesh, to double-check for any signs that he might be attached. Then maybe she'd pop back for a spot of spying over lunch.

It was a bit of fun, she told herself.

Flinging back the covers, she made her way to the ensuite with its grey-tiled walk-in shower and adjusted the temperature before stepping under the powerful flow and feeling yesterday wash from her skin. Travelling always made her feel sticky, dirty and far from attractive – not quite the look she was hoping to for today and even after a shower last night, she'd still felt slightly dishevelled.

Duly cleansed, she stepped into a simple pair of linen trousers, teamed with a white T-shirt. She dried her hair, taking a little more care with the ends than usual, curling them under to give herself a sleek appearance. Or at least, comparatively sleek, she thought, noting that her careful efforts were already starting to fail as her hair began to fall into its usual shape. Still, she thought, Pierre had liked her hair when they'd been together, and it wasn't so different from the way it'd been then. Just a little shorter. And sans butterfly clips and crimp marks – which could only be an improvement. She liked to think that the couple of grey hairs that had appeared over the last few years were fairly well disguised by her highlights – she hadn't yet opted to fully dye them.

She applied her make-up, adding an extra coat of mascara for good measure, then inspected the result. Not bad, she thought. Not bad at all. She wondered when she'd stopped making quite such an effort when she was with Rory. But that was how things went. At the start of a relationship, you want to be your best self, but as the years wear on, you start to let all the sides of you seep out, and the veneer of perfection is gone. It wasn't so much that she'd let herself go; she'd just relaxed, confident in the long-term nature of her relationship.

It was daunting, this idea of starting over, but she was trying to calm the nerves that already fizzed in her chest by telling herself that it was actually exciting and thrilling and lots of other positive 'ing's instead of downright terrifying.

As a final flourish, she spritzed on some perfume, which likely Pierre would never smell but made her feel fabulous nonetheless, and nodded in the mirror. This was as good as it got. If Pierre was really 'The One', he'd love her 'just as she was' – at least, if the romantic comedy movies she binged on occasionally were to be believed.

She stuffed some euros into her purse, pulled her handbag onto her shoulder, grabbed the key and opened the door onto the white-skied morning. It was fresh, probably about twelve degrees, but pleasant. The clouds, such as they were, didn't look threatening, but hung white and light in the air, their edges blushed with golden sunlight.

It wasn't quite summer on the Med, but it beat October in Hertfordshire hands down, she thought, as she began to walk the route she'd planned to Pierre's office.

At times as she walked along, it was as if she stepped outside herself, looked at herself as a casual observer. What was she actually doing? But she carried on. Because she was here, she'd made her choice and she had to follow things through now.

Plus, she reminded herself, this was not a major mission. Just a cup of coffee in a café. How nervous did she have to be for that?

As she approached her designated café, she was disappointed to note that all the outside tables were already taken. People in office-wear sat talking earnestly over tiny black coffees. A woman was talking on her phone, tapping the table with her fingers as she spoke. A man in a beret sat on the final of the four outside tables, scrolling the internet on his mobile.

Damn. Without a front-row seat, she didn't have a hope in hell of spotting Pierre. As it was, the road between the café and the whitewashed office where the headquarters of the bakery chain was based made it a slight challenge – inside, she'd be completely shielded from the view.

She was about to turn and wander around the block a couple of times hoping for an opening when a shaft of sunlight broke through from behind the light cloud, playing on her face. And almost simultaneously, the man with the beret rose, checked his watch, slipped his phone into his pocket and took his empty cup inside the café.

Probably, he was going to leave, she thought. It was possible, of course, that he was going for a refill and she was slipping into his place too quickly. But the sun's rays illuminating the spot, the man's fortuitous leaving, obstacles clearing from her path... maybe this was a sign? If she didn't take it, someone else would and she was tired of skulking in the shadows, both literally and metaphorically.

She set her bag on the table territorially, and almost instantly, a waiter in jeans and a grey T-shirt appeared at her side. 'Oui madame?' he said, pulling out a notepad with a slight sigh, as if by gracing the café with her custom, she was making his life just a little bit more tedious than it had been already.

She smiled at the waiter, hoping to break him. And he returned a small grin. 'Can I have a black coffee, please,' she said with her best French accent, picking up the menu from the table. 'And do you have any croissants left?'

'But of course,' he said, adding, 'your French is very good, madame.'

It was a compliment, but in a way insulting, as she'd hoped in her naivety that by using French, she might pass for a native, at least when the conversation was limited to ordering caffeinated drinks. Clearly, her British accent shone through despite her efforts.

'Thank you,' she said graciously, scared afterwards to say much at all in French in case she shattered his illusions of her 'very good' language skills.

After the waiter took her menu and disappeared, Nina glanced over at the office building. It was a large premises, several businesses perhaps housed inside. A few lights already bloomed at the windows, but much of the building was still gloomy and unlit. Once in a while, a person would arrive, type in a code and enter through the security doors. But so far, nobody had looked even slightly like Pierre.

Her order arrived and after eating her croissant, she sipped her coffee slowly, hoping it would last for at least three quarters of an hour. She drew her book from her bag and rested it on the table as a decoy, angling herself so that a casual observer would think she was engrossed with the page rather than staring at the entrance of the office block opposite like a private detective on a stake-out.

As time went on, more and more people seemed to enter the building. The sliding doors were activated and people came and went without the need for security codes. Lights appeared in all of the windows and she could see people inside moving past, too small and indistinct and fleeting to be identified.

Perhaps she'd missed him. Perhaps he worked from home. Perhaps the website she'd found had been out of date. Perhaps he was already in and she simply hadn't recognised him so many years after the fact. She began to get restless – the coffee not helping and her croissant a distant memory.

The moment she tipped the final dregs of her cup into her mouth, the waiter appeared at her side again. 'Madame,' he said. 'Can I get you anything more?'

'Yes,' she said. 'A tea, if you have it?'

'What kind?'

'Just ordinary,' she smiled, turning her attention back to the office block.

'But what is ordinary?' he asked, confused. 'We have earl grey, mint tea, English breakfast, camomile...'

'English breakfast please,' she said. 'With milk.'

He nodded, his brow furrowing slightly as if she'd made an unusual order and once again vanished into the café's interior.

She glanced back over at the offices, without much hope. She'd finish the tea then take a walk along the front, and maybe come back later. And if that didn't work, well, she'd think of something else. It had been a long shot to think she'd come across him on the first day, be able to pin him down so easily.

But, just as she was resigning herself to the fact her initial mission had failed, someone caught her eye. It wasn't the face that she recognised first, but the walk. Something distinctly his, that her conscious mind had forgotten but her memory had stored somewhere. A jaunty, confident walk, his arms swinging by his sides. She allowed her eyes to travel up to the walker's face and almost gasped.

Because it was *him*. And she realised she'd have recognised him anywhere. Yes, she'd been studying pictures of him on the internet, she'd known how his features had changed, how his face had widened, his looks had matured. She'd been more or less aware of how the man she was seeking would look twenty-three years after she'd last glimpsed him in the flesh.

What she hadn't realised was how she'd still see traces of the boy he had been beneath the man he'd become. The turn of his head, the way he held himself. That walk. It was him. *Her* Pierre. Two decades on, yet still somehow the same.

She watched as he strode purposefully through the sliding doors and was swallowed up inside.

'Madame?' a voice broke through her reverie and she realised the waiter was back at her table, holding a mug on the tray.

'Here is your milk and your teabag.' He lay an English breakfast teabag in a packet next to her.

She looked at the cup, full of milk clearly warmed with the cappuccino machine, touched the side to feel that it wasn't much more than tepid, wondered what a 'tea latte' might taste like, and almost sent the whole thing back. Then found herself smiling and saying 'thank you' as if it was actually just what she'd ordered.

Because it didn't matter, at least not that much, she thought to herself as she sipped the strange, milky, slightly browned drink moments later. She might not have got what she ordered, but she'd definitely got what she came for.

17

Nina had heard the expression 'walking with a spring in her step' before – but had never really known what it meant. But making her way back to Jean-Luc's, she felt euphoric and every step felt lighter, more purposeful than it did usually. Seeing Pierre and feeling for that moment that whatever else had changed, the essence of the young man she'd loved was still there, made her feel that her plan wasn't so ridiculous, that her quest wasn't so pointless. That actually, just maybe, she might be on the cusp of a brilliant adventure.

The mild air felt pleasant and she turned her face slightly to feel the rays of the sun, weak but still warm, play on her skin. Breathing deeply, she felt it all fall away: the divorce, the job she may or may not return to, the worries about her age, the time she felt she'd wasted. For a moment, none of it mattered and she felt light and free and younger and full of possibilities.

At the very least, she had a month ahead of her in this glorious place, taking the time to re-explore the destination of her childhood, to enjoy the clement(ish) weather, to take in the scenery and thoroughly reset. At best, well, it seemed in that moment, anything was possible.

Turning onto the empty street that led to Jean-Luc's, she noticed that something had changed. There was a van – an ancient VW camper in a mid-blue colour – parked haphazardly against the kerb, one wheel on and the rest off, making the poor machine lean at an odd angle. It was probably someone visiting one of the neighbours, but it seemed odd that the camper had been parked directly outside the home she was borrowing for four weeks.

She increased her pace, the spring disappearing momentarily, until she reached the end of the pathway that led to the house's front door. There on the step was a woman who looked to be in her twenties, her hair bundled on top of her head, wearing khaki combat trousers, a vest top and with an enormous rucksack at her feet. She was smoking a cigarette and staring off into the mid-distance, and at first, she didn't notice Nina at all.

'Are you OK?' Nina said in French. She wanted to say a sharp, *Can I help you?* as she might in English; the sort of phrase that looks fine written out, but delivered with the right tone can actually mean *What the flip are you doing on my front steps?* But she lacked knowledge of current French sarcasm and wasn't sure whether the words would work in translation. She'd probably end up having to help the woman with something by default.

The woman looked up, blowing a plume of smoke out of the side of her mouth. Nina had never smoked, and never wanted to, but just for a minute, she wished she could look as cool and nonchalant as this woman did as she regarded Nina and casually expelled a cloud of fumes.

'No, perhaps I can help you?' she said. 'Are you here to see Jean-Luc?'

'No,' Nina replied. 'I'm staying here at the moment.'

The woman arched an eyebrow. 'Then you are Jean-Luc's friend? A special friend, perhaps?'

Nina wondered why the woman felt entitled to ask her any questions at all. She was staying here legitimately, and if this person – an ex-girlfriend, perhaps? – didn't even know Jean-Luc well enough to have learned he was away in the UK, she couldn't have that close a relationship with him.

'Not at all,' she said, trying to keep her tone cool. 'I've... Jean-Luc has offered me his house to come on holiday.' She felt the inadequacies of her language. What was the current French vernacular for 'house swap?'

'He let you stay here?' The woman looked surprised. She stumped the cigarette out on the step. 'But you are not friends.' A dark curl fell forward from her hastily gathered bun and brushed her cheek. She tucked it behind her ear. She was petite, with deep, brown eyes, long lashes and the kind of face that didn't need a slick of make-up to make it beautiful. Her skin looked naturally tanned and her dark, curled hair had a hint of gold from time spent in the sun.

'I'm sorry,' Nina said. 'But why is this any of your business?'

'I don't understand,' the woman said. 'I do not have a business.'

Another language faux pas. 'I mean,' Nina said, her French faltering, 'well, who are you? And why do you need to know?' She brandished the key. 'I'm just going to go in now,' she said. 'I'm sorry, Jean-Luc isn't here, so I'm afraid you've had a wasted journey.'

The woman laughed. 'I think it would be a good idea to let me wait inside with you. I will call him and when he gets home, we can talk with him.' She seemed unfazed by Nina's coldness.

'Jean-Luc is in England,' Nina said. 'He won't be back until next month.'

'Oh, *merde*,' the woman's shoulders slumped for the first time.

'Why does he not tell me this? He has a phone,' she was talking to herself rather than posing a question to Nina.

'I'm sorry,' Nina said, her tone softening. 'I think it was quite a last-minute decision for him, if that helps.'

The woman looked up and fixed her deep, brown eyes on Nina's face. She shook her head. 'My brother has always been like this. He is a little careless sometimes.'

'Oh, you're his sister!' Suddenly, Nina had to adjust her thinking. 'He didn't tell you he was going?'

'No,' the woman said. 'And I have been driving for three hours to see him, the stupid boy.'

Nina smiled sympathetically. 'That's awful,' she said. 'What about your other brother, Antoine?'

'Yes, perhaps I can see him. But he will be working now. Perhaps we could make a coffee, and I could wait?'

Nina looked at the woman. She only had her word that she was indeed Jean-Luc's sister. And she didn't particularly want to invite this stranger inside. 'What about a coffee shop?' she said brightly. 'You could wait at one of those lovely cafés near the front?'

The woman eyed her, taking another drag of her cigarette. 'It is OK,' she said. 'I understand. Of course you are not able to invite me.'

'Understand what?'

She took her time, blowing yet another stream of smoke into the air. 'It is your British nature, I think,' she said. 'You are awkward, yes?'

'I am not!' Nina found herself saying.

'Then you are suspicious? You think that I might be a criminal, perhaps?'

'Well, no. Of course not, but... oh look,' Nina said. 'Of course. Come in. Sorry.'

'Thank you,' the woman stubbed her cigarette out on the step and lay the stump neatly at the corner of the concrete, evidently with the intention of throwing it in the bin when it had cooled. 'I am sorry to be a bother for you.'

'It's fine,' Nina said, opening the door and gesturing the woman in and wondering quite how the invitation had come about.

Ten minutes later, they were installed on the cream sofas, Nina slightly worried at the state of the woman's boots and the fact they were drinking rich black coffee, but too polite to object. Surely Jean-Luc's sister would know the house rules he usually lived by?

'So, we should start again,' the woman said. She stuck out a hand. 'I'm Sabine, sister of the useless Jean-Luc, who told me I could come anytime for a break, but did not tell me he was leaving the country.'

Nina laughed in spite of herself. 'I'm Nina,' she said, giving Sabine's cool hand a quick shake. 'We're doing a...' she lapsed into English, 'house swap?'

'Oh, so he is in your house?' Sabine said, clearly familiar with the English expression. 'And you have his?'

'That's right.'

'For how long?'

'A month.'

'*Merde*,' Sabine said again. 'I'm sorry to have troubled you. I will sleep in the van and then I will go tomorrow. Or perhaps, as you say, I can stay with my other brother, Antoine. But he lives in a very small apartment,' she mused.

Was she hinting that Nina should offer her a bed for the night?

'Yes,' she said, quickly. 'Happy to have the van on the drive for a night.' The last thing she wanted was for her solitude to be interrupted – this was meant to be her moment to find herself again, carve out a little space for herself.

'Of course, it may seem a little odd to the neighbours to have me stay there,' Sabine continued, as if simply musing aloud.

'I'm sure they won't mind,' Nina said, firmly.

'Yes. You are right. And perhaps it is for the best. I am not sure you are the kind of person I could share a space with.'

Nina found herself bristling. 'What do you mean?' she said, affronted.

'Oh, but do not take it the wrong way. You are a little uptight? A stressed person? And I am relaxed; I like to take things easier. You would probably be very difficult to stay with.' Sabine smiled as if sympathising with Nina; it must be hard to be such an awkward, fussy person.

'Not at all!' Nina said. 'I'm relaxed! I'm chilled! I'm not uptight!' She realised she had sat up straight and raised herself up to say this and tried to relax her posture more. 'I don't mind people staying with me.'

'You don't?' Sabine said, looking at her craftily. 'Well, if you are sure?'

'What?'

'Yes. I will take your invitation to stay. If you are sure. I am sure Jean-Luc would approve,' Sabine said. 'Thank you.'

'But...'

'I will get my bags.' Sabine said, standing up and placing her cup on the coffee table. 'Perhaps you can help? I have jewels in the van – I make things with silver – and I do not want them to get stolen.'

An hour on, the living room was filled with debris from the van, and the pair were sitting down to another coffee that somehow Nina had found herself offering and making for Sabine.

'Thank you for letting me stay,' Sabine said. 'I will not be more than perhaps a week or two?'

'I thought you said overnight...?'

'Oh yes, a few nights,' Sabine said, as if agreeing with Nina.

'Just a few or seven perhaps, or...' she trailed off. 'It is kind of you. You are truly a kind person.'

Am I? thought Nina.

'And I am sorry – because I should have called Jean-Luc before I came. But he is normally here; he is not like me. I am never still. I like to take a risk, to do things, like a shot to the head.'

'Like a what?'

'Oh, it is an expression,' Sabine said, smiling, 'you know, under a moment's impulsion.'

'Oh, I understand,' Nina said. 'Like suddenly, we say in English, "on the spur of the moment",' she said, lapsing into English.

Sabine nodded. 'Yes, like a spur,' she said.

'I'm the opposite usually,' she found herself saying. 'This is a once-in-a-lifetime thing for me.'

'A holiday?'

'Well, no. I do go on holiday, I suppose. But a month, on my own, you understand?'

Sabine nodded. 'I am your opposite too then perhaps,' she said. 'I have been travelling,' she waved her hand towards the enormous rucksack and scattered bags, 'for three months now. I was with a friend but she quit me – she got a job somewhere and wanted to take it. It is fine, but I came to Jean-Luc's for a break to consider what to do next.' She looked suddenly sad.

'Oh, I'm sorry,' said Nina instinctively, sipping her coffee. 'What do you think you will do? Get a job too? Do something else?'

'No,' Sabine shook her head, losing some of her hair from its messy bun. 'I will carry on travelling. It is my passion. I just need to take a little time to plan first for once. I am lucky – I have a good business with my jewellery and of course I can sell it from everywhere.'

'Must be nice,' Nina found herself saying. 'You know, to do what you want at any moment, please yourself.'

Sabine shrugged. 'It is selfish, perhaps. But I feel that life is short and it is up to us to live it properly. Of course, it helps, too, if you have a successful brother with a nice house where you can come to collapse when you need.'

'So a week, then?' Nina asked cautiously.

'Yes, a week or two then probably I will go. I want to travel to Vienna by Christmas – to see the markets and drink *Weihnachtspunsch*. It is wonderful, they say, in December. I would like to take my time to get there, not to waste the places I pass through.'

It sounded suspiciously as if Sabine was putting down roots.

Nina nodded. 'Don't you usually sleep in the van?'

Sabine nodded. 'Yes, I always sleep in her when I am on my travels in Europe. When I travel by plane, I sleep where I can. Maybe in a hostel, or some camping.' She shrugged as if it wasn't important. 'And of course, when I am close to family, I stay with them.' She looked at Nina pointedly.

'And it's probably a bit cold this time of year,' Nina said, her practical side kicking in.

Sabine laughed. 'I hope not. I have done some work on insulation! But if it gets too bad, I can stay in a *chambre d'hotes* or something. I will find my way, do not worry.'

Nina glanced at her watch. It was almost lunchtime. Pierre would possibly be leaving his offices and going to a café. She wanted to see where he went, what he did so she could engineer a 'chance' meeting with him. But she wasn't quite sure how to get out of the conversation without having to explain what she was doing – and probably make Sabine believe she was completely mad.

'But I am keeping you?' Sabine said, noticing the glance.

'No, it's fine. I'm... I was going to go to lunch. It doesn't matter.'

'But it does! You must go and do your plans. I will not get in the way. But if you want, I would like to cook you dinner this evening. To thank you. I will prepare something special for us, if it is OK?'

'You don't have to...' Nina began, then, 'Yes. Yes please,' she said. ''That's kind of you.'

It was, after all, the least her rather unwelcome guest could do.

18

THEN

'*Ca va*?' he asked her, falling into step as they approached the classroom together.

'Oui, merci,' she replied politely. To her horror, she realised she was blushing.

'Because Brigitte, she seems not to spend much time together,' he said, in imperfect English.

It was true. Brigitte, although perfectly polite, had disappeared when they'd arrived at school, seeking out a group of friends who weren't part of the exchange programme. At first, Nina had wondered whether she ought to follow her, but something about the way she'd slipped off almost secretively stopped her – she'd sensed she wasn't welcome.

It didn't bother her that much – she had the rest of the exchange students to hang out with. A lot of them had clustered together, and she wasn't the only one without a pen pal at her side. But Pierre was right: she did feel a little out of sorts.

'It's OK,' she lied.

'Perhaps,' he said, 'we can sit together?'

She wasn't used to boys being so direct. Her only two relationships so far had both involved a friend of the boy in question telling Bess he liked her and asking her out via whispered messages.

Everyone said that French boys were more sophisticated. Perhaps this was what they meant?

'OK,' she said, shrugging slightly but inwardly delighted.

19

NOW

By 3 p.m., Nina had drunk so much caffeine, she probably wouldn't sleep for several days. She'd had a few problems getting her order right. She kept asking for black coffee, but finding instead of the larger cup she'd expect back home, she'd be given a tiny, thimble-sized espresso. Each time, she'd vow to remember to ask for *café allongé*, but she was so distracted by her mission to spy on Pierre, whenever the waiter returned she'd simply say 'un café' and the whole process would repeat.

How many espressos, she wondered, sipping her third, would it take to induce some sort of mania? She felt a tingling in her fingers and decided that this simply had to be her last. Of course, she could order a tea (or a tea latte) but the thought wasn't tempting. She'd had a bowl of lunchtime soup at the start, but they stopped serving food at 2 p.m. And there were cold drinks on offer, but after more than two hours of sitting and waiting, she was ready to leave. Clearly Pierre ate his lunch at his desk, or perhaps there was an in-house canteen or a back entrance? Either way, she wasn't going to get lucky twice in one day.

It was a bit of a blow – she was hoping to find his favourite eatery and another lunchtime, 'accidentally' bump into him there. It would be harder if she simply had his workplace to go on – what could she do? Register as a new client? Follow him into reception? She was familiar enough with romance novels to know that meet-cutes can happen almost anywhere, but had yet to see a believable romance which started by the heroine going into the reception of a bakery head office.

This was hardly a romantic situation, in any case. It belonged more in a documentary about amateur detectives, she thought glumly as she drained her tiny cup, ate the chocolate the waiter had put on her plate and – feeling thoroughly sick – went to pay for her mistakes.

She wobbled onto the street and decided to take a walk before going back to Jean-Luc's. She needed to clear her head of thoughts and her body of stimulants, and it seemed like the best way to do both. Gone was her earlier positivity at seeing Pierre, and as well as still feeling slightly sick, she also felt slightly silly.

When she arrived at the seafront twenty minutes later, she began to regret her decision not to bring a jumper with her. While the weather was still mild, the sea infused the air with a nip of autumn coolness, and goosebumps appeared on her arms in almost instant protest. She folded her arms across her chest and found a bench overlooking the water where she could sit and think and shiver for a moment before heading back.

Behind her, the pathway was wide, allowing for cyclists, walkers and even the odd skateboarder to drift by with ease. A couple of women glided past on rollerblades, laughing and moving effortlessly. There was something wonderfully free about it. She hadn't ever mastered her blades as a child, but then she'd had gravelled paths, potholes and kerbs to contend with. This smooth path would be ideal for giving it another go. Perhaps something else for her list.

She breathed deeply, feeling the freshness enter her lungs. People said sea air was good for you – she wasn't sure if there was any science behind it, but she always felt better for spending some time in close proximity to a beach. Was it the air itself, or the feeling of timeless restfulness that the sea evoked in her? Its large, ever-changing, half-living expanse – full of mystery and depth that humans had yet to fully explore – made her feel small. The same way she'd sometimes feel when laying on her back looking up at the stars on a summer night. Tiny, insignificant.

The thought of her own inconsequentiality was terrifying in some ways, but reassuring in others. The little risks that she was taking really didn't matter. Whatever happened would happen. And when it had, she could always come back to the sea. And the sea would be there, waiting, restless yet calm, dangerous yet enticing, timelessly pulling itself back and forth from the shore.

She'd read about cold water swimming recently – the idea that submersing yourself in icy water was good for your health. The article she'd found had been in a Sunday supplement and contained a huge photo of women of a certain age standing and shivering together at the water's edge. Rather you than me, she'd thought.

But she did like the sea. And although the water would be cool this time of year it – probably – wouldn't be freezing. Perhaps she should grab her cossie one morning and give it a go. After all, she was here to have new experiences, not simply hunt down a man from the past.

For now though, she felt herself begin to shiver and decided it was high time to make her way back to the warmth of Jean-Luc's place, or at least to grab a thicker jumper from her suitcase. She stood and turned, taking in the unusual sight of a sculptured shoal of fish, in enormous, undulating, wrought iron behind her. She knew that Cagnes-sur-Mer was a former fishing town and supposed that the fish in some way marked that important part of their history. But she wondered too whether it was a sign – the idea of fish in the sea, that there would be other 'Pierres' in the future if this didn't work out. Then she laughed at herself – the sculpture, she read, had been installed in 2006. It was hardly likely that the universe had inspired a sculptor to create iron fish, that the local council had paid a no doubt enormous sum to erect the things, all because some crazy forty-year-old English woman might have a crisis of romantic confidence close to twenty years later.

She made her way back towards the centre, passing white apartments with immaculate balconies, topping restaurants and shops and bars below. The place had a holiday feel; despite the fact that it was low season, there were still unmistakable tourists walking towards the front or browsing in the shops. As she got further from the shore, the apartment blocks grew smaller and houses began to pop up – a variety of shapes and sizes, most painted in white or peach, with terracotta roofs.

She turned into a street with patchwork paved walkways and again into another, expecting any moment to see Jean-Luc's house – which would be a relief as she'd been walking now for thirty minutes and the back of her shoe was starting to rub. Only when she reached what she thought was the right street, she realised she must have taken a wrong turning somewhere.

Pulling her phone from her bag, she flagged up Jean-Luc's address and discovered to her horror that she'd somehow drifted off course. She'd been so sure she'd been going the right way, even congratulating herself on her sense of direction, but had actually been heading diagonally away from where she wanted to be.

Damn. She considered trying to hire taxi, but it seemed excessive. The walk would do her good, she tried to persuade herself, and turned in the right direction. Her phone, oblivious to its surroundings, barked out a command for her to turn left, and she quickly muted it, blushing.

By the time she reached the front again, she was limping and reconsidering her thoughts about taxis. She sank onto a bench outside a shop and pulled off her shoe. The back of her ankle was red-raw, rubbed beyond blisters by the walk. Admitting defeat, she picked up her phone to see whether her Uber app would work on the French Riviera.

'Are you OK, madame?' a man's voice behind her said.

She jumped, knocking her shoe from the bench to the ground.

The man rushed around to pick it up and, kneeling, offered it to her. It would have been almost fairy tale like, his handing her the shoe as if she was Cinderella. If only there hadn't been blood on the back, and if the shoe had been delicate and feminine rather than the rather sweaty white sandal she'd favoured today. 'Thank you,' she said, taking the shoe from him quickly, hopefully before he saw the state of it.

He was dressed in blue overalls and smelled of petrol and grease and no doubt came from the garage on the corner. Perhaps he'd seen her tending her foot and suspected there might be a broken car for her to fix. At the same time, he looked disarmingly familiar, and she felt her brow furrow as she tried to place him.

'It is Nina, oui?' he said.

'Yes, but...'

'Antoine,' he said, indicating the badge on his shirt, as if she'd expect him to prove his identity. 'You are staying at my brother's house?'

Her confusion melted away as she recognised the man who'd shown her the house the previous day. Dressed in his work attire, he'd looked both familiar and different at once.

'Oh, yes. Of course,' she said.

'And you are hurt?' he said, concerned.

'Oh, no. Not really,' she lied, reaching to pull the shoe back onto her foot. As she did so, her phone slid from her lap and hit the pavement with a sickening crack. She picked it up, to see the screen had become a spiderweb of shattered glass. 'Oh no!' she said, thinking of the expense. Then 'Oh, bugger,' she added, remembering she'd been about to order what was probably a life-saving taxi.

'*Mince!* I am sorry,' Antoine said, looking at the broken phone in her hand.

'It's not your fault,' she said, horrified to realise there were tears pricking at her eyes. *It is only a phone*, she tried to tell herself sternly. *And it is only a blister. And I am only thirty minutes from Jean-Luc's*. But it was no use. A tell-tale tear ran down her cheek and she rubbed it away, annoyed to have let her guard slip.

'Can I help you?' he said. 'Do you need to make a call?' He pulled his phone from his pocket and looked at her expectantly.

'Oh,' she said, looking at her phone. 'It might still work, but well, if you don't mind. Perhaps. I was about to call a taxi. I'm know Jean-Luc's isn't far, but...' she gestured to her foot and grimaced.

'Oh, but there is no need!' he said, breaking into a smile. 'I can take you!'

She looked at him, at his badge, at his earnest face. You weren't meant to get into cars with strange men, were you? But then he wasn't strictly a stranger.

'Are you sure?'

'Of course,' he said. 'Wait here.' He disappeared at a trot.

The air had warmed slightly, or perhaps she was just warmer from exertion; either way, it felt quite pleasant to be sitting on a bench in the autumn sunshine knowing that she was waiting for a car to pull up and take her home; that she wouldn't have to walk on her sore foot any more and could consign her ruined sandals to the bin when she got back. She watched people move past, some hurried, most strolling; noticed a flock of birds making shapes in the sky as they moved and gathered and grouped for a flight to even warmer climes.

She was still smiling when she turned her head and saw Antoine again – wheeling what looked to be a heavy, black push-bike. Her face dropped. His remained resolutely upbeat.

'But this is...' she said, indicating the bike... 'A bike?'

'Yes, a bike,' he said. 'But don't worry, it is electric and it has enough space for two.' He indicated the rather small seat which could probably manage to accommodate two rather modest bottoms and she eyed it dubiously.

'It is fine,' he said. 'I have given my sister and my friends many rides.' He handed her what looked like a flimsy bike helmet.

Not quite knowing how to refuse in the face of his beaming positivity, she took the helmet and fastened it as best she could on her head. Antoine stepped onto the bike and indicated the tiny space behind him. Carefully manoeuvring to ensure she didn't flash her knickers, she lifted her leg and climbed on behind him, feeling embarrassed as he guided her hands around his waist.

'Hang on, haven't you got a helmet for yourself?' she asked.

'I will be fine,' he said. 'I'm very experienced.'

It wasn't particularly reassuring. But before she could say anything else, he flipped the bike's stand and with a 'Hold on tight!', began pedalling precariously onto the walkway then further on to the road.

Despite the bike's electric capabilities, Antoine seemed up for a challenge and elected not to put on the power. Instead, he pedalled furiously, puffing his cheeks out with effort and guiding them along the rather bumpy, smaller roads towards her holiday house. Finally, just as the bike began to wobble on a slight incline and she was about to tap him on the shoulder, he pressed something with his foot and a tiny motor kicked in.

The power was similar to that of a milk float, and the bike buzzed loudly under its heavy load as they negotiated the streets. She found herself clinging on to Antoine more and more tightly as they rounded corners and made their way over drain covers. Her foot had ceased to hurt, but she was pretty sure she was going to have to soak her bottom in a warm bath later if she wanted to sit down on this holiday again.

Finally, she began to recognise small elements of her surroundings, until at last, she saw Sabine's dented VW parked up on the roadside and breathed a sigh of relief.

Antoine drew up to the kerb and switched off the engine, leaning his leg against the pavement to keep the bike steady as she clambered off, almost falling. 'Voila!' he said proudly.

'Thank you,' she said, trying to resist the urge to put her hand on her bum and inspect the damage. 'Do you want to come in for a drink or...?'

But he was staring at the van. 'Sabine is here?' he asked, seeming incredulous.

'Yes. Sorry, I assumed she'd have told you.'

Sabine appeared on the doorstep, looked at them both, her face breaking into a wide grin when she recognised her brother. 'Antoine!' she said, waving and running towards him.

He walked quickly to meet her, scooping her in his arms and giving her an affectionate kiss on the top of the head. 'You are here! Why didn't you call me?' he said.

'But I have! You do not check your phone,' she slapped him lightly on the chest and laughed. 'Too busy with your head in a car engine, perhaps?'

Antoine laughed. 'Yes, probably. And sadly, I must go and do that again,' he said. 'But I will come later and see you – or you can stay at my place if you want?'

'On your futon?' Sabine said, crinkling her nose. 'No I think I prefer it here at Jean-Luc's.'

'But I hope you will not be causing troubles for Jean-Luc's guest?' Antoine asked her, an eyebrow arched. 'She said you can stay, but I hope she really wants you to.'

'But of course!' Sabine said. 'She is very kind.'

'And you will not make troubles?'

She slapped his chest playfully. 'I never make troubles,' she said. 'Unlike my terrible brothers! Anyway, Nina asked me. It was her idea!'

Antoine laughed. 'Perhaps anyway I will take you out later, just in case – to give Nina a little space, no?'

'Yes, OK,' Sabine smiled.

'But now, I must go.' He climbed back into the saddle, gave a small salute, then kicked the bike back into life and buzzed precariously down the street, turning the corner at the end, almost running into the side of a rusty Citroën.

Nina shook her head, smiling. She wondered what Bess would make of her new housemate and the unconventional journey she'd just taken home and gave a little laugh.

'You are OK?' Sabine said from the step. 'Come inside. I am starting to cook.'

20

As soon as she'd staggered up the stairs and tended to her poor, injured foot, Nina changed into more comfortable clothes and picked up her phone. The cracks on the screen weren't quite as bad as she'd originally thought, and she could still use the touch screen to negotiate her apps. There was a message from Sal – asking something about the washing machine for Jean-Luc – and she replied quickly, explaining the overcomplicated settings the washing machine needed in order to perform its primary function. Then she saw a note from Bess.

BESS

So how's it going?

NINA

Yes, good. Jean-Luc's sister has turned up. And I just had a white-knuckle ride on a wobbly motorbike...

BESS

What?!

NINA

Will update you later… But yeah, it's lovely here and the weather's not bad. So…

BESS

But, what about Pierre? Did you find him? Has he confessed his undying love? WHEN IS THE WEDDING?

NINA

Yes, no and ha!

BESS

??

NINA

Yes, I found him. No, we haven't spoken yet. (I'm sure when we do he will definitely confess the undying love, etc *smiling emoji*)

BESS

You FOUND him! That's huge. Is he still gorgeous?

NINA

100 per cent. But I've only watched him so far. No contact.

BESS

Never thought I'd be praising someone for 'stalking' but yay! Go you!

NINA

You realise I have that in writing – so if this ever goes to trial, you're an accomplice.

BESS

If we're going down, we're doing it together. Thelma and Louise all the way!

NINA

No offense, but if you decide to drive off a cliff, I might bail…

BESS

Don't blame you. By the way, your Jean-Luc guy is pretty hot.

NINA

He is?

BESS

Yeah. Well, according to Sal anyway. She's pretty much taken over all the checking up on him/helping him out detail.

NINA

I've met his brother – he's not bad himself.

BESS

Nina! You are on a MISSION. Do not get distracted. One gorgeous French man is enough. Don't be greedy!

NINA

Haha. Don't worry. I've also met his sister actually. She's staying at the house for a bit.

BESS

Hang on, I thought you were going to be the only one there?

NINA

Yes, but she showed up and she's sort of staying here now.

BESS

And that's OK with you? I thought you were keen on the glorious isolation aspect.

NINA

Yeah, it's OK. She's very persuasive. I sort of found myself agreeing. But you know what? She seems OK and from what I can smell, she's a very good cook!

BESS

Silver linings and all that.

NINA

Exactly.

BESS

And Project Pierre is still on?

NINA

Very much so. I'm fully focused! Pierre looked amazing and kind of just the same, even though he was older obviously… But gorgeous!

BESS

Fab. Although… you know, be careful.

NINA

Oh, don't worry… I've told myself that whatever happens, it's a great place to have a holiday. Any more, well, icing on the cake! Thinking of trying a bit of rollerblading!

BESS

Rollerblading? That's not very French… or sensible. But hey, why not. Anyway, keep me posted on all developing events. I'm up to my eyeballs at work and could do with the distraction.

NINA

Will do. Speak soon.

BESS

Yep. TTYL xx

Smiling to herself, Nina opened up her email and checked her latest messages.

Hi Nina,

Glad to hear things are going well on your holiday!

Quick question: you mentioned the house sale is going through – so I've started getting your room ready! I have all your old bedding – do you still like NSYNC? If not, I can always put the duvet cover on inside out.

We're off out to the theatre tonight. The am-drams are putting on a performance of *The Full Monty* at the Acorn Theatre. Front row tickets! I've managed to persuade Dad to come, even though he thinks he won't be able to sit through the performance what with his scratched derrière. I suggested he bring a rubber ring, but he was having none of it!

Rupert sends his love. He's very settled – here's a snap!

Anyway, must go.

Speak soon.

Mum xx

The attached picture showed Rupert stretched luxuriously on her parents' couch, a feline smile on his fluffy face. That cat knew how to make himself at home. Nina smiled, shaking her head, as she typed a response.

Hi Mum,

Have fun at the theatre.

Things are good here – just settling in and finding my feet. Give Rupert a stroke for me!

Lots of love,

Nina x

Nina closed her emails then, unable to help herself, opened up a chat to Sal.

NINA

Bess tells me Jean-Luc is quite the hotty!

SAL

Really? I haven't noticed *winking emoji*

NINA

Is this why you've volunteered to wash his smalls?

SAL

Nina! No, he just asked me for some info on the washing machine. Hot or not, I'm not going near someone's underpants. But he has asked me to give him the tour of St Albans.

NINA

Are you going to? You don't have to you know. Don't feel obligated or anything.

SAL

I am! But don't worry, it's not any sort of obligation. He's just a nice guy, good company. Speaks good English thankfully. So I thought – why not?

NINA

Well, have fun. And don't do anything I wouldn't do.

SAL

That's a pretty wide remit these days!

NINA

Good point. Well, have fun.

SAL

Oh I will!

A delicious smell curled up the stairs from the kitchen and Nina put her phone down and made her way towards it. In the kitchen, Sabine was standing over a stove, dipping in a wooden spoon and lifting it to her mouth for a taste. She looked up as Nina entered the room and smiled.

'I hope you like chicken in red wine,' she said.

'It smells delicious. Thanks for doing this.'

'Ah it is no problem – thank you for letting me stay.' Sabine poured wine into a large glass and handed it to Nina. 'Now sit! It is almost ready.'

It was seven o'clock and after a brief rest and catch up on her messages, Nina was more than ready to eat. Thanking Sabine again, she moved from the kitchen to the table and slid onto one of the benches. Taking a sip from her red wine, she felt it warm her mouth as it made its way to her stomach. Today had been a little derailed, sure, but it had been a success more than anything. She'd found Pierre and something about seeing him, the way he was still recognisably himself, had given her hope that maybe he'd remember her and there might be something still between them. Plus, she'd had another first – a ride on the back of a motorbike. Well, almost a motorbike. A hybrid. And that would do.

Sabine came through from the kitchen with two enormous plates, each with a chicken portion and red wine sauce served with green beans. Each plate had an enormous chunk of bread on the side, torn from a fresh loaf. She smiled as she placed Nina's in front of her.

'This looks delicious,' Nina said, feeling her stomach growl and remembering she'd only managed a bowl of soup for lunch.

'Thank you. It is my mother's recipe,' said Sabine. She lifted a piece of chicken to her mouth and chewed, her eyes momentarily closed. 'Mmm,' she sighed. 'It is nice to have a meal cooked properly after eating in the van for so long.'

'Don't you have a stove in there?' Nina asked.

'Yes, but I cannot cook much – there is nowhere to store any leftovers. So really I eat mainly bread and drink coffee,' said Sabine with a shrug. 'Ah, and I go to buy food in restaurants of course, but it cannot be every day. Jewellery sells well, but it is not a fortune.'

Nina nodded. 'You must make sure you eat properly now then, before you go out again.'

Sabine laughed – an infectious sound, slightly high-pitched. 'You sound like my mother.'

Nina felt her cheeks get hot. 'Oh,' she said.

'No, it is good. My mother is – well, was – wonderful. And she cared so much for people,' Sabine said earnestly. 'She died a few years ago. But I still hear her voice in my mind sometimes.'

Nina nodded. 'Sorry,' she said.

'For what?'

'For your loss.'

'Oh,' Sabine nodded. 'But I do not think it was your fault, eh?' she said, her eyes sparkling with mischief suddenly. 'British people, they like to apologise!'

Nina laughed. 'It does seem to be a bit of a habit, yes.'

'It is OK. She was not young. She had a good life. But it does not stop me missing her,' Sabine said, taking another mouthful.

Nina nodded, vowing to spend more time at her mum and dad's when she got back.

'So do you have many plans for your holiday?' Sabine asked. 'I hope I am not ruining anything for you?'

Nina shook her head. 'You won't be,' she said. 'I mean, it's not strictly a holiday, in the usual sense...' She found herself trailing off, unsure of how to finish her sentence.

Sabine looked at her. 'Not a holiday? Does this mean you are here for work?' she asked, her brow furrowed.

'Well, not exactly.'

'So then it *is* a holiday?'

Nina felt herself get red. 'Well, yes, I suppose so.'

Sabine looked at her and took a sip of wine. 'I do not understand,' she said. 'You say it is not a holiday, but next you say that it is?'

Nina had not planned on telling anyone about her Pierre mission. It was far too difficult to explain in English, let alone French, and if she was honest, far too embarrassing. But with Sabine's confused eyes on her, she felt she ought to clarify.

'I suppose what I mean is, while I'm not working. I am... well, I'm here to do something.'

'Really?'

'Sort of a personal mission, I suppose.'

'Ah you are challenging yourself. To improve your French, perhaps?'

'Well, yes.' Nina said, wondering whether she should leave it there. But something about Sabine's frank openness and the evening and the wine and the fact she hadn't really had a decent chat with anyone for a while prompted her to go on. 'My French isn't as good as I want so I hope to improve that, but that is not my main reason.'

'You do very well, with your French. Your accent is good.'

'Thank you,' she smiled. 'Oh, God. I can't believe I'm going to tell you this... but I'm here to find a man.'

'You want to find a French man to love?' Sabine looked interested. 'You have run out of British ones, perhaps?' She grinned.

'Well, yes. He *is* French. But not any man. A specific man.' In for a penny, thought Nina, and filled in the blanks for her new friend in French, with occasional lapses into English. Her divorce, her significant birthday and the letter she'd revisited. Then finding Pierre online and suddenly having the urge to see him and find out whether they had, after all, been fated to get together.

'So, here I am!' she concluded.

Sabine was silent for a moment and Nina had a sudden lurch

of fear. What if she seemed completely crazy? Saying it all out loud, and in her faltering French, it had sounded slightly bizarre.

She was about to say something to mitigate her confession – such as, *Just a bit of fun, though!* But before she could, Sabine clapped her hands together loudly, making Nina drop her fork right into her pile of green beans.

'Ah, but I *love* it!' she cried, her eyes sparkling with excitement. 'It is so romantic. That you have him in your heart after so many, many, many, many years.'

No need for quite so many 'many's, Nina thought, wondering how old Sabine was. She looked about twenty-five – probably forty seemed completely ancient to her. 'Well, it's just—' she began.

'And I can help you to do this,' Sabine carried on. 'We can find Pierre, find a way for you to meet him, as if it is just a coincidence. And to see whether he feels anything too.' She seemed inordinately excited. 'And my brother! He can help us! He works near there. Maybe he already knows Pierre!' She drew out her phone and began to type.

'No, honestly,' Nina said, reaching a hand out and putting it on Sabine's arm. 'I'd rather just keep it a secret. It's just… it feels a bit silly really, I suppose.'

'Pah, nonsense,' said Sabine, who clearly had the bit well and truly between her teeth at this point. 'This is love. Love is many things, but it is not silly. It is wonderful!' She wiped a rogue tear from her eye. 'Now I must stay for some time for this project – and Antoine, he will help us to think of ways to do this. And you will be together.' She clasped her hands in rapture. 'And it will be the most wonderful love story.'

'Or he'll reject me completely. Or I'll find out he's married,' added Nina.

'No. I am certain. This will not happen,' said Sabine. 'Because it is written in the stars, no? And the stars, they never lie.'

Nina wondered whether Sabine had ever read her horoscope in the *Daily Mail*, but kept schtum. She sensed that she was fighting a losing battle. This was no longer her secret mission; this was Sabine's project and no longer completely in her control. She took a deep drink from her wine. Embrace it, she thought. I'm meant to be embracing life. Risk. Making things happen.

Her stomach gurgled hesitantly. Nina sometimes wondered at the expression 'go with your gut.' That was meant to be about taking risks, acting decisively, wasn't it? But her stomach seemed to curdle at any sign of trouble – if she listened to it too much, she'd never leave the house. Or possibly the bathroom.

Sabine's phone beeped and she seized it, scrolling quickly with her thumb. 'Antoine, he says yes, he will help. He does not know Pierre, I am afraid. But he works with a lot of people. Someone will know something.'

'Oh God. Please tell him not to involve anyone else!' Nina said, her stomach finally overruling her heart.

'Ah, he will be discreet,' said Sabine. 'He knows that it is a secret, just for us.'

'OK. Thank you,' Nina said.

Sabine reached over and clutched Nina's hand in a surprise gesture of friendship. 'No, you do not need to thank me,' she said. 'This is something that I long to be a part of. Life is an adventure, and love is an adventure. And I live for adventures.'

21

THEN

'You want to come to the beach?' Brigitte asked her that morning. It was Saturday and their day to spend with their families. In all honesty, Nina hadn't been looking forward to it. 'Some friends are coming.'

'OK,' she said.

Brigitte nodded. 'Bring your costume.'

Conversation between them was a little stilted. She'd learned over the last few days that Brigitte's English was a little behind the others – perhaps the reason she'd sometimes preferred to absent herself from Nina's side. In fact, truth be known, Brigitte hadn't wanted to participate in the exchange at all – her parents had forced her, she'd admitted. It had made Nina feel a bit weird – like she was in the way. But after Brigitte's confession, her pen pal had become a lot more friendly – perhaps less conscious of her attempts at English and more assured that Nina's French was advanced enough to keep the conversation going.

They went to the main beach, which was pebbled. She winced as she made her way across the unforgiving stones to the water's edge. But once there, spreading out their towels, they lay in the warm sun, Nina could imagine that she was on a far more luxurious holiday – perhaps in an exclusive Spanish resort, or further afield – somewhere like Greece or Italy or all the other places she hoped to travel to eventually.

And then he was there too, with a group of friends, throwing a ball and splashing in the water. With her sunglasses on, she was able to watch him undetected.

Eventually, he came over. 'Swim?' he asked, looking at them both but glancing mostly at Nina – or at least it felt that way.

'Oui,' she said, self-conscious as she slipped off her beach dress to reveal her bikini, but feeling awfully grown-up at the same time.

22

NOW

The following morning at 6 a.m., Nina found herself sitting abruptly up in bed, her heart racing. She took a moment to adjust to her surroundings, steady her breathing, before leaning back again against the soft, feather pillows. Whether it was the dream or the fact that she'd had rather too much wine last night, she wasn't sure. But she was definitely awake and with so much adrenaline coursing through her veins, seemingly unlikely to go back to sleep.

She'd left her shutters open last night, choosing just to pull the curtains across and tumble into bed after staying up later than planned, putting the world to rights with Sabine. She'd learned that her new friend had been travelling for almost a year – that she was determined to see the world selling her jewellery before she settled down to a regular job (if she ever did). Nina had shared anecdotes about her own life, but they'd seemed quite dull in comparison. That she'd 'almost' gone travelling. That she'd got a sensible job and married instead. That life had spat her out at the age of forty, suddenly directionless and full of regret.

They'd talked about her French exchange from so many years

ago – how she and Pierre had had what had seemed like an instant connection. How she'd kept his letters in a box, along with a necklace he gave her, despite having decided not to stay in touch. How this whole adventure had come around. Sabine had listened, rapt, as if Nina had been telling a story of far-flung places and out-of-this-world adventures. Perhaps that had also been the wine.

Sabine had shared her own stories: about taking a gap year after university and never really settling down. 'I lived in New Zealand, Australia, South America,' she said. 'I worked for maybe six months, maybe eight. And sometimes, I thought – yes, this is it! This is where I wish to settle. But then my feet got restless and I knew I needed to get back on the road.'

The conversation had been so consuming, so entertaining, that Nina had barely noticed the hours go by. It was only when Sabine received a phone call from Antoine – who'd excitedly told her that although none of his friends knew Pierre, one of them worked in the same building – that Nina had realised it was gone midnight and suddenly felt the tiredness in her limbs.

She listened on speakerphone as Pierre told Sabine how his friend had often seen Pierre at Café de la Place not far from their offices. 'Perhaps I will go there tomorrow,' he'd told Sabine.

'Tell him not to speak to him!' Nina had mouthed desperately.

Sabine, her eyes sparkling with mischief, had told her brother to be discreet. 'Just follow him, don't speak to him. You are not Jules Maigret, remember? You will blow our cover.' She'd seemed delighted with the idea of her brother in the role of TV detective and once she'd hung up, had clapped her hands together excitedly again. 'This is fantastic!' she'd said. 'We will soon know where he goes, and we can arrange for you to bump into him. And voila! The rest will be history!'

Last night, Nina couldn't help but smile, despite her anxiety. But today, she felt a little less sure of things. This was meant to be an undercover mission – something she could do without humiliating herself if it all went wrong. Now, it seemed, there were others on the case. Not only did this mean she couldn't get out of it; it also meant that if Pierre didn't remember her, or rejected her, or saw through any flimsy 'Meet-Cute Plan' they might concoct, she'd have witnesses to her embarrassment.

Feeling nervous, she tossed the covers back, stepped out of bed and into her dressing gown. Opening the curtains to let the dull, early-morning half-light into the room, she looked out over the dotted rooftops, nestled in greenery, and beyond to the horizon. She couldn't see the sea from here, but she'd definitely walk down later and have a promenade. Perhaps with more comfortable shoes this time, she thought.

She'd steer well away from the Café de la Place – she'd looked it up on Google Earth last night: a small brasserie located on a street corner a few roads away from Pierre's office. It was tempting to head down there herself, but she'd die of embarrassment if she bumped into Antoine or Pierre at this point. Better to let things work themselves out and take some advice from her new friends. Probably.

Downstairs, all was quiet. Sabine wasn't yet up, so Nina made herself a cup of coffee and leaned against the kitchen counter, looking out over the garden. It was clearly well loved – the grass was neat and the little line of trees at its edge was obviously recently pruned. She imagined the space in the sunshine, the pool uncovered and invitingly warm; pictured a far-fetched scenario where she ended up living in a house like this with Pierre – her happy ever after. Would it be as wonderful as she imagined? Or would she, like Sabine, get itchy feet after a while?

She picked her phone up from the kitchen counter and scrolled through social media, then went onto WhatsApp – Sal had sent a picture of herself outside Nina's house in St Albans, grinning.

Looking after things for you!

It said, with a winking face.

Thank you

She replied, with a smiling emoji.

* * *

Later, after a day of exploring the town, and an afternoon walk on the beach, Nina was more than ready for a meal. But this time, she rejected Sabine's offer to cook. 'I'll take you out,' she said. 'My treat.'

Sabine had asked if it was OK to invite Antoine, and she hadn't been able to say no – even though she was a little embarrassed now that he was in on the 'plan.' 'Thank you,' Sabine had said when she'd agreed. 'Antoine he is divorced, like you, and sometimes I worry he gets lonely.'

'Oh, that's sad,' Nina said, wondering if a similar fate awaited her. 'Do you ever think of inviting him on your travels?'

Sabine found this suggestion hilarious. 'I am sorry,' she gasped, 'but I cannot imagine Antoine in the van. And of course, he has his job. And his son too – Theo. He is thirteen now and I do not think Antoine would leave him.'

'Oh, he's a dad?'

'Yes, but Theo he lives with his mother. Antoine sees him at the weekends only. It is quite sad.'

* * *

By seven o'clock, they were walking, in a strange trio, to the seafront, Antoine pushing his bike alongside him after deciding to walk with them. 'He is crazy to ride such a bike,' Sabine said. 'I went on that thing once, and once is enough.'

'Oh, it's not that bad,' Nina had said, feeling desperately embarrassed. 'But, if you're walking... well, it'd be nice to chat,' she'd added hurriedly before Antoine thought to offer her his spare seat.

'I will walk the bike to the restaurant then I can ride her home,' he'd said.

'Well, you must not drink then,' Sabine had told him firmly, then added conspiratorially to Nina, 'He rode after one glass of wine once, and he crashed into a tiny wall and broke his nose. He is not so good after a drink, I think.'

Nina had laughed a little, conscious that Antoine's face did not register amusement at the memory. And then they were there, seated at a small table with a linen tablecloth, scouring a delicious-looking menu with a waiter hovering nearby.

They made their order and then, once Antoine had poured them each a generous glass of white wine and put a couple of inches into a glass for himself – despite Sabine's protest – he smiled at Nina and said, 'So you wish to meet Pierre Dupont.'

'Well, yes,' she said, feeling her hands get hot. Something about the way Antoine was looking at her, his eyes sparkling, unsettled her. Perhaps he was laughing at her, thought her ridiculous. 'Just... I mean, it's just a bit of fun... I...'

Antoine raised an eyebrow, 'Ah so when my sister say that it is very important – a question of life and death – she is perhaps not being quite truthful?'

'Life or death?' Nina repeated, looking at Sabine. 'No, it's not quite that important.'

'Pah!' Sabine said, a smile on her lips. 'But love is the most important thing! It is what life is about.'

Nina and Antoine exchanged a glance of mutual amusement.

'My sister is very romantic,' Antoine said. 'Probably because she has not yet been disappointed in love. If she had been married to Bernice like me, I think she might think a little differently.'

Sabine slapped his arm playfully. 'And you are so old and disappointed and no longer have hope,' she said. 'But some of us, we still believe in a one true love. In fate.' She looked at Nina for solidarity.

Nina smiled at the pair of them. She didn't have any siblings and envied for a moment their clear mutual affection. 'I wouldn't call him old,' she said, smiling. 'What would that make me?'

They looked up. 'I don't understand,' said Sabine.

'Well if he's old at, what, I'm guessing thirty-three, thirty-four, maybe, then me being forty must make me practically an antique!' she said.

They laughed. 'Ah, all our family have baby faces,' said Sabine. 'He is forty-two, and very old.'

'Oh, he seems much younger,' Nina said, surprised.

'But perhaps that is because old is not to do with age, not really. It is to do with in here,' Sabine patted her chest. 'Here we are as young as we allow ourselves to be.'

Nina nodded. 'Well, you might have a point,' she said, still surprised that Antoine was older than she was. Perhaps it was all the sea air. People used salt as a preservative, didn't they? Perhaps it worked on humans as well as food?

'Anyway,' Antoine said as the waiter leaned in with the dishes – salmon for him, chicken for Sabine and steak for Nina. 'I am happy to give fate a helping hand for you. And I have found that Pierre goes to the restaurant almost every day at 11.30 a.m.'

'That early?' Nina said, realising that was why she hadn't seen Pierre the day before.

'Yes. He eats at twelve and always walks there. Anyway, I accidentally bumped into him when he was paying and spoke to him for a moment, about the brasserie, what food he recommends,' he said. 'He told me that it is his daily habit. So it's certain that if you wish to meet him, you could do it almost any day.'

Nina's heart thundered. So she could actually 'bump into' Pierre tomorrow – or whenever she wanted.

'Thank you,' she said, cutting her steak without really paying it much attention. 'That's amazing. Really.'

Antoine blushed. 'No problem,' he told her, attempting to stick his fork into a new potato which skittered around his plate.

'We can help you with a plan,' said Sabine. 'We will find a way for you to meet him, but it seems like an accident!'

Nina nodded, feeling slightly sick. 'Thank you,' she said again.

She raised her fork to her lips and felt an unexpected cold and clammy feeling. The meat was soft and chilly... and raw. Horrified, she spat into her napkin then looked at her plate. Her steak, the one she'd assumed would be at least seared on the outside, was a mass of curled fronds of raw meat. 'My... I...' she said, looking at Sabine with panic.

'What is the matter?' said her friend, concerned.

'It's... my meat hasn't been cooked!' she said.

'But you ordered steak tartare!' said Sabine. 'That is raw steak.'

Nina had spent so many years being afraid of undercooked meat since a bout of food poisoning at a birthday barbecue in her teens – the idea of eating it raw was horrifying. 'But... why, I don't...' she said. She'd seen steak tartare on a menu before but had had no idea what it actually was. 'I can't...'

Then she saw the two of them exchanging an amused glance. Sod it, she thought, forking the meat into her mouth and trying to chew. I'm meant to be taking risks. Plus the last thing she wanted to look was uncultured, unfamiliar with what was probably a perfectly ordinary dish. Just one she hadn't had the pleasure to try before.

But... no. Moments later, she flagged the waiter down and ordered a safer option.

Risking it all for love was one thing, but chewing raw meat and risking a day on the toilet was quite another.

23

BUMPING INTO PIERRE

Pros:
Maybe he will remember
Maybe he's single
Happy ever after…?
At least I will know

Cons:
What if he doesn't remember?
What if he's not single?
Could be embarrassing

It had taken three days for Nina to work up the courage, find the right outfit and get her confidence in check, but she was finally at the entrance of the brasserie. She'd waited, with a giggling Sabine, outside for a bit – out of sight, close to a shop window – until she was sure Pierre had entered. And now she was here, Sabine at her side, ostentatiously to get a bite to eat, but in reality, to potentially change her life/embarrass herself beyond all measure. It was hard to know which way things would go.

Inside the bistro, there was a quiet murmur of conversation. Several of the tables were already filled with people in various types of attire – those clearly on a lunch break from work, others who might be meeting friends or who were there on holiday dressed in shorts and jeans and sweatshirts. As they entered, a waiter came up to them and nodded when they asked for a table for two. 'We have just one more,' he said and it occurred to Nina that they probably should have booked.

Thankfully, the table was in an excellent position – towards the back of the dining area, in a corner, unobtrusive, but with a clear view of all the tables in the restaurant. Nina glanced quickly around and noticed Pierre sitting with a group of five other men, talking earnestly to an older man in a suit on his right. She felt a flutter and for a moment wondered if she might be sick. But it was just nerves, she told herself, nothing else.

When the waiter came to serve, she quickly ordered the *plat de jour* – turkey with haricot verts – and water for the table. Sabine took a little longer, then settled on some sort of sausage dish. As the waiter nodded at their excellent taste and took their menus, Sabine gave her a nudge. 'So,' she said. 'Are you going to go and talk to him?'

Nina looked over. She was so close – Pierre was just a few metres away, looking just as gorgeous as she remembered. But the last few metres between them were somehow enormous. What was she actually going to do? Walk up and ask him if he was Pierre; explain that she was there on holiday and she'd just happened to recognise him?

'I will,' she said, taking a sip of her water. 'I just... maybe in a minute. He seems busy.'

Sabine nodded. 'What will you say?' she said.

'I thought I'd just... well, introduce myself,' Nina said.

Sabine shook her head vehemently. 'No, this will not do!' she said.

'What do you mean?'

'Well,' she said, wrinkling her nose slightly. 'It is not very romantic, is it? Just to say, "Oh hello, how are you and do you remember me?"'

'I'm not sure what you mean?'

'Just think,' Sabine said, leaning forward conspiratorially, 'when you tell your children, your grandchildren about how you meet, do you want to be telling them that you said hello in a restaurant? You need something more memorable.'

'I do?'

Sabine nodded. 'Definitely. And you want to get his attention, no? So you need to do something that will stay in his memory too. So when later he thinks about it, he thinks about you. And he wonders... whether perhaps it was fate that brought you together!'

'OK,' Nina said, uncertainly. Perhaps Sabine had a point. Maybe she ought to do something a little less direct, but more memorable. Pierre might be embarrassed if she introduced herself out of the blue. And what if he didn't remember her? She wanted him to notice her for all the right reasons, to fall in love with her again. 'But what do you suggest?'

'Ah!' said Sabine, a little too loudly, as if an incredible idea had just presented itself. 'Perhaps you can faint onto him? You can go to the bar, or as if to the toilet, and when you are close, act as if you feel dizzy. You can sink down towards him. He will catch you! It will be so very romantic!' She beamed at Nina in triumph.

'No,' said Nina shaking her head. 'I just... I can't do that.' Her acting at school had never been anything to write home about, and she didn't want to end up making a scene in the restaurant. She'd probably knock a glass of wine over him or break his chair or something in any case. Or, knowing her luck, be so very good at playing the part that she'd get carted off in an ambulance.

'No?' said Sabine as if she couldn't quite believe anyone would turn down such a fabulous idea. 'OK, perhaps something more subtle? You tell him that you are being followed, or that the waiter, he is pestering you for a date. Please can he help you?'

Nina shook her head. 'He'd think I was mad,' she said. 'Why would I pick him, out of all the men in here to rescue me? Most people would probably just leave or call the police or whatever.'

'True,' Sabine nodded as if Nina had just imparted some sage advice. She drummed her fingers on the linen tablecloth. Then, once again, inspiration struck. 'Ah!' she said, all smiles. 'Perhaps you can go past and just drop something, and he will pick it up and chase you?'

Nina considered. 'Actually, that's not a bad idea,' she said. She could probably handle dropping something and walking quickly past. He'd have to come to her with it and she could suddenly recognise him.

The waiter arrived with two steaming plates of delicious food. Thankfully, this time, Nina's meat was cooked to perfection. She took a forkful, considering. 'But what can I drop?' she said, thinking of the meagre contents of her bag. Her purse, her phone, a few dirty tissues and a tampon. She couldn't easily drop either of the former items and pretend not to notice – they were large and would make a noise on the floor. And she wasn't going to start scattering sanitary products or snot rags in her wake.

'Maybe a bracelet?' Sabine said. She removed a brown, beaded bracelet from her wrist and gave it to Nina. 'This one, it is large. It falls off sometimes. It will be easy to drop.'

Nina eyed the tiny, carved, wooden beads and slipped the bracelet onto her wrist. It was perfect. She looked over at Pierre, who was eating the same meal as she was – a sign? she wondered, until she remembered it was the dish of the day. He was still engrossed in conversation with the men at his table and she wondered whether he'd even notice a dropped bracelet.

'What if he doesn't even notice?' she said to Sabine.

'Pah, then we try something else,' she said. 'We can pick up a bracelet ourselves, right? And Pierre, he is not going anywhere.'

It was true. This could be the perfect meet-cute. The Cinderella-esque returning of an item of clothing, slipping it back on her wrist for her; their eyes would meet and she'd say, *Do I know you from somewhere?* She could see it all now.

'OK,' she said, taking a deep breath. She wiped her mouth with her napkin and smoothed down her hair. 'Do I look OK?'

'Beautiful,' Sabine said, her mouth stretched into an excited smile. Nina hoped she wouldn't clap or let out a squeal as she walked past Pierre.

Her legs feeling a little wobbly, she stood up, steadied herself and began her walk across the restaurant floor, towards the stand of condiments. She'd pretend she was going to get a salt pot or a napkin from the stand, weaving her way past and just happen to brush against him slightly. She slipped the bracelet down to her hand in readiness, keeping it in place with a finger until the crucial moment.

Walking across the room, she felt as if everyone must be watching, wondering what she was doing, even though, in reality, several people had risen from their tables at various points, to collect items or make their way to the bathroom.

Her heart hammering, she let the bracelet slip further and, just as she passed Pierre, allowed it to fall to the ground. To her, it made an enormous clatter as the wooden beads hit the parquet, but nobody around seemed to flinch or notice the noise at all. Making sure she didn't obviously react, she made her way to the condiments where she could browse little packets of salt and pepper and look back subtly to see what happened next.

To her disappointment, Pierre didn't move; didn't seem to have noticed the jewellery by his chair. He was saying something earnest to the man to his left, his hand on his shoulder. Both men roared with laughter moments later.

Look to your right! Nina wanted to tell him. *Notice it!*

The bracelet lay just a few inches from Pierre's slightly pointed leather shoe. He moved his foot a little and came painfully close to touching it. But nothing. Across the room, Sabine was looking too. Nina gave her a shrug – what else could she do?

Pierre broke away from the conversation and had a deep drink of water. His eyes wandered around the room, and rested on Nina for a second. She thought she might have seen his brow furrow a little, wondered if he recognised her but couldn't place her. But before he could work it out, one of his colleagues tapped his shoulder. Turning, he placed his glass back down and put his cutlery together on the table, and started looking around – probably for a waiter. Surely, he'd see the bracelet in a second? she thought, picking up more napkins than an ordinary person probably would. Surely, he'd pick it up and realise what had happened. Surely...

The door to the restaurant opened and a man entered, looking around, searching for someone. With a start, Nina realised it was Antoine. He noticed her by the stand and a large smile spread across his face. Walking towards her, his foot kicked the bracelet slightly and he bent down to pick it up after it had skittered a little on the floor. He looked at it then flagged down a passing water and handed it to him.

Pierre had now attracted the attention of his own waiter and was talking to him earnestly, possibly about coffee or desserts or something completely different. The moment, the opportunity had passed.

Antoine arrived at the condiment stand, 'Hello' he said.

'Hi. I didn't know you were coming.'

Antoine nodded. 'I came to join you for coffee after your meal – Sabine said you'd be here.' He looked over and saw Sabine, who'd gone to claim her bracelet back from the waiter.

Nina smiled. 'Well, nice to see you,' she said. She didn't tell him he'd blown her meet-cute. After all, there was no way he could have known how important it was to leave the bracelet near Pierre. And there was always tomorrow, she told herself, walking with him past Pierre – so painfully close yet so far away – and back to their little corner table.

Sabine was shaking her head. 'Ah, Antoine, you have terrible timing!' she said.

He glanced at his watch. 'But it is one o'clock like you said.'

Sabine rolled her eyes at Nina. 'Ah, but I mean... well, you came just at the moment when... Oh never mind.'

Antoine pulled out a chair. 'I am not interrupting?'

'No,' said Nina quickly. 'Not at all. Honestly.' She watched as Pierre checked the time, and pushed his chair back. He shook hands with the man next to him and made his way to the till to pay. Then, popping his wallet into his jacket pocket, he strode out of the brasserie without a second glance.

'Ah, she missed her chance!' said Sabine, frustratedly. 'He is gone now.'

'It's not Antoine's fault,' Nina said quickly. 'Anyway, it's fine. There's always tomorrow. Always somewhere else we can go.'

'And that is why I am here,' Antoine said excitedly. 'I have the perfect opportunity for you.'

24

THEN

They'd met up beforehand to come to the disco en-masse – Nina, Bess, Brigitte and a few of her friends, and Bess's pen pal Lili. Already the hall was fairly full – the whole of Year 12 had been invited, and people were dancing or sipping sparkling apple juice from plastic cups. Some kids preferred to huddle in corners, talking. A couple of boys ran around, skidding on their knees when space allowed.

It looked amazing.

Bess had convinced Nina to wear her cropped top with her combat jeans. It was a high crop and revealed all of her midriff. She'd carried it around with her since buying it three months ago, but never actually felt brave enough to wear it. Now she tugged at it a little, knowing she'd have to slip off her jacket when they got into the warm hall and reveal her belly button – and more – to the world.

But several of the girls were dressed similarly. Perhaps it wouldn't be so bad after all.

Inside the disco, it felt warm and sticky and sweaty, and they had to push through the dancers to get to the drinks stand. She and Bess sipped their apple juice and leaned against the wall, trying to look nonchalant, sussing out the dynamics of the party before fully participating.

'I thought you wouldn't come,' said a voice in her ear.

She turned and felt a flash of pleasure. Pierre. They'd spoken several times over the past few days – once for almost twenty minutes. And she'd felt what she thought must be a 'connection' – the feeling that she'd known him for years. She smiled, then jumped slightly as he grabbed her hand without her realising.

'Come with me?' he asked.

She looked at Bess, who tipped her head 'yes.'

Delighted, she allowed herself to be gently guided back through the dancers to the double doors and out into the night.

25

NOW

'OK,' said Antoine, holding the heavy, silver boule in his hand. 'You push up your wrist and you flick.' He tossed the ball in an arc towards a black, target ball and it landed in the grass with a thump.

'Right,' Nina said.

Yesterday, at lunch, Antoine had told her that he'd seen Pierre's name on an emailed list – Antoine's firm had sent around an email about a pétanque club – they were trying to get a team together, and Pierre's name had been down on a list of existing club members.

When pétanque had first been mentioned, Nina hadn't known what Antoine was talking about. But he'd explained the game and it sounded very much like carpet bowls, but with balls being tossed rather than sedately rolled.

'Anyone can play!' he'd said, excitedly. 'And you can just go and say you are interested to try. They play each Sunday, and after, they go for some drinks, yes? So, it is perfect!'

'Except...' she'd said.

'Except?' he'd asked, with a wide-eyed optimism similar to his sister's.

'I have no idea how to do it,' she said with a shrug. 'And I'm rubbish at sports.'

He'd shaken his head. 'It's not true,' he said. 'Nobody can be truly bad at pétanque. Not so bad as not to play in any case. You do not need to beat him. Just talk to him.'

She'd nodded. And somehow agreed that when Antoine had time off from his work, she would let him teach her. 'I taught Theo when he was just eight years old,' he'd said. 'I am sure I can help you.' He'd suggested they go to the pétanque courts at the park, but she'd asked instead if they could start with some basic throwing in the garden. She wasn't ready for any sort of audience yet.

She'd treated today as a holiday while waiting for her 'lesson' and it had been fun. She hadn't gone stalking Pierre, or carrying out any sort of amateur sleuthing, but spent her day exploring Cagnes-sur-Mer, visiting the beach and the beachfront shops, having lunch in one of the restaurants on the front. She'd taken a few selfies – one by the statues of fishes was a particular favourite – and sent them to Sal and Bess. She'd quipped:

> Well, you said there were plenty more fish in the sea. Love you.

Sal had sent her own picture back, snapping herself looking great and almost as if it might be a date.

> Taking Jean-Luc out for a traditional English pub roast

Nina had enquired:

> Oh, yes? Anything I should know about?

She'd just received a winking emoji in response.

Now, she steadied her arm and eyed the target ball, trying to gauge the amount of effort she ought to put into her throw. Then, she breathed deeply and launched. The ball rose into the air then thudded down, about five metres wide of target.

She looked at Antoine, and briefly saw a horrified expression on his face. He quickly rearranged his features into a more neutral expression.

'OK!' he said. 'Good for the first throw. But maybe we should try it again.'

'Definitely,' she said.

Antoine had arrived at 5 p.m., having managed to get out of work early – and it was already quarter to six. The evening was mild and cool, bright, but with a dusting of cloud across the white sky. She sighed, wondering if this was going to be another romantic dead-end. She wasn't there to become world champion at pétanque, but she needed at least to be good enough not to embarrass herself too much in front of Pierre. Or to make it obvious that she'd just joined the pétanque group just so she could bump into him.

Taking a deep breath, she tried again; this time, her boule landed closer to the target – not close enough, but a definite improvement. She threw her third – again, a small improvement – and walked to pick the balls up for another go.

'It is not so bad,' Antoine told her. 'You need to angle your arm more to the centre.'

'Like this?' she asked, holding a boule in her hand and moving her arm.

'No,' he said, and came to stand behind her. 'Do you mind if I...'

'It's fine,' she said, feeling his arm slide under hers for support.

'You pull back like this,' he said, guiding her arm backwards. It felt strange, the skin of his arm touching hers – intimate. His breath was on her neck. 'And then you thrust!' He pushed her arm forward at a slightly different angle than the one she'd tried previously. She released the ball and it arced perfectly in the air, landing directly on the target ball.

'Wow!' she said. 'That was amazing.'

'Ah, a happy accident, I think,' he said. 'I do not usually land quite so well. But perhaps you felt the difference when I was holding your arm.'

'I did,' she said, glancing at him. 'I felt the difference.' Their eyes locked for a second before he turned away, picking up another boule from close to her feet and holding it out to her.

'Perhaps it is good to try again, while you still have this feeling,' he said.

'Yes,' she said. 'Yes, good idea.'

She held out her arm and steadied it, before focusing on the target ball. This time, the ball arced more cleanly through the air. It landed less than two metres from the target – much closer than she'd achieved before. 'Yes!' she said, exhilarated.

'Bravo! And another,' he said, holding another boule in his hand.

Once again, the shot was a success. And suddenly, she realised she had a feel for it – that she now knew how to play pétanque at least well enough to visit the club without shame. She'd continue to practice over the three days between now and the Sunday club and hopefully when she turned up, she'd have a game and then go about seeing if she could catch Pierre's eye. According to Antoine, the club was very informal – a group of locals gathering to play together each week. Anyone who turned up would be included, and some would stay on afterwards to socialise.

'Thank you,' she said to Antoine, 'I think I've got it. Or at least enough to fool Pierre into thinking I like pétanque.'

He smiled. 'No problem. And he is very lucky, this man, to have someone like you working so hard for him. I am guessing you have some wonderful memories together?'

She smiled. 'Yes,' she said. 'Lots of them.' She racked her brain for an example. There was the time when he'd grabbed her hand at the disco. The time they'd got the giggles in the classroom. Once he'd sent her a scribbled note saying she looked good. None of those moments quite lent themselves to anecdote though, she thought. They sounded, if anything, a bit juvenile from the outside. Not enough to explain her longing for him now.

But it was impossible to put into words how Pierre had made her feel. That rush of love and excitement whenever she'd seen him. The way his eyes had looked into hers and made her feel special and magical all at once.

Antoine looked at her for a second, perhaps sensing she was going to say something else. When she didn't, he smiled and spoke. 'Perhaps you wish to practice more?'

'I think I've probably done enough for tonight,' she said, rubbing her shoulder. 'But thank you so much. Would you like a drink or something?'

He shook his head. 'No thank you. I need to go. But another time?'

'Of course,' she said, 'another time.'

He nodded. 'And perhaps we can try on Saturday at the courts?' he said. 'Or at least watch some pétanque there?'

'Good idea,' she said. It was so kind of him to help her, be so invested. He must really be a great brother to Sabine.

He picked up his bike helmet and, with a little mock salute, put it on his head and went to grab his electric pushbike from where he'd leaned it against the wall. He kicked the engine into play and it stuttered and emitted the strange, tinny sound she remembered from the other day. And then he was gone, waving his hand as he disappeared from view.

She stood for a second, holding a boule and watching the space he'd just left. Then righted herself and collected the pétanque kit together before making her way into the house via the back door.

Sabine was there, stirring something on the stove, her back to her.

'Well,' said Nina. 'I think I might be closer to mastering pétanque.'

'Oh yes?' said Sabine. 'That is good news. And Antoine, he was helpful?'

'Very helpful,' she said. 'You're lucky to have a brother like that.'

'Ah, but he is not always like that,' Sabine said with a grin. 'He is very nice, but I'm not sure he would give up his time so easily for me!'

'Oh!' Nina said, blushing at the implication. But surely Sabine must be wrong. He couldn't find her attractive, or it would make no sense for him to be helping her to meet another man. 'Well, it's very kind of him,' she managed at last.

'Anyway,' Sabine said, switching the heat from under the saucepan and covering whatever she'd produced with a lid. 'Antoine helped you with the sport part, but perhaps I can help you with what you do next?' She turned to Nina with an enormous grin on her face. 'I can help you with the love.'

'Oh no!' Nina says. 'I'm... I think I'll be OK. And I don't think we'll be at that stage for a while...' But then her new friend laughed, seeing the look of horror that must have flitted across her face.

'Ah no, not the making love – the sex tips, that is up to you!' she said, delighted. 'But I could help you with what to say. Perhaps we can practice?'

Nina smiled. 'I think I'll be OK,' she said. 'It might be better to just let things be natural.'

Sabine's brow furrowed. 'I don't think so,' she said. 'It might be too difficult for you, especially in French. Because you have to prepare for so many different outcomes? He might remember you. But perhaps not. Or perhaps you will have to fill in the details for him a little? Or maybe he will fall into your arms and you will be happy ever after. But we cannot be sure.'

Nina felt something flutter in her chest. Sabine was right. She had no idea whether Pierre would remember her in the same way. Their relationship had been intense, but it had been short. And they'd both been young.

'I see that you are thinking about it!' Sabine said. 'But don't worry; I was bored today and so I wrote some ideas down for you!' She pointed to a notebook on the oak table. 'Would you like to practice?'

Nina didn't feel as if she had much choice in the matter, so allowed herself to be led to the table. The notebook was filled with ideas and although she was a little overwhelmed at how much thought Sabine had put into it, she really felt as if she owed a lot to this young woman, who'd plonked herself down in Nina's life and seemed to be so invested.

'Wow,' she said, looking at the notes. 'You really *were* bored.'

Sabine shrugged. 'Well, I like the action,' she said. 'I am not used to being still! Perhaps I am ready to travel again.' She grinned. 'But also, it is nice, helping you with this. I suppose I am a romantic at heart,' she said, touching her chest. 'And your story touches me.'

'Well, thank you,' Nina said. 'I wish...' She trailed off and Sabine looked at her interestedly.

'You wish what?'

'Well, that I had your confidence. I seem to doubt myself the whole time.'

'Don't be silly! You are here, alone. That takes confidence, even if you are also a little nervous,' said Sabine.

'Maybe,' Nina said. 'It's just... I wanted to come here because I never took risks before. Things hadn't gone so well for me and I suppose I thought I'd try to be the opposite. Someone who says yes to everything!'

Sabine nodded.

'Only, I'm still the same person inside,' Nina said, touching her chest. 'A coward.'

'That is ridiculous! You are doing so many brave things.'

Nina shrugged.

Sabine shook her head. 'It makes me sad that you see yourself like this,' she said. 'But there are ways to build confidence.'

'Your notes?'

'Yes, perhaps. But other ways. By taking more risks and finding things turn out OK. Tell me, what is something else you wish to do but perhaps you feel too scared?'

'Sky diving?'

'OK, anything else?'

'Rollerblading?' she mooted.

'OK.' Sabine nodded, thoughtfully.

'Cold water swimming?'

'Yes!' Sabine's cry almost made Nina jump. 'Yes, wild swimming in the sea, yes? I have done this and it is magical.'

Nina nodded. 'See I've never dared.'

'But it is not too late! We have definitely cold water here!' Sabine said. 'And we can go tomorrow!'

'Oh I don't think...'

'Yes! I must leave soon. We have to seize the day. This will be good for you. For your confidence before you see Pierre.'

'I just don't think...'

'No, it is settled. We will do this,' Sabine nodded firmly. 'And

Nina, you will find your confidence.' She passed Nina a sheaf of notes. 'Now, let's practice.'

In some ways, it was wonderful, having this strange, kind brother and sister duo helping her. In others, it was odd – she felt propelled forward rather than taking things at her own pace. But perhaps that was a good thing. Perhaps otherwise she'd never move forward at all.

26

'Good morning!'

'Wha... Where... Am I...?' Nina shot up in bed, rubbing her eyes. The air was cold in the bedroom and even though her shutters were slightly ajar, there was no light yet visible outside.

Sabine stood in the doorway of her bedroom, resplendent in a pair of multi-coloured yoga pants and a baggy, white jumper. Her hair was gathered into a messy bun.

'Come on lazy girl, it is time to get up! We must make the most of this opportunity!' she cried. 'Let's go!'

Nina, still not one 100 per cent sure whether she was dreaming, gazed blearily at her new housemate. 'What's happened?' she asked. 'Why have you...?'

'Pah! Nothing has happened. And nothing will happen if we stay in bed for all the day,' Sabine said, scornfully. 'Today, we are going wild swimming! Remember?'

Somewhere in the back of Nina's mind, a memory stirred. 'Today?' she said.

'Today. We talked yesterday, remember? This is the way you will find confidence. You will know that you can achieve anything!'

Nina remembered being vaguely enthusiastic last night, but the cold morning darkness had drained her of this completely. *All I'm going to achieve is hypothermia*, she thought but managed to stop herself saying.

'Oh yes,' she said. 'But I didn't realise we were talking about this morning specifically...'

'We didn't,' Sabine admitted. 'But it is so important to take the chance! You told me you longed to do it. So why not this morning!'

Nina could think of a few reasons, but none of them could be expressed without several curse words. 'Um,' she said.

'So come on! Up! Up! Up!' Sabine cried, clapping her hands and reminding Nina of a particularly driven PE teacher at school.

She found herself climbing out of bed, self-conscious in her small T-shirt and knickers, and picking up a pair of jogging bottoms from where she'd slung them on a chair.

'Right. Five minutes. Coffee,' Sabine said, sternly. Then she gave a cheeky wink and disappeared from view.

Nina had to use all her self-resolve not to collapse back into the bed and pull the duvet over her face. *You're a grown adult!* she told herself sternly. *You are allowed to say no to things!* But whether it was her tendency to people please, Sabine's forthright instructive persuasion or the fact she had made a promise to herself to try something new, she found herself instead rifling through her drawer for her swimming costume. She found it – shrivelled and black and slightly worse for wear – tucked behind a pair of warm socks and slipped into it. Then pulled on jogging bottoms, a T-shirt and a thick hoody, laced up her trainers and looked in the mirror.

She looked exactly as she suspected she'd look. Dishevelled. Doomed.

But taking a breath, she turned and made her way downstairs. *It'll be a good anecdote*, she reminded herself, *if I survive.*

Moments later, they were in the VW, chugging down to the

front. The van smelled of petrol and cigarettes, its seat sank beneath Nina's bottom and she could feel stiff, unyielding springs under the upholstery. Sabine was chatting away, but only twenty minutes into her day, Nina found it hard to concentrate. Instead, she took in the sights of early morning Cagnes-sur-Mer – lights sprinkled in windows, a few cars moving along the road in the semi-darkness. The shops and cafés on the front were mostly illuminated, but still closed. It was only six o'clock after all.

That was the problem, she thought. She'd said she might like to try cold water swimming. But she hadn't said anything about six o'clock in the bloody morning. Was this part of it? Was the early hour meant to enhance the confidence-boosting properties of an icy swim? At least there'd be no one else on the beach, she supposed.

In almost no time, Sabine stamped on the brake and expertly guided the van into a car parking space on the front. They'd driven to a sandy stretch of beach close to the main promenade. At least, Nina thought, she'd been spared the prospect of pebbles. She hardly recognised her surroundings in the dark – was this the beach she'd walked to, or another one entirely? And was it really safe to swim in the sea when you barely knew where you were on dry land?

'Which beach is this?' she asked Sabine.

'Ah, it is La Plage du Grand Large,' her friend replied.

'A big large?' Nina said, wondering whether the name had been chosen to honour the bottoms of women like her, dragged to the beach to humiliate or freeze themselves in the ocean.

'Ha yes,' Sabine said, smiling. 'Because the sea stretches for miles.'

'I know how he feels.'

Sabine gave her a smile and pulled on the handbrake noisily. 'Come' she said. 'Bring your towel.'

At this time of the morning, the air was bitingly cold, blowing in from the surface of the sea and reminding Nina that although sometimes in the day it felt quite summery, it really was the cusp of autumn. Sabine seemed undeterred, striding towards the water's edge, smiling. 'Ah, I have forgotten how amazing this can be!' she said.

She lay her towel on the sand and, then sat on it and took off her shoes, placing them on each side of the towel. 'For the wind,' she said. Then she stripped off her top and trousers as if it was a summer's day and she couldn't wait to be rid of their pesky warmth.

Nina slowly copied her, removing her trainers, jogging bottoms and finally her hoody. Then looked properly at her friend and gasped.

Sabine was now entirely naked.

'Oh,' her friend said, as if just having an ordinary, casual conversation, not standing in front of someone on a chilly beach in the semi-darkness entirely naked. 'You have decided to wear a costume. I find it is more free with nothing at all.'

'Er, I think I prefer this,' Nina said, covering herself with her arms as if Sabine might at any minute encourage her to rip the suit free and run into the sea as naked as a newborn. 'This time at least.'

Sabine shrugged, then turned and ran to the shallows, splashing in as if they were a clement temperature until she was up to her thighs. Then she turned. 'Come! Nina!' she said. 'It is truly wonderful!'

Unconvinced and already about as cold as it was possible to get, Nina followed – stepping into the tiny ripples at the edge of the sea and finding the water to be far from wonderful. Deadly would be a better description.

But she'd said she'd do it. And she'd promised herself that

she'd be brave and bold and all the things you say when you're feeling at one with the world and a couple of red wines down. So she pushed each foot forward, grimacing as the water lapped at her shins.

In front, her naked friend seemed to have no such sensibilities and was already waist deep (which in some ways was a relief) and splashing in the water like a toddler on holiday.

Nina had read articles extolling the benefits of cold water swimming. It would improve her mood! Her immune system! Help her to burn calories! She would feel exhilarated! Cleansed! Invigorated! Fit! So far, she seemed simply to be in danger of hyperthermia and in need of the largest cup of hot... anything she'd ever had. But it was now or never. She'd made it this far and she couldn't imagine ever putting herself through it again. She didn't want to be the person who fell at the final hurdle. So somehow, she managed to step a few more paces and push herself forward and...

...and she was swimming! As her arms moved through the water, she realised that some sort of defence had kicked in in her body and she no longer felt the extremity of the cold. She felt fresh, and while not invigorated, she hadn't died of the shock – so better than she'd thought she'd be.

Sabine was ahead, doing a gentle breaststroke and watching the edges of the clouds begin to lighten as the sun finally dragged itself from slumber and began its slow ascent towards its place in the autumn sky. She glanced back at Nina. 'See!' she said. 'You love it!'

'I wouldn't go that far!' Nina said, swallowing a gulp of seawater in the process.

'Ah but you do! You are smiling.'

And Nina realised that although she hadn't been aware of it, her lips were stretched to a smile. Unless it was rigor mortis, she was actually – on some subconscious level – happy.

Half an hour later, they were shivering in the van. Sabine pulled a flask from a string bag and passed her a plastic cup. 'Now,' she said, 'we get warm. It is important.' She filled the cup with dark, strong hot chocolate and as Nina sipped, she felt her body shudder in gratefulness.

'You are OK?' Sabine said, looking at her sideways.

Nina nodded. Her face and body felt stiff, as if in defence against the experience she'd just put it through. But inside, her heart, her body felt light. It was an odd combination.

'When we get back, you must take a bath,' said Sabine. 'We do not want you ill for your date.'

Nina managed to nod again.

Sabine drank deeply from her own hot chocolate mug. 'And thank you,' she said.

'Thank me?' Nina asked, incredulous.

'Yes, for wanting to do this. For coming with me. Ah, yes, maybe I am an adventurer. But it is not always easy to get the motivation up to do something like this alone. It helped me that you wanted to come. And now I remember why I loved the water so much,' Sabine said, smiling and seemingly not at all cold. Her cheeks and nose were pink and her fingertips wrapped around her cup, were not pale as Nina's had become.

'Well, thank you too,' Nina said. 'I'd never have done it without you. I can't actually believe I've done it *with* you, if I'm honest.'

Sabine laughed. 'Then perhaps I am a bad influence on you. I get you into all sorts of danger,' she said.

'No,' Nina said, feeling the muscles of her face relax a little as her core temperature began to build, 'I actually think you're really good for me.'

'Then we are good for each other,' Sabine said. 'It's easier for me to be strong when someone needs my help. And perhaps right now, you need someone like me to encourage you. And the result is now we have both enjoyed a swim before the rest of the world even have their trousers on!'

Nina snorted. 'I suppose we have.'

'And now you can be brave. To meet Pierre. Because there are difficult things in life, but that does not mean we cannot do them. We can do the difficult things if we really want to.'

'As long as there's hot chocolate afterwards?' Nina said.

'Yes, *exactly*. With a hot chocolate, we can do anything!'

27

Sunday morning, Nina woke up early. She felt a little sick – as if the day ahead was far more momentous than it really was. She tried to remind herself that she wasn't getting married, or going to a job interview; she didn't have to perform on stage or go for a hospital appointment. She was simply going to have a game of amateur pétanque – something she was now reasonably proficient at – and perhaps get the chance to chat with an old friend. That was all. That was *all*, she told herself sternly. Still, her heart continued to beat at what felt like a rapid rate.

The pétanque group wasn't due to meet until 11 a.m., but now, at 6.30 a.m., she knew she had no hope of going back to sleep. The most sensible thing to do would be to distract herself as best she could. Quietly making her way downstairs so as not to wake Sabine just in case her adventurous friend fancied another ice-cold dip, she made herself a strong coffee and sat scrolling through her phone.

There was a message from Sal.

Oh my God. Jean-Luc asked me to take him to the theatre. So we went to Les Misérables at the West End. Nina – I'd forgotten how much I loved going into London on a night out. And seeing it all with Jean-Luc, it felt brand new! But that's not the best bit.

What's the best bit?

There was a pause but then the circle next to Sal's name went green. Her friend was online.

At the end, we kissed! And Oh My God it was something!

She replied, finding herself smiling.

Amazing!

It was kind of nice to feel that even if her bizarre plan failed to end well, she'd given Sal a little bit of happiness by sending Jean-Luc to her. She hoped he was as nice as his siblings seemed to be. Sal deserved a bit of luck romantically.

She thought back to her self-pitying, drunken rant on her birthday. Telling Bess and Sal that they were lucky. Sal hadn't taken her to task on this, but she'd have had every right to. It wasn't as if her friend had had it easy – and being a mother didn't repair all the different hurts Sal had experienced over the years. When she was home – whatever happened here – she resolved to be a better friend. Less selfish.

There was another email from Mum too.

Hello love,

I hope you're having a lovely time in France. Have you sent us a postcard? We keep checking the mail, but nothing's come so far. Do think to send us one if you get the chance! Dad keeps them all you know.

Our news is that Dad's bought a bench press. Reckons he's going to build muscle. I said he'd have to do more with it than he did with the exercise bike. That's still in the corner of our bedroom. I use it to air my smalls. I've said he can keep it in your room, but only until you arrive! We can't have him huffing and puffing in the corner when you're trying to settle in.

Rupert's taken to sitting on Dad's stomach when he tries to lift weights. Your father always asks me to move him, but I think Rupert's taken quite the shine! I call them gym buddies.

Anyway, ta ta for now.

Much love,

MUM

Alongside Sal's message, Mum's email and an advert from her local Indian restaurant, there was a note from the solicitor, saying that they were approaching exchange and it looked as if completion was likely to be in a month's time – a little sooner than she'd originally asked for. She replied that this was fine. She'd be back by then to move her things out, maybe put some into storage. Then, if no better offer had come her way – and it didn't look likely – it would be back to Mum and Dad's, her childhood room with its single bed and faded posters.

The lack of panic she felt surprised her. Perhaps it was the image of Dad up that ladder, wobbling away or the thought of him straining himself pumping iron. Maybe it was Sabine's wistful words about her own mother. It wouldn't hurt Mum and Dad to have a little help from her now.

An hour later and two coffees down, she went upstairs to take a shower. She'd chosen her outfit – something pétanque friendly, and that didn't look as if she was 'trying too hard' – and laid it out on the bed now. Some three-quarter length jeans and a well-fitted black top, a loose cardigan over the top and her favourite necklace. Something she'd feel smart but still herself in.

She wondered how Pierre would feel if he knew how momentous this day felt to her. Would he be excited too? Flattered? And was he with someone? Nobody, even her two French friends/amateur detectives had been able to tell her this for sure, but hopefully that was a good sign.

She wished she'd been able to scroll fully through his Facebook page – which was private other than the key details she already knew – or find a little more out about his history. Whether he'd been married before, as she had, or stayed single all these years (which seemed unlikely). Did he have children out there somewhere? Was he a part-time dad? Or was he happily married, settled and completely besotted with a gorgeous, perfect wife?

She expelled her breath sharply and tried to stop her mind wandering. It would be disappointing, she told herself, but it wouldn't matter. She needn't tell him anything more about why she was there than felt comfortable. She'd probably never confess to him the lengths she'd gone to track him down and arrange a meeting – not until much later in their relationship if they ended up having one.

She thought back to the scenarios she'd rehearsed with Sabine. The first, that he'd recognise her instantly, had felt farfetched – especially as he'd definitely seen her in the restaurant and hadn't immediately been able to place her. The worst-case-scenario – that he had no idea who she was and in any case was in a happy, committed relationship – had been much easier to buy into.

But Sabine, clearly a hopeless romantic at heart, had told her that she believed things were going to happen for Nina and Pierre. 'I feel it,' she'd said, clutching her hands together in front of her heart and looking briefly to the heavens. Or at least in the direction of them. 'I feel that this is going to be truly magical.'

Could people really feel things? Nina had always been deeply sceptical about the idea of anything approaching psychic powers or gut feelings about people or places. But something about Sabine's enthusiasm was infectious.

She imagined herself now, walking up to Pierre. How his face would change a little as he felt something stir in his memory. How it would light up when he realised who she was. They'd disappear together, talking non-stop to catch up on their years apart. And everything would fall into place. *Well, why not?* she thought. *Why shouldn't that happen for me?*

She and Rory had met in a lecture at university – they'd been sitting together and she'd had to borrow a pen. After the lecture, she'd forgotten to return it, and had had to track him down in the student bar where he'd bought her a drink. They'd been friends first – something people told her was a Good Thing. Then one night, he'd leaned in and kissed her and she'd thought, why not?

There had definitely been attraction there, chemistry between them. And in many ways, too, he'd been a best friend. But it had never been the all-consuming pull she'd felt for Pierre. They'd moved in together at twenty five and when he'd asked her to marry him a few years later, it had seemed like the logical step. Their relationship hadn't been a disaster. It had been great, at first. Then good. There just hadn't been quite enough between them to keep them together 'till death do us part.'

Deep down, it had probably been her fault, she thought. Because she'd experienced something so strong and life-affirming with Pierre in that magical week. She'd put her feelings for him to one side, of course. Gone to university, met Rory. Felt completely committed when she'd been saying her 'I dos' and had looked back on the French affair with a kind of fondness for her former self. But perhaps on some level she'd always held a torch for him?

She pulled on her clothes and brushed her hair into its usual shape, then applied a little make-up: some tinted moisturiser, a touch of mascara – nothing too outlandish that would look out of place at a casual pétanque meet.

Both Sabine and Antoine had offered to join her, but she'd refused; this was something she really needed to do on her own. Having an audience would make it excruciating.

It was only 9 a.m., but she decided to take a walk to steady herself. Sabine was still snoring steadily in her room, and the silence of the house was driving her mad. She opened the door as quietly as she could and stepped into the morning air.

The days had fallen into a recognisable pattern. Each seemed to start with a slight mist in the air, the temperature cool but not cold. Then, around ten or eleven, the autumn sun would burn this off and the day would come into itself. Once or twice, the temperature had reached the high twenties – summer weather where she came from. Most of the time it settled at a comfortable twenty-three. She'd been praying the rain that was predicted for some time in the next few days would hold off and it seemed that her prayers had been answered – today, beyond the light mist, there didn't seem to be a cloud in the sky, apart from a few fluffy white specimens that looked no threat to anyone.

She breathed in and was about to step forward, heading probably for the front as she often did, when she heard a strange buzzing sound. She looked along the road to the corner and saw a man on an electric bike making his way towards her at barely more than a snail's pace.

Antoine. She shook her head and smiled at his slow progress. What was he doing here?

She stayed put and waited for him to draw up. As he did so, his bike wobbled and almost fell, and he performed a strange, jumping and staggering manoeuvre until finally getting his balance back and standing up, red-faced, to look at her.

'You alright?' she asked, nodding at the bike to acknowledge his near fall.

'Yes,' he said, removing his helmet, his hair squashed flat against his head. He smiled at her and it was impossible not to reciprocate.

'Sabine's still asleep, I'm afraid,' she told him. 'I can...'

He put a hand on her arm. 'No, please don't. It was you I came to see.'

'Me?'

'Yes, I am on my way to my friend's house, but I want to stop and wish you good luck,' he said. 'I hope all goes well with your pétanque and with Pierre.'

'Thank you,' she said, her mouth feeling slightly wobbly. It was great that Antoine and Sabine seemed so invested in her love life – and sometimes quite a comfort to know she had people rooting for her. But there was a pressure there too; because if today went badly, people would know about it. They'd see her foolishness for what it was.

She had a sudden urge to book a taxi, jump on a plane and write it all off as a huge mistake.

But that was old Nina talking. New Nina took risks, seized the day. Did all that *carpe diem* stuff. Or at least, she was trying to.

'Do you want...?' she said, making an obligatory gesture towards the house and hoping he realised that she meant coffee rather than breakfast or something less wholesome.

But he shook his head. 'I must go,' he said, lifting his helmet ready to slide his head inside. Then he stopped, closed his eyes and took a breath, expelling it in a sudden, enormous sigh. Opening his eyes again, he fixed his gaze on her. 'But I want to say, too, that if this Pierre... if he does not fall at your feet, then he is a fool,' he said. 'I wanted to say this last night but my words would not come.'

'Oh!'

He shrugged. 'But of course. You are beautiful, Nina. You are brave and clever and you came here for him. There are many men, I am sure, who would want to trade places with this man.'

She began to scoff. Then she realised that there was something behind his eyes, something underneath his words that he was trying to tell her. 'Oh,' she said, more softly.

He looked over her shoulder and for a moment, she followed his gaze, confused. But it seemed he was looking at nothing, thinking, perhaps about what to say next. 'Sabine tells me that you are trying to be braver,' he said. 'With your naked swimming and your rollerblading.'

'I wasn't actually nak—'

'And I will try to be brave too,' he said. 'Nina, I know you have your heart set on someone else. That you have this dream of Pierre. But since I first saw you, I felt something. As if,' he stopped, a look passing over his face, 'as if I have already known you for many years, but also as if it is the first time. It is hard to explain.'

'Oh,' she said.

'I do not expect you to say anything now. It is the wrong time to tell you this. And if Pierre, he feels as you do, I hope that you will find happiness. But if not, perhaps you will find in time, there is room for someone new,' he said. 'And I'd like to be that person, Nina.'

She opened her mouth to speak but closed it again.

'You came here looking for an old love,' he said. 'But maybe he is not what you remembered. And perhaps you are not the person you used to be either. Maybe it is time for a *new* love. Someone who sees you as you are now and thinks that you are perfect.'

'Antoine… I…' she began, not quite knowing what she was about to say, her heart thundering against her ribs and a tremble moving through her body. She recognised his words, she realised. Almost as if she'd known what he was going to say.

He slid his helmet on. 'It is OK, you do not need to say anything. I know that this is something you must do,' he said. 'It is important to see Pierre and find out – answer this question. But I cannot help it if I hope for a different ending to your story,' he shrugged. 'Love is always complicated!'

She nodded, finding her voice. 'It is,' she said. 'It really is.'

Moments later, he'd disappeared around the corner in a buzz of low-powered battery noise, and she was left stunned. She'd been so sure that Antoine was just an attentive brother, just helpful to her because of Sabine. But perhaps she'd misread the signs all along?

28

THEN

'Where are we going?' Nina asked breathlessly as she half walked, half ran behind him into the dark courtyard. She knew it was misguided to disappear with a boy she barely knew, but something about Pierre made her feel safe. She would trust her intuition.

Around the back of the hall close to the school field which lay in almost complete darkness, he stopped and turned to her. Distant lights shone on the road beyond the playing field and she could hear the traffic make its way along the nearby road. They were so close to civilisation, so close to everyday things. Yet this was... well, it felt magical and amazing.

Then his lips were on hers. Gently, softly, taking his time in a way none of her previous boyfriends had done. They'd been all tongue and braces and hopeful, groping hands. He kissed her like they were in a movie.

'Nina,' he said, pulling away. 'I think I am in love with you.'

She laughed, not because she thought it ridiculous but because nobody had ever said that to her before, and she couldn't believe that this handsome, popular boy even liked her, let alone loved her.

'Sorry,' she said, and she looked at him. What was love? She wondered. Because if it was this indescribable pull towards him, the feeling of completeness she felt when they were together, the fact that the idea of leaving him made her feel wretched, then she must feel it too. 'Me too,' she said, softly, uncertainly.

Then he kissed her again. Deeply and for longer than before, and she felt beautiful and grown-up and like the type of girl boys fall in love with all the time.

It was typical that she should meet a boy who loved her, whom she loved too, in a place so far away from home.

Tomorrow, they were due to leave. But she was determined to make the most of tonight.

29

NOW

After Antoine left, she sat for a while – almost stunned by what he'd said and not entirely sure how to feel. The morning, which had started so promising, had become white-skied with a hint of rain in the air. The weather was turning, just slightly, reminding her that even in this place that felt like summer, autumn was on its way.

Nina liked the autumn, ordinarily. Liked the feeling of snuggling up in the warm, gently lit cosiness of her living room, hot chocolate in hand, pyjamas on by nine o'clock and a film streaming on the TV. But here, in this strange place she'd begun to see as different and exotic, the autumnal feel was a little unsettling. It was as if the British weather had cottoned on to her plan and was saying, *Hey Nina! You belong in England; what are you doing here?*

Antoine's words had made her feel strange, less certain about what she was doing. Was he right? Would Pierre be changed beyond recognition? Was she being foolish? And why had she felt so suddenly drawn to him when she'd read that old letter? Was it because she'd felt something similar beneath the surface or – and more likely – was she just so needy after the rejection of divorce that she was ready to swoon into anyone's arms if they expressed enough enthusiasm?

Before she'd left for pétanque, an email had arrived from Jemima – cheerily efficient even on a Sunday. Not mentioning work. More of a 'just wondered how it's all going?' message. But somehow, it had thrown her – pierced through the bubble she'd been living in and reminded her that there was a real world with a job and responsibilities and the necessity to move boxes back into her childhood bedroom shortly.

She'd replied – because she couldn't ever bring herself to ignore someone, however inappropriate it was for them to interrupt her holiday – giving a generic, cheery 'having a great time' response, and hoped that Jemima would now leave her alone until the end of her break. She hadn't mentioned that she'd considered not going back at all... Although she'd composed a message along those lines a couple of times in her head, her fingers simply refused to seize the day and tell her boss. It was sensible, she'd told herself, keeping her options open.

What about taking a risk? her mind had pointed out.

But there was no point taking a risk in this situation, she'd decided. There was nothing much to be gained by flinging her safety net from under her. Not yet. She'd only been here a week and a bit – although somehow, it seemed longer – and hadn't even spoken to Pierre yet.

Last night, she and Antoine had wandered down to the 'boulodrome' – she'd been terrified at the word at first. It sounded like an enormous arena or something: the kind of place that might feature in a *Mad Max* movie, not somewhere an amateur would dare to venture. But Antoine had laughed and told her it was simply a rectangle of pétanque courts where people could turn up and play when they wanted.

'Sometimes, people just go there with friends,' he'd said.

'Sometimes, there is a group, like the one Pierre is part of. But don't worry. Nobody is professional. People are not all young and fit.'

She'd smiled at his reassurance, although later wondered whether he was suggesting that she was neither of those two things.

They'd arrived, pétanque balls in hand, and watched for a while from a café opposite the courts. The boulodrome consisted of around nine courts, laid out neatly within a slightly raised rectangle, surrounded by trees and shrubs, parking spaces and eventually a line of cafés and shops. Antoine had been right – it seemed that everyone and anyone could play pétanque. She saw groups of teenagers in jeans and a group of smartly dressed office workers. A couple on a date, who threw half-hearted shots and laughed and fell into each other's arms after each failure. There was a family: parents, grandparents and two young children occupying another of the courts. The atmosphere felt relaxed and the play was definitely not all on a professional level.

She'd tried to imagine herself walking up to one of the groups, as she would have to the following day, and felt that she could picture it. That it wouldn't be, after all, so very terrifying.

She'd sipped a white wine and felt herself relax a little about the prospect of the next day. And when Antoine asked her if she wanted to try the courts out, she'd felt fine about it, joining the other mismatched teams on the boulodrome, and finding a spare court where they'd flung a few boules and she'd found that she felt relatively confident about that side of things now.

'Thanks,' she'd said to Antoine afterwards, shortly after turning down his offer of a 'lift' home – she knew now what that meant. 'You've really helped.'

'Good,' he'd said, lifting his hand as if to brush some hair from her forehead, but hesitating then dropping his arm. 'And remember, if you do need me to walk with you or even come to play pétanque, then I am free tomorrow and you only have to call.'

And here she was, looking at the pétanque courts and feeling slightly unsettled in her stomach. She was slightly early but a group were already gathering, standing and talking in rapid French by the entrance, one or two carrying bags that probably held boules and a target ball. Some were dressed in shorts, which seemed a little optimistic based on the weather forecast. There was an elderly man leaning on a cane, two older women, a couple of younger, and three men, none of whom was Pierre.

Part of her was relieved not to see him. She could turn up, play pétanque and go home without having to face potential rejection – scenario three of Sabine's suggested outcomes. The other part felt disappointed – but then it was early. There was still time.

Feeling herself quiver slightly inside, she threw her shoulders back, tried to walk confidently and approached the group. She tapped one of the women on the shoulder and when she turned, said, 'Is this where the pétanque club meets?' with her best French accent.

'Yes,' said the woman. 'Are you going to join us?'

'I hope so, if that's OK?'

'Yes, we will need to get you the forms to join the club. But you can do that later. Today, you can try, if you want?' the woman said.

'Thank you.'

'We will start soon,' the woman added.

They fell into an awkward silence.

'I'm Nina, by the way,' she said.

'Oh, yes. Sorry. I am Anne-Sophie,' said the woman, with a smile. 'You are English?'

Was it really so obvious?

'Yes,' Nina said.

'So you are on holidays?'

'Well, staying here for a while,' Nina said, not quite sure how to brand her visit and not wanting to be told the club wasn't for tourists. 'I have friends who live here,' she added, which was true now, she supposed.

Anne-Sophie nodded. 'That's nice,' she said. 'And you have played before.'

'A little,' Nina said, shrugging her shoulders and realising she may well have reached 'Peak French' in that moment. Since being here, she'd noticed how modest people could be – especially when it came to their language skills. Occasionally, she'd been in a shop or restaurant speaking French, only to have the staff member speak back to her in flawless English. No matter how amazing their level was, when she asked them 'Oh do you speak English?' they'd always replied with 'A little.'

The group stood together, with small conversations breaking out between various members – exchanging kisses of greeting, shaking hands.

'OK,' said Anne-Sophie, 'I think this is all now.'

She said something quickly to one of the men who'd nodded. 'Let's start?' he suggested, looking at the group. There were twelve of them in all now, but no Pierre. The man quickly divided them into groups of four and they moved to separate courts to start their play.

Nina had just resigned herself to the fact that this was not going to be her day when there was a screech of tyres. A small, silver convertible pulled into one of the empty spaces. Its door opened and there he was, *her* Pierre, looking slightly unkempt and rushed. He locked his car and walked quickly to the man who'd assigned the groups, who gestured at the three teams, two of which had started their matches. Nina's group had not quite got there yet.

Pierre nodded to the man, and walked quickly to her group.

That was the end of Nina's game. With Pierre close, she found each time she threw the pétanque ball, it landed embarrassingly far from the target. But in her defence, she felt every sinew of her body respond to the fact that Pierre was there, playing pétanque with her. They stood together in a little group of four while the fifth had their turn, and made general conversation. But nobody had introduced her to him, and she didn't quite know where to start.

The kind of conversation that bubbled up in their small group was the kind made out of the side of the mouth while the eyes remain fixed on the court. Comments about the player's performance, the weather, something about politics that she got lost completely trying to follow. Still, she was a little disheartened by the fact he hadn't recognised her yet. Then again, she told herself, making yet another disastrous throw, he'd barely looked at her so far, and the last thing he'd be expecting at a pétanque club in his hometown would be the ex-girlfriend from his teens suddenly turning up brandishing a boule.

She had to do something to make this happen. Not simply linger on the periphery of his vision and hope that he did all the hard work for her. She'd come this far – flown to his hometown, taken a month off work (or maybe quit altogether), planned and schemed and dreamed. She was right next to him, had a legitimate reason to strike up a conversation. Surely this was the moment she should seize, and if not, what had she done all the other things for?

She thought back to the wild swimming – how difficult it had been at first, how she'd almost run screaming as the icy water had lapped around her thighs. But how she'd pushed herself forward and suddenly found herself swimming.

As she returned to the group, blushing a little at her lack of skill, she made sure to stand next to him.

Their bodies were almost touching. He was wearing dark jeans and a T-shirt, his arms bare. He'd thickened since they'd met –

hardly surprising that he no longer had the physique of a seventeen-year-old boy – but in a good way. He looked fit, strong, tanned. His hair was a little unkempt, but then he'd clearly rushed to the club this morning, and it had sprung into slight curls. He had a smattering of stubble where he'd had no time to shave. She looked up at him, hoping to catch his attention, and suddenly, his eyes were on her, an expression on his face that registered slight confusion.

'You're new, I think,' he said, holding out his hand. 'I'm Pierre.'

She took it, wondering if he too could feel the electrical charge pulse between them. Was memory ever held in the body? she wondered. Would his skin recognise her touch even if his brain couldn't quite place her?

'Nina,' she said.

He paused, his eyes studying her face so intently that she almost felt she should glance away. She tried to keep calm, hold his gaze.

At last he spoke. 'I am sorry,' he said, 'but you look very familiar. Have we met somewhere before?'

30

Anyone watching from the outside probably wouldn't know the momentous thing that had happened to Nina. Had she been seven years old, she'd probably have skipped and danced all the way home. But that sort of behaviour from a forty-year-old woman would probably lead to someone calling the police or psychiatric support.

So she was walking. But boy, inside, she was skipping. Because everything she could have possibly hoped for had happened.

'I came to Cagnes-sur-Mer a long time ago,' she'd said, 'on French exchange.'

He'd done a double take, looked at her face – she hoped she'd managed to pluck that stray chin hair that came to visit every few weeks – and then said. 'You're my Nina?'

'Hang on,' she'd said, trying to give the impression of someone also racking her brain. 'You're not... is it Pierre Dupont?'

'Yes!' he'd said excitedly. 'That is me!'

'Oh my goodness!' she'd feigned. 'I never imagined you'd still be living here! I just... I remembered the great time I'd had here and wanted to visit the town again. But…' she trailed off under his intense gaze.

'But we found each other. Perhaps just by chance, by our love of pétanque,' he'd smiled.

'Um, yes.'

He'd reached up his hand that until that moment had been tucked in his pocket and brushed her hair slightly from her face. 'And you look just the same,' he'd said. 'If not, even more beautiful.'

She'd felt her face get hot. 'So do you,' she said. 'Look the same, I mean.'

Then it was his turn to throw his boules. It was almost painful waiting for him to return. But as soon as he'd thrown his – remarkably accurate – shots, he'd been back at her side. 'We must catch up!' he said. 'I do not remember why we did not keep talking all those years ago.'

She decided not to fill him in on the fact that, she supposed, she'd ghosted him, although at the time, it wouldn't have been called that. 'Uh huh,' she'd said, as if for her, too, the reason she hadn't come to him had been lost in the mists of time.

'You are single?' he said, nodding towards her left hand. 'Or are you here with your husband or boyfriend, perhaps?'

'No,' she'd said. 'I mean, no husband, no boyfriend.'

It seemed almost too easy. His asking her that upfront so early on in their conversation. As if he wasn't afraid of revealing his hand. Of revealing that he was still interested even after all these years. 'And you?' she asked, emboldened by his courage.

He'd held up his hand. 'No ring, sadly,' he'd said. 'Perhaps, as they say, I have been waiting for the right person.' And he'd held her gaze long enough for her to feel a quiver inside.

Then it had been her turn to throw boules. And she'd completely lost any semblance of an aim she'd had – one of her throws ended up on another court. But although it had been embarrassing, it hadn't mattered. He was here, he remembered her and, in some ways, it was as if she'd never left him.

She'd hoped he might stay afterwards, ask her for lunch or a drink or to walk somewhere, but he'd had to go. But not before he'd arranged for them to meet for an evening meal the next night and exchanged phone numbers. She had a date with Pierre. She. Had. A. DATE. With. Pierre!

She practically burst into the house, desperate to either see Sabine or to ring Bess or something – she had to let the joy and nervousness and the unreality of it all out to someone. So, when she saw her friend, dressed in pyjama bottoms and a vest top, her hair scruffy from bed, drinking coffee at the table, she was so glad she was there to confide in she almost jumped into her arms.

'Sabine!' she gasped, causing her new friend to almost slop coffee all down her front.

'*Oh my God!*' Sabine said, placing the mug on the table and looking up. 'You have almost killed me.' She peered at Nina's face, her brows furrowing. 'Is something the matter?'

'No!' Nina almost cried. 'No! Just the opposite!'

She sat down, realising she was trembling slightly with it all, and recounted the details of the morning. Her initial nerves, Pierre's late arrival, her struggle to talk to him and then the moment they connected. 'And he remembered me!' she said. 'As soon as I mentioned that I was here once on French exchange, it all came back to him!'

'And was he mad at you for stopping the letters? For not coming to be with him?'

Nina shook her head. 'That's the best bit!' she said. 'He seems to have forgotten all about it, or if he hasn't, he's forgiven me and doesn't want to bring it up.' She realised she was babbling but couldn't seem to stop. 'Sabine, he's single and he's invited me on a date tomorrow evening!' She felt almost giddy at how easily, how readily things had fallen into place. Perhaps fate did exist. Perhaps she'd been so sure of herself, so convinced that things never really happened for reason, that she'd blinded herself to signs, to life events that had pushed her to exactly this place. A second chance, twenty-three years after what might have been the worst mistake of her life. She thought back to the lucky dog and bird poo incident. Perhaps fate had been trying to give her a clue after all? Then again, perhaps it was better to think of it as written in the stars than spelled out with animal excrement.

'This is wonderful!' Sabine said. 'I am so very happy for you! And we must choose you something beautiful to wear, no? I have started to pack some of my bags, but I have a scarf that perhaps you can borrow?'

Nina felt something sink. 'You're packing?' she said.

'Yes, I am starting to. I am not leaving for a small time but I will need to start thinking about it, if I want to visit all the places I wish and be in Vienna for the markets,' she said. 'And I have the fidgets.'

'The fidgets?'

'Yes, an expression. For needing to go. I do not like to sit still for too long.'

Nina nodded, wondering why she felt suddenly flat.

'But do not worry! I will help you for this date, and I can go knowing that you have everything you came for!' Sabine said brightly. 'I will leave with a smile on my face, and I can tell everyone that romance does exist because I have a friend with a magical story.'

Nina smiled. 'Thank you,' she said.

They were silent for a moment.

'You know, I envy you,' she said, unaware until she spoke that she'd been about to express this thought out loud.

'Me? You are jealous?' Sabine put a hand on her chest as if to double-check Nina understood what she was saying. 'But this is ridiculous! Why do you say this?'

Nina shrugged. 'I don't know. I suppose I had the urge to travel – like you – before. And I gave up some opportunities. Gave up on too much, really. And you look back when you're older... Well, it's hard not to wish you'd made different choices. Been freer. Maybe if I was your age, I'd be travelling too,' she said.

Sabine covered her mouth, her shoulders shaking slightly. For a moment, Nina thought she might be crying. Then realised she was actually laughing. 'I am sorry,' she said. 'But it is so drole, so funny.'

Nina flushed. 'What? You don't think I'm being honest with you? Or...?'

'No,' Sabine's hand was on her shoulder. 'I am sorry, I'm not laughing at your wishes and dreams, don't worry. But because you think I am so very, very young.'

Nina looked into the bright-eyed face in front of her. She's going to tell me she's all of twenty-five, she thought, because people in their twenties think that's ANCIENT.

'I am not so much younger than you,' Sabine said.

Nina smiled. 'I suppose fifteen years or so doesn't seem much. It's just in terms of... well, the kind of opportunities open to you. It's a lifetime, really.' Sabine would probably understand more when she got to forty. How all the avenues you felt would always be open seemed somehow closed. How opportunities and chances dried up as you aged. And you found yourself – not stuck, necessarily – but fixed. You became the person you'd been working towards being. Only you hadn't realised the chances to change your fortunes would start to disappear until it was too late.

Sabine grinned. 'I am very flattered that you think this,' she said. 'Because you have told me you are forty, and this must mean you think I am very young.' She shook her head. 'Nina, I am thirty-seven. And I do not think that in three years, I will give up travelling because the calendar says so.'

Nina looked at Sabine's face again. And started to see it differently. Not to imagine wrinkles that weren't there, but to truly see her for the first time. And she realised that perhaps she and Sabine didn't look so very different in age in terms of skin or hair or emerging crows' feet. It was something in Sabine's eyes that projected this aura of youthful energy. It was her spirit, not just her skin, that made her seem so much younger. She felt free, so she was free, at least from the kind of concerns that anchored Nina to the spot.

'Wow,' she said at last. 'Well, you'll have to share your skincare regime secrets with me!'

Sabine laughed. 'I find that being happy is great for the complexion, no?'

'Well,' Nina said. 'I think you're amazing.'

'Pah! Well, do not say this to my brother. Jean-Luc, not Antoine. He thinks that I am a catastrophe. I don't own property. I don't have a career. I make my money from small jobs, and from selling jewellery and besides – I do not need much. But he wants me to get married, to have a job and a house...'

Nina frowned. 'It's not really his business though, is it?'

Sabine smiled. 'Oh, but do not think too badly of him. He loves me. He means the best for me. And he worries because he has so much money already and he compares us. And he thinks that one day, things will not be so good for me. But I tell him that I will be fine. I have time. Maybe one day, I will find a husband. But there is no hurry.'

Nina nodded. 'That's a great attitude,' she said. 'I always feel in such a rush about everything. I mean, I had Pierre... then walked away, but met Rory soon after. And he was a nice guy and it seemed to be the right time. Some of my friends were engaged... Sometimes, I think if I hadn't been in such a rush to tick all the boxes, things might be completely different now.'

'The boxes?'

'Yes, I mean, to...' Nina struggled for words. 'To do all the things that people expect.'

Sabine nodded. 'Yes, I know these things.'

'Yes, and I think I saw them as... marks of success or something? Like things I should be doing. So I did them. It didn't occur to me that... I had the time to pause and get it right.' She smiled.

'But you do.' Sabine said.

'Well, I *did*.'

'No, my friend, you *do*. You have the time now to pause and do what you wish.'

'And to date attractive men I met twenty-three years ago?' Nina joked.

'But of course!' Sabine put a hand on Nina's arm. 'And please do not think that I am always happy. I sometimes wake in the van and I think I must be crazy. And other times, my money runs out and I am eating a stale croissant for breakfast like a dog.'

Nina wasn't sure even French dogs ate croissants, but she kept quiet.

'And I look at my brothers with their homes and their jobs and maybe soon wives and babies and I think there must be something wrong with me,' she said. 'But then I sit with myself and I think about life and I realise that I can choose to be happy or choose to be sad. And I choose to smile,' she said, her mouth stretched wide. 'Because life is short and I enjoy smiling.'

Nina smiled now. 'Well, I think your brothers should be jealous of you,' she said.

Sabine smiled widely. 'That is very kind to say.'

They were silent for a moment, then Sabine said. 'So, let's find you the perfect outfit, yes? Then before I go, I can know that you have your dream.'

31

THEN

The next day, as they waited for the coach, Brigitte's parents assumed that Nina was crying at the prospect of leaving their daughter. 'It has been a pleasure to have you, Nina,' her mother said. 'I am sure that Brigitte will miss you very much too.'

Nina hadn't the heart to correct them. It was just that she'd hoped more than anything that Pierre would come to say goodbye. But of course, he couldn't. He was in lessons – only the French exchange students had been allowed a reprieve to wave their English counterparts off on their journey.

'Come on,' Bess said, giving her a nudge as they were called to the coach. 'I bagsy the window seat.'

Nina nodded. She hadn't told Bess everything that had happened – they'd barely seen each other since the night of the disco. She didn't know exactly what Nina was leaving behind.

Then, just as she began to step up into the coach, there he was, running and red-faced and glancing behind him as if he knew he shouldn't be there.

Pierre! She hoped for a moment that he might sweep her up

and kiss her last night, but of course that wasn't possible. What he did do was slip a letter into her hand, smile briefly, then run back towards the classroom block.

32

NOW

NINA

Guess who I've got a date with?! PIERRE!

BESS

You're kidding!

SAL

Really? No!!

NINA

The very one. He remembered me!

BESS

Blimey.

SAL

French guys are SO romantic.

NINA

Here's hoping. I'm just so glad I found the confidence to bump into him!

BESS

The confidence you found frolicking half-naked in the sea at some ghastly hour of the morning?

NINA

Haha. Hey! Don't knock it till you've tried it!

SAL

I still can't believe you did that! Skinny dipping!

NINA

For the last time, I was in a swimming costume.

SAL

Not when I tell people the anecdote you weren't!

NINA

laughing emoji In all seriousness, I'm pretty nervous though.

BESS

So how are you going to prepare for the date?
More confidence building?

NINA

I hadn't thought. I don't think I could cope with another cold water swim right now, but maybe I'll try something.

BESS

Well, keep us posted.

SAL

Yes! And photos or it didn't happen.

NINA

Of course! Seriously though, it's amazing how open he was about his feelings too.

SAL

Ah, French guys are super romantic. As I'm beginning to find out… *winking emoji*

BESS

Oh God, here she goes. See what I have to put up with? *smiling emoji*

NINA

Ah, I think it's sweet.

SAL

Thanks Nina! And you having a date with Pierre – well, that's… brilliant news.

BESS

I don't know. With you and Sal getting it on with your handsome French men, I'm wondering whether I ought to get in on the action!

NINA

You're happily married, remember?

BESS

An insignificant detail *winking emoji* Happy for you though. When is the date?

NINA

Tomorrow.

BESS

Eek! Squeaky bum time!

SAL

Or hopefully not.

BESS

Quite.

NINA

Haha

SAL

Send us a pic?

BESS

Yes. We need to see Pierre! Explain. He'll understand!

NINA

I'll see what I can do.

Nina was smiling as she came off the chat. It was lovely to have made new friends here, but these two women who always had her back had almost evolved beyond mere friendship. They were her family. Especially now Rory was gone. She lay back on the sofa and sipped her coffee, feeling at one with the world and ready to step into a beautiful future.

* * *

By six o'clock the following evening, she had completely lost her Zen. She was standing in a room covered with clothes, still wearing her underwear and almost completely out of options. Some outfits had looked OK but seemed too dressy, others too dressed down. Some trying too hard, others not trying hard enough. She'd managed to create about eight different combinations from the holiday clothes she'd brought and unless she decided to go on the date dressed in her joggers – the only item she hadn't tried on – she was all out of options.

'Don't panic,' she told herself. Then ignored her own advice. There was just an hour to go until she would need to leave and she could hardly strut up to Pierre in her M&S nude basic underwear ensemble, could she? She was all for complete honesty within a relationship but some things are better kept under wraps.

There was nothing else for it. She grabbed her dressing gown from the back of the door and scuttled along the corridor to Sabine's room. Earlier, when Sabine had offered once again to help her find the ideal outfit, she'd thanked her but turned her down. Sabine was in the process of packing and she hadn't wanted to interrupt really – she knew her friend wanted to get on her way in a few days. Plus, she'd been convinced that within the few favourites that she'd packed, she'd find the ideal outfit. Her luggage allowance had been modest, so she'd made sure to only include things she felt great in.

Correction: had *once* felt great in. Now, everything she looked at looked old, tired, ill-fitting or ill-advised. She knew, deep down, it was probably her nerves talking. But every time she'd turned to the mirror after wriggling into something new, she'd felt horrified. Was this drab-looking woman really her? What had Pierre been thinking when he'd asked her out? Should she simply ring him and cancel?

Mirrors had never been her friend. They always seemed to reflect how she felt inside more than how she actually looked. And these feelings defied logic. She knew from experience that often in the morning, she'd feel she looked overweight or baggy-eyed, but that later, she'd look at herself and realise she was fine. Or that sometimes, she'd get dressed up for a night out and feel fabulous, only to catch a glimpse of herself in the bathroom mirrors in a bar and feel less confident.

Objectively, her appearance couldn't change that much over the course of a few hours, she'd often reasoned with herself. She knew it was an emotional reaction more than anything else.

But she also couldn't shake the belief that if she could just find the right product, the right outfit, the right lighting, she would feel better. Which had led to a lot of product buying over the years, until she'd discovered that her bank balance was the only thing seemingly altered.

Now, after standing in the rubble of her wardrobe for ten minutes in near despair, she ought probably to slip into a dress she knew usually looked good, and simply put her self-loathing down to nerves. But she couldn't resist getting a second opinion at least; this date was too important to mess up.

'Sabine?' she said, knocking on the door and opening it gently.

Sabine's bed was covered with clothing, which she was folding and placing into an optimistically small bag. She looked up and smiled, but Nina could see that her friend's eyes were a little wet.

'Are you OK?' she said.

'Ah, yes,' nodded Sabine, flicking the tears from her eyes as if they were a nuisance. 'It is strange for me, as I enjoy travelling but I also hate to say goodbye to people, to places. So I am feeling sad to leave even if I am excited to go.'

Nina nodded. 'I understand,' she said. 'Sometimes, you want to be in two places.'

'Yes,' Sabine agreed, putting the T-shirt she was folding back on the bed. 'I am happy to travel, very happy and lucky. But sometimes I think, am I doing the right thing? Should I be somewhere else? Should I be with my brothers... my friends? Am I selfish to do this all the time?'

'I understand.' Nina nodded. 'But it's not selfish to live your life the way you want – after all, it's what they're all doing!'

Sabine looked at her. 'You are not much older than me,' she said. 'But you are certainly wise. What you say – it makes me feel better.'

'Well, I'm glad,' Nina smiled.

The pair locked eyes for a moment.

'You have already become a good friend to me,' Sabine said. 'I hope we can stay in touch.'

'Of course!'

Sabine's lip wobbled again. 'Oh *mince*!' she said. 'Why must my eyes rain all the time? I am just a little overwhelmed, I think. And it will be difficult perhaps on my own without my friend. But we will see.'

They fell into silence, each of their faces stretched into a sad smile. Nina felt a little awkward to have come to Sabine with such a seemingly insignificant problem and made to leave.

'But wait, why have you come to see me?' Sabine said.

'Oh it's nothing. Just... well, not sure what to wear,' Nina said. 'But I'll figure it out.' She gave what she hoped was a confident smile.

'Are you OK?' Sabine said, her voice concerned. 'Your face has gone a little strange.'

'Yes. Yes, I'm fine.'

'Good. Anyway, you must *not* go. Because I want to help you. In fact, I was about to come to your room. I have found a dress in my bag that I think will look better on you than me.' She lifted out a summer dress from the seemingly too-small bag. It was three quarter length, black with a red floral pattern, a nipped-in waist and scooped front. It was, indeed, beautiful.

'Oh,' said Nina. 'I mean, it's lovely. But are you sure?'

'Pah, it is just a dress,' Sabine smiled. 'Try it!'

Whether it was the new outfit choice or simply Sabine's enthusiasm when she stepped out of her room a few minutes later, the soft material swinging perfectly at her calves, Nina wasn't sure. But suddenly, her feelings of self-loathing vanished and she was able to meet the eye of the woman in the mirror with confidence.

'You look beautiful,' Sabine told her.

And for once, rather than deflect the compliment, Nina simply thanked her.

Twenty minutes later, her taxi arrived. She had been going to walk, but the weather had had other ideas. Light rain was falling – the first proper rain since she'd arrived almost two weeks ago now – and the pavements glistened in the fading evening light. Sabine had invited Antoine around for drinks and had offered to ask him to give her a lift, but she'd smilingly turned him down. She hadn't been 100 per cent sure whether Sabine had been joking, or whether she hadn't considered just how Nina's hair and outfit would fare in the combination of rain and the turns and sway of an impromptu bike ride. Plus, it seemed cruel to ask Antoine to transport her to a date with Pierre after what he'd said.

Sitting in the back of the taxi as it made its way to the restaurant, she felt sick with nerves. Somehow, this was more daunting than trying to meet Pierre on false pretences at pétanque. Because this time, she didn't have a backup plan, perhaps. Or because she knew that whatever spark they'd felt might brighten or dull depending on how the evening went.

Neither of them knew how the other had fared over the past two decades. What had passed. Marriages, children, jobs, illnesses, family – they had so much to find out about each other. She wasn't the same person Pierre had fallen in love with – how could she be? Nobody could stay seventeen forever. And she wouldn't *want* to be that person either, she realised.

Life had dealt her a few curveballs and a few 'boring' balls (if that was a thing; she wasn't up on her sport analogies), but each one had shaped her, changed her. Even the bad things that had happened had sometimes made her better in some way – sometimes stronger, more emotionally resilient, or more respectful of others' feelings. She still had her moments, but essentially, she liked herself now; was comfortable with herself in a way that would have seemed impossible back then.

How had Pierre changed? Had he become a better, stronger version of the boy she'd known? Had life shaped his personality, likes and dislikes?

If she'd got on the plane years ago and they'd married, perhaps they'd still be together – against all odds. But the difference would be that they'd have grown together; had shared experiences that bound them to one another. And they'd have witnessed the changes first-hand, as they happened.

By the time the taxi pulled up against the kerb ten minutes later, she was practically a nervous wreck. She tried to give herself a good talking to (in her head at least). *Come on Nina; this is Pierre! Your bond goes way deeper than that.* The inner core of him would still be the same – they'd find the connection; she was almost sure.

The restaurant Pierre had chosen was a brasserie – not his habitual lunchtime one, but another, tucked away down a side street so narrow, the taxi had to drop her at the top of the road. 'I am sorry,' her driver told her. 'But I am worried I will not be able to turn.'

She understood. Her heels clacking on the cobbles, she staggered towards the small awning and the rectangle of yellow light spilling from the window into the autumn half-light. She tried to steady her breathing, determined to keep her cool – to be her best self for this date, no matter how much her stomach churned.

Negotiating her way down the alleyway, she was almost taken out by a young guy riding a longboard. She stumbled and turned angrily, only to realise that it wasn't a young guy as she'd thought, but a woman with shortish grey hair. The woman made a steady pace on the board, seemingly untroubled by the uneven ground below. As Nina looked, the woman raised her hand apologetically and Nina nodded her forgiveness then stepped through the open glass door of the restaurant.

Inside, Pierre was already in situ, drinking a glass of red wine at the table. He was dressed smartly in a crisp white shirt and black jeans. His hair was gelled and he'd shaved the stubble he'd been sporting last time they'd met. As he looked up, their eyes locked and his face broke into a smile.

And all the worries about the date melted away. Suddenly, she felt younger, remembered the pull they'd felt between them. And hoped he was feeling it too.

She walked across to the table with a smile and said, in a jokey voice. 'May I join you, Monsieur?'

And the once love-of-her-life looked up with his deep brown eyes and said, 'Beautiful Nina. I thought you would never ask.'

33

As Nina slid into the chair opposite the potential love of her life, she realised she was beaming. She tried to temper her smile a little – after all, she didn't want him to think she was insane. 'It's good to see you,' she said, feeling about twenty years younger and slightly flustered and embarrassed and overcome with the urge to brush the little clump of hair that had fallen slightly out of place back from his forehead.

'And you,' he said, smiling. 'It has been too long, Mina.'

'It's Nina.'

'But of course! I am nervous, I think,' he said, giving her a grin. 'It is such a surprise to see you again. I couldn't believe it when I recognised you at pétanque. Of all the towns in all of France, you decided to come back to this one.'

'Well, I had such great memories from French exchange,' she said. 'A long time ago now, though. And I can't believe you still live locally!' she lied, not wanting him to know that she'd made absolutely sure of his location before she'd booked her tickets. One step at a time, she thought. No need to scare him away with too much truth all at once.

A silence fell over them which at first felt comfortable, but began to stretch – her mouth was dry and she couldn't think what to say. In the end, 'I was almost run over just then!' she blurted, nodding towards the window as if to indicate the location of her close call.

'Really? But there are no cars usually?' he said, looking concerned and surprised at once.

'No,' she said. 'By a woman on a skateboard, or longboard or whatever you call them. It's fine really. It was funny, once I'd got my balance back.'

'Funny?'

'Yes. So strange to see an older woman on a board instead of some young teenager.'

Pierre smiled. 'I know this woman. She is my old teacher, I think. She rides her board to work and after she rides home. For many years now.'

'Wow, well, that's one way to travel, I suppose.'

'Yes! She is very good at it. People tell her to stop but she says she will continue on her board as long as she can stand upright,' he said.

'Good for her!' Nina said. Proof, if it were needed, that age was just a number.

The waiter came and they ordered a bottle of red wine and water for the table, then sat back and looked at each other over the tops of their menus. 'Ah, so you must tell me about your life,' said Pierre laying his down as if food really wasn't his priority. She promptly lowered her own. 'What has happened since we last met?'

How much should she tell him? 'Well, I got a degree,' she said. 'And I'm working now – as an office manager. And, well, I met a guy and got married. But it didn't work out.'

He nodded. 'I am sorry to hear that. But then, of course I am not sorry. Because otherwise, you wouldn't be here with me.'

She felt herself blush. 'And you?' she said. 'What happened to you afterwards?'

'After?'

'After we lost touch.'

'Ah, after,' he said. 'Well, I passed my baccalaureate and went to do some training. And then I came into a little money. I invested in my friend's patisserie and the rest is history.'

She nodded. 'Amazing.' His eyes were boring into her and she felt almost weak. 'Look, I'm sorry—' she found herself blurting out.

'For what?' he said, confused.

'For not replying to that last letter you sent. For not getting in touch at all when I promised I would,' she told him. 'I guess it would be easier these days, you know, with Facebook and mobile phones and things. But I shouldn't have just left you hanging. I should have been upfront with you. Especially after... well, you know.'

'After...?' he prompted.

She flushed. 'Well, you were my first. I thought...'

'Oh yes, and you were mine, Nina,' he said, nodding his understanding. 'It meant a lot to me.' He shook his head. 'I was sad when you rejected me. But it was a long time ago. So it doesn't matter. We are different people now.'

'Yes!' she said, almost too enthusiastically. 'We are different, and I guess I know what I want now in a way maybe I didn't then.'

'But of course,' he began. Then the waiter interrupted them, hovering with his notebook poised in anticipation of an order.

'Oh sorry,' began Nina, 'we haven't...'

'I will have the steak,' Pierre interrupted – his tone harsher and his French more rapid when speaking to the waiter. 'With the frites, and green salad.'

'Oh,' Nina said, panicking that she hadn't yet made her own choice. She'd assumed he'd laid his menu down because he was too taken by her, but clearly he had made his choice. She quickly scanned the menu, then simply said, 'I'll have the same, please.' She was pretty sure he hadn't said steak tartare, so she ought to be safe.

The waiter nodded and took their menus, poured Pierre a small amount of red wine to taste and watched him swill it expertly in his mouth.

'Yes,' said Pierre at last. 'It is good.'

The waiter, who looked about nineteen years old, nodded as if deeply respectful of Pierre's expertise, then half-filled both their enormous glasses. Then he went off to the kitchen to pass their order to the chef.

The brasserie was filling up now and Pierre kept looking around every time another couple or party came to sit nearby. 'I did not realise it would be so busy tonight,' he confessed.

'It's OK. All adds to the ambiance,' she smiled.

'Yes, that is true. But it is not intimate,' he said, sadly.

There was something a little well, intimate, about his using that word. She smiled at him again. 'It's great,' she said. 'A lovely place.' Although, in fairness, the brasserie was a little run-down compared to some of the restaurants she'd visited and passed during her time here and she wondered a little at his choice. Now she understood – he'd thought it would be quiet so they could talk.

They were silent for a moment, looking at each other. 'I am sorry,' Pierre admitted. 'I can't remember what we were speaking about. I think it's because it is hard to focus when I am with you.'

She blushed again – perhaps she really was becoming her seventeen-year-old self – and said, 'I was just apologising. You know. For not returning that last letter. I've sometimes wondered what might have happened if I'd come over – if we'd seen each other again.'

'Do not worry about this,' he said. 'You were young. We were both young. Twenty is far too young to be making grown-up decisions. It is practically still a child.'

'No, seventeen,' she corrected.

'*Quoi?*'

'We were only seventeen,' she said. 'Not twenty. Because you were still at lycée, and I was at school.'

Pierre laughed. 'I am terrible at maths!' he said. 'So now you know my secret. I would never be able to manage an office like you. I am confined to using my patisserie management skills instead.'

She laughed along too. Although it didn't take a maths whizz to work out that twenty-year-olds don't tend to go on school French exchange. Perhaps he was as nervous as she felt.

She longed to ask Pierre if they could take a photo together so she could send it to Sal and Bess, but decided that asking for a selfie would make her seem as if she'd never properly left high school. Instead, she asked Pierre to tell her about his own intervening years.

'Ah, I did not marry like you,' he said, a little wistfully. 'But I tried. I made love to many, many women.'

'Oh,' she said.

He grinned, clearly pleased with the revelation. She felt a little odd about it – was she the right person to be boasting to? But perhaps it was only a turn of phrase rather than anything else.

'That's... good,' she said at last.

'Yes, but I was never in love,' he said, sadly. 'I see beautiful women and we have a lot of fun in the bedroom. But I never found my love. My true love.' His hand crawled across the table towards hers and suddenly, their fingers were touching. She felt a tingle run up her arm and met his eye.

'I…' she began.

But then, typically, their food arrived. Two thick steaks with chips and a side salad which both looked and smelled delicious. They laughed and tucked in.

'So, tell me. If you had written this letter to me. Where do you think we might be now?' he said, his eyebrows raised.

'Oh,' she said. 'I don't know.' She didn't want to tell him the kind of life she'd fantasised about – their glorious beachside wedding, the house close to the sea. 'What do you think?'

'Oh, I think we would have been very, very happy,' he said. 'But then we are still young, yes? It is not too late!'

If someone had told her a few weeks ago that Pierre – *her* Pierre – would be saying these things to her, she'd have barely believed them. Things couldn't be going better if she'd scripted the encounter herself.

Conversation flowed between them over the next hour – she told him about life in St Albans (mostly boring) and he about life in Cagnes-sur-Mer – (it is a good place). She told him about Bess and how they were still friends, but he couldn't really remember her. 'I only had eyes for you, I think,' he'd said, with an embarrassed laugh. 'I cannot remember anyone else who was on this exchange.'

When the time came to pay, she insisted on paying her way – and although he put up a little fight, he acquiesced. 'Shall we go for a walk?' he said then. 'It is a little dark, but not so very cold. And I do not think it is raining any more.'

'I'd love to,' she said.

She felt a little like a teenager linking arms and going through the restaurant door into the dark street. As if they might sneak an illicit kiss on the beach, and stay out way past curfew. Not that either of them had one any more.

She was about to express this to him when there was the thud of someone running behind. At first she thought they were being mugged and clutched her handbag. But instead, it was the waiter from the restaurant, still dressed in his white shirt and black tie, holding something in his hand. 'Monsieur,' he said. 'Monsieur Dupont!'

Pierre turned, smiling. 'I am sorry,' he'd said. 'Is something the matter?'

The waiter panted for a second, out of breath from his sprint, then pulled a gold band from his pocket. 'You dropped this,' he'd said. 'Under your table.'

Pierre looked at the ring, his forehead furrowing. 'No, you are mistaken.'

'Are you sure? You are the first to sit there since we opened so...'

'Perhaps it belongs to a staff member,' Pierre said. 'Or perhaps to my friend here, Nina.'

'Oh no,' Nina said. 'It's not mine.' She smiled. 'Thank you, though. It's nice of you to try to return it to us.'

The waiter shrugged. 'Perhaps it rolled from another customer,' he said.

'Of course!' Pierre said. 'That's what it must be.' He smiled. 'Actually,' he said, pulling a ten euro note from his pocket. 'I forgot to leave a tip, I think. So this is for you. For your kindness.'

'Merci, monsieur,' said the waiter, taking the note. 'If you are sure?'

'Of course!' Pierre said. They turned and the waiter slow-jogged back into the brasserie.

'That was nice of you,' Nina said. Her father had always told her that the mark of a man (or woman) was how they treated waiting staff in restaurants. In which case, Pierre had just earned her father's approval.

'Ah, he is just a boy with a difficult job. And it was kind of him to try to return the ring,' said Pierre, shrugging. Then a look crossed his face. He patted his pocket. 'Ah *mince*!' he said.

'What is it?'

'I'm sorry, but I left my phone in the restaurant, I think. *Merde*. I hope nobody has taken it. It is for my work too.'

'I'm sure it will be fine. Shall we...' she began.

'No, you stay. I will get it quickly,' he said, jogging off in the waiter's wake.

She smiled and shook her head, checking her own phone was in her bag for good measure. It was, so she pulled it out and messaged the girls.

NINA

Date's gone BRILLIANTLY. We're off for a walk on the beach!

She took a quick selfie of her smiling face, with the restaurant in the background, then slipped her phone back in her pocket as she noticed Pierre leaving the restaurant holding his phone triumphantly. She'd read any responses later. For now, she had better things to do.

34

THEN

Dear Nina,

I am sorry for my English! But I want to write to you in your own language, because it makes me feel close to you.

I am so sad that you are going. I did not sleep last night after the party. All I could think about was you!

I hope you can write to me. I hope you feel the same way that I do!

Perhaps we can find a way for you to come back, if you want? So we can spend more time together. Maybe forever…

Until then, bisous,

Pierre x

35

NOW

The first thing Nina did when she woke the next morning was reach for her phone, set on the bedside table. Had Pierre sent her a message? And there it was – *sleep well, ma belle* – a little text he must have sent when he'd arrived home.

Their walk on the beach had been fairly short-lived. Although it was beautiful and indeed not raining as Pierre had said, a strong sea breeze cooled the air, making it feel chilly. But just as she'd wondered what they were doing there, standing in a secluded spot on the beach, Pierre had reached a hand around her back and pulled her to him, kissing her deeply. She'd practically melted into him. Before, she'd never understood exactly what that expression meant. But now she knew the feeling of completely surrendering to a kiss – leaning into him and feeling the softness of his lips against hers, the firm grip of his arms behind her waist.

She'd wondered whether he might invite her back to his and had spent the rest of their short walk trying to decide how she'd respond if he did. But in the end, he'd been quite the gentleman – ordering her a taxi and arranging another date. She'd driven away feeling a little disappointed, but relieved all at once. It would probably have been too much if they'd gone home together tonight – and potentially they had the rest of their lives, so there was no rush to jump into bed together.

He's such a gentleman! she'd told Bess and Sal on WhatsApp.

She scrolled onto her social media and looked at a couple of updates. Sal had posted a picture of her tour of St Albans with Jean-Luc and another of them eating dinner together. Jean-Luc, she saw, had the look of his brother, yet his face was wider, less attractive than Antoine's. A few people had commented underneath – *Who's the hot guy?* and, *Great place for a date.* But Sal had corrected them. *Just a friend*, but added a smiling emoji for good measure.

Nina hoped that Sal wasn't rushing into anything – the last thing she wanted was to be responsible for her friend's heartache.

Then opening her email inbox, she had a heart-sinking moment. She hadn't checked in for a few days and of course her inbox was full of the usual spam: adverts for websites she'd never signed up to receive information from, an email to confirm some theatre tickets she'd booked in a few months' time. And, there nestling between the junk was another message from Jemima.

She'd had a couple over the almost-fortnight since she'd arrived – one to tell her (once again) to have a great holiday but with a note asking how to refill her office stapler – and one with details of the long-distant Christmas 'do' that had been sent to everyone. So she assumed it would be a message in a similar vein when she clicked to open.

But, no.

Hi Nina,

I hope your extended holiday is going well. I'm afraid things have been a little difficult in the office in your absence. It has been hard for the temp we've employed to pick up the reins, so to speak, and I must talk to you on your return about noting down procedures in order that any leave can be covered more effectively in future.

With this in mind, I am writing to see whether you might wish to cut your holiday a little short. While the additional leave was given in good grace, it has been clear to me that the efficiency of the firm has been affected greatly by your absence.

Knowing your commitment to the firm and your usual high performance, I'd like to suggest you consider taking one more week and then return to work. We can negotiate some further unpaid leave later in the year should you still feel the need.

I trust that you have had time to rest, and look forward to hearing back from you.

Sincerely,

Jemima

Nina threw the phone face-down on the bed. But it was too late, the damage was done. Her boss had reached into the bubble that she'd created for herself on this holiday and pierced it – and now her work brain had been activated. She started wondering what Jemima meant about 'noting procedures.' Was this a dig at her for not writing down, step by step, every aspect of her job for someone who needed to cover? Because in all honesty, it wasn't really her place to do that. When she'd arrived, it had been Jemima herself who'd shown her the ropes and those ropes had remained more or less intact for fifteen years.

On the face of it, the email was polite – Jemima was always professional in that way. But when Nina read between the lines, there were accusations there. That it was Nina's fault the temp couldn't cope. That the company was struggling without her. That she ought really to have had enough holiday by now and get back to the real world.

She knew what her friends and family would tell her to do. Ignore the email, carry on with the holiday – or remind Jemima that she had originally wanted to leave and request that her resignation be accepted. She shouldn't allow the boss of a company she'd dedicated years of her life to, a company she'd clearly made herself indispensable to, treat her in this way.

But thinking things and feeling them were two very different things. Could she afford to lose this job? What would she do if she left for good? Would she get a bad reference if she didn't go back and save the day? What were her rights? How might Jemima make life difficult for her if she didn't acquiesce and hop on the next plane?

When Nina had started working at the firm, it had been run by a guy called Colin – an older guy who had been in the business for years and was relaxed about things. One of the reasons she'd chosen her role was because the firm had a real family atmosphere. People would go out for lunch together, pop to the pub after work. Everyone got their jobs done, but always had time to stop and chat by the coffee percolator or during lunch at their desks. Jemima had been there, but as an assistant, rather than running the show.

When Colin had retired and Jemima had been promoted into his position four years ago, everything had changed, including Jemima's whole attitude to work. She'd come in wearing business suits and a tight, brisk smile and started talking about bottom lines and cash flow and social media presence and building their customer base. None of these things were new – Colin had managed the firm well and it had grown incrementally each year: new staff members, a new website; they were always pitching to new clients. But Jemima brought all that to the surface – the importance of raising the company (which had operated very well for fifty years before she'd taken over) and that workers were professional and didn't waste time. Ever since then, both output and morale had seemed to plummet.

Then Covid had hit and they'd all worked from home, and since then, the office had been manned by a transient staff – some in three days, some fewer. You never knew who was going to be there, and work become something you did on your own, with the main communication via email.

The combination of this, and Jemima's leadership, had changed the job entirely, Nina realised. It had sucked the heart out of the firm and reduced them to a disparate group of people rather than a team. It had made people edgy and paranoid and afraid of making a mistake. It had dried up any small talk as each person focused on their own workload and the need not to be seen in an unfavourable light.

If Colin had made this plea to her, she probably wouldn't have minded going back to save the day. But then Colin would never have done this, she realised. He'd respected the fact that while he expected a level of dedication from his employees, the firm would never be their entire lives. 'And it shouldn't be,' he'd used to say. 'What would I want with a load of one-dimensional employees? You need to have a life outside of this place in order to give your all when you're here.'

Now Jemima, with her focus on growth at all costs, in tandem with Covid-19, had changed her place of work into something unrecognisable. So why was it so hard for Nina to just walk away? How did she still have this hold over her?

She started to type:

Hi Jemima,

I am sorry to hear that the firm is struggling with the new temp. However, all the procedures involved in the office management are clearly outlined in my job description and I am sure other members of staff can assist.

After careful consideration of my situation, I have decided I wish to honour my original intention and leave at the end of my notice period. As this is two weeks, and I have this amount left on the unpaid leave you signed off on 15th October, I will not be returning to work at the end of this month period.

I wish you all the best in the future.

Regards,

Nina

Her finger hovered over 'send.' *Do it!* Her mind urged. But then she thought about the house sale – how until completion, you never really knew for sure if it would work out. She had some savings, but they would run out eventually. What if Jemima turned on her and made it difficult for her to find another job? She wouldn't put it past her. Yes, she was meant to be taking risks, but this was a risk too far.

QUITTING

Pros:
Putting myself first
No more Jemima!

Cons:
Jemima might not give a reference
What if I can't find another job?
No idea what I want to do
Will I find something I like doing more?
Cutting off my nose to spite my face?

She deleted her draft email then, not quite knowing how to respond, put her phone away and tried to get her mind back in the moment. She was here, in France. Last night, she'd had a meal with the man who could be the love of her life – they'd kissed and had plans for tomorrow. If she put Jemima out of her mind, the world could be her oyster (hopefully, an oyster with a pearl in it, rather than the sloppy, mucous-y kind that made her retch).

The anxiety that had awakened in her made it impossible for her to lay in bed any more. She quickly got up and slipped on some jeans and a T-shirt. Pushing her hair back with a headband, she washed her face in the ensuite and applied a bit of tinted moisturiser.

Downstairs, she was relieved to hear the sound of the radio chattering in French and noticed the smell of coffee in the air. Sabine was up and about and she needed the distraction.

She found her friend at the oak table, a map spread in front of her. She was marking something with a pen. When Nina entered she looked up.

'Morning,' she said. 'Did you sleep well?' Her eyebrows raised in mischief. 'Sweet dreams, I bet?'

Nina smiled. 'Yes,' she said. 'Very well.'

She'd been surprised last night to find that Sabine had waited up for her. She'd found her on the sofa watching TV wrapped in a blanket. When the door had clicked, she'd looked up immediately. 'You are home!' she'd said, almost overjoyed. 'You must tell me everything!'

So Nina had relived the evening that was already a contender for the most romantic of her life. On paper, perhaps it was an ordinary date – a meal followed by a walk on the beach and a kiss. But in her life, it was momentous. Twenty-three years had passed and yet she'd still felt that passionate pull towards Pierre.

Sabine had been thrilled. 'I knew it!' she'd said. 'It is so romantic!' She'd hugged her and pulled back, her eyes shining. 'Now I can leave with a smile on my face,' she'd said.

Sabine had earmarked Friday for the start of her trip – one she planned to take six weeks completing. She would arrive in Vienna by December having taken her time stopping at some of the places she longed to visit. 'I will go to Genoa, perhaps even further into Italy,' she'd said when she'd explained her plans. 'I want to see as many beautiful places as possible – and it is important to go slow, as my van cannot do too many miles at once.'

Nina had listened rather jealously. She'd longed to visit Italy for years and it seemed ludicrous that in all that time, she hadn't booked a weekend away there. Perhaps once she'd settled either here or back home, she'd save up for city breaks to the places she thought she'd love. It wasn't as 'free' and authentic a trip as Sabine would have, but it would be something.

'I am starting to pack the van today,' Sabine said, putting the top back on her pen with a click. 'I need to clear everything out and start again, I think.'

'Shall I help you?'

'I am sure you have better things to do than help me with this dirty van,' Sabine grinned.

'Actually,' she said. 'I don't really. And... well, I sort of need to be busy today.'

Sabine nodded. 'It is hard to wait until your next date, I think?' she said, looking at Nina from the corner of her eye and smiling.

'Yes,' she said. 'That's probably it.'

'Perhaps you should try something else – something new. It will distract you – and like you say – you are here for an adventure, not just for love,' suggested Sabine. 'You mentioned rollerblades – Jean-Luc, he has a pair if you would like to borrow.'

'Maybe later,' Nina said, imagining the spectacle she'd make of herself rolling along. Then she thought of Pierre's teacher, how nonchalant she'd looked on her longboard, how unashamed. Was it really ever too late to do something new? And should she be so worried about what she looked like, especially in a town full of strangers? Perhaps she'd give it a go after all.

For some reason, though as she stepped out onto the driveway and began to lay items from Sabine's camper on the ground as they sorted the possessions she'd need and ones she could do without, Nina couldn't shake the feeling that something was about to go horribly wrong.

'You are alright?' Sabine said, handing her a box of kitchen utensils. 'You seem a little, sad?'

'Yes, I'm fine, just thinking,' she said.

'But these thoughts, they make your face look troubled,' Sabine said. 'I can help, perhaps?'

Nina shook her head. 'It's just a work thing. Nothing interesting – I'm just trying to get my mind off it, to be honest.'

Sabine smiled. 'I understand. I will say no more.' She mimed zipping her mouth shut. 'But I will say,' she added, 'that if you do need advice, I will try to help. Or Antoine. He is more experienced at work problems.'

'Thank you.' Nina sighed, looking at the interior of the van and thinking how cosy it must be to nestle inside it for the night, how nice to be able to meander and stop where you wished – with no one emailing you snotty missives and making you feel at fault. 'I sort of wish I could swap places, you know,' she found herself saying.

'Swap? With me?'

'Yes. Setting off on an adventure. Being completely free. The... well, the uncertainty of it all – it must be exciting to think you can do whatever you want.'

Nina shrugged. 'Perhaps. It is not easy sometimes. Money can be a problem. Getting a little work. I suppose, for the most part, you are right. But also, I don't understand.'

'Don't understand what?'

'Why you say you are not free. You are as free as I am. If you like, you can come with me. I have space,' she said, gesturing the interior of the van. 'It is close, but you will find it is not too hard to live in.'

Nina laughed, then stopped when she realised Sabine wasn't joining in.

'What is funny?' her friend said.

'Sorry, I didn't realise...' she said. 'Oh, Sabine. I'd love to be the sort of person who could do that. But it's not for me. I just don't think I could... cope. But maybe I will fly to Vienna, meet you at the markets when you are there.'

'Yes, of course,' Sabine said. 'But the offer is there. You can travel in style!' She grinned as she passed an overflowing laundry basket to Nina. 'We have all of life's luxury right here.'

'Yes, I can see that!' Nina said, looking at the pile of dirty clothes protruding from the basket.

And then they both laughed, and Nina thought how wonderful it was to have made such a great friend.

36

They were sitting together, companionably, at the outdoor table sipping a mid-morning coffee when Sabine announced, 'Yes, I will definitely go on Friday.'

'OK,' Nina said, her heart turning over. She'd got used to seeing Sabine's smiling face around the house – it would feel empty when it was once again 'just hers.'

'I have a few more things to sort out and of course I want to see my brother a little more. And my new friend,' she said, looking at Nina across the top of her coffee. 'But it is time, I think.'

Nina nodded, trying not to show her disappointment. After all, she only had a couple of weeks left here herself: while she dreamed that things might go well with Pierre, it was unlikely she'd be settling in Cagnes-sur-Mer just yet – more likely that they'd travel back and forth for a bit. Weekends in Paris, perhaps. Then, as they grew closer – well, who knew?

'Are you alright?' Sabine asked.

'Just dreaming really.'

'Ah, about your new lover?'

'Well, yes. I suppose,' Nina said, embarrassed. 'A little,' she shrugged. 'And you know, I'll miss you too.'

'You will?' said Sabine, seemingly surprised.

'Of course.'

'But you will have a lot of fun, I think when I am gone,' Sabine said. 'You will have the holiday you expected to have without someone's sister turning up.'

Nina smiled. 'I suppose you're right. But it's been nice having you.'

'Well, likewise. And Pierre, he is taking you out again tomorrow?'

Nina smiled. 'Yes. This time we're going to Le Petit Grill,' she said, trying to roll her r's the way a French person might and – to her horror – showering the table with a few drops of half-consumed coffee. 'Sorry,' she added, wiping the table with her sleeve.

Sabine laughed. 'It is OK. We French, we like to make the most of our "r"s!'

'You'll have to help me choose my outfit again,' Nina said.

'For Le Petit Grill?' Sabine's nose wrinkled slightly. 'I do not think you have to dress up for this place.'

'Oh.'

'It is perhaps not the most luxurious place to go,' Sabine said. 'You can wear just your jeans I think.'

'Oh.' Nina hadn't thought it would be a home of haute cuisine, but she had thought that Pierre might have chosen a nicer restaurant than last time. Perhaps, again, he was hoping that they'd have the space and quiet atmosphere to talk?

'Sorry, I am sure it will be wonderful,' Sabine said. 'Just because a man does not spend lot of money on a date, doesn't mean he is not falling in love.'

Nina blushed at the idea of love. 'Yes,' she said, decisively. 'Maybe it just means he's comfortable with me or something.'

'Or maybe he likes Le Petit Grill?' Sabine said. 'It is not to everyone's taste perhaps, but some people must go there.'

It didn't sound like the most positive of reviews. Nina sat back and looked across the garden. The rain that had pattered on the roof last night had cleared and the sky was a wash of blue and white. While the air had a touch of cold in it, it was mild enough for them both to sit in the fresh morning air in a light jumper rather than a coat.

The other problem, raised by the fact that Sabine had mentioned jeans, was that the only real pair of jeans she'd brought were her old faithful, baggy pair – used for slopping around the house or doing the gardening. She hadn't brought anything figure-hugging or smart-casual. She'd have to pop out later to do some shopping. Still, hopefully that would be a pleasure.

* * *

That afternoon, she set out with her credit card at the ready, hoping that some of the shops along the front would sell suitable clothes. She was just making her way to the corner when she heard the pounding of feet on the pavement. Turning, she saw Sabine racing after her, holding something in her hands.

'My God, what's wrong!' she said.

'Nothing!' Sabine grinned, panting and leaning over slightly. She held up her hands and Nina could see now that she was holding a pair of plastic rollerblades with adjustable straps. 'Jean-Luc is just a size 42, and these adjust to smaller feet too,' she said, looking delighted with herself. 'Now is your chance to build your confidence and have a little fun!'

'Oh, no,' Nina said. 'I don't think so. I'm just going around a few shops.'

'But you will need a break too!' Sabine countered. 'And you can try these along the front, like you said.'

Nina felt her face get hot. 'I'm not sure,' she said.

'Because you are worried what people think?'

'Because there's every chance I might break something,' Nina said, only half joking. She'd not been close to a pair of rollerblades for at least two decades, maybe more.

'But there is more chance that you will just have fun, an experience!' Sabine said. 'Perhaps I will meet you, yes? In an hour or when you find your clothes. And I can cheer you on?'

'Maybe,' Nina said, feeling already that Sabine interpreted 'maybes' as 'yeses.' Damn her very British need to let people down easy. It simply didn't compute this side of the Channel.

After strolling around a few boutiques, she ended up purchasing not the elaborate outfit she'd imagined, but something altogether more chic but quite casual. The shop assistant helped, selecting cuts that Nina wouldn't have been drawn to, explaining the fit of each top and how the colours might work.

So she was feeling quite buoyant when she received the message from Sabine.

I AM COMING TO THE TOWN. YOU FORGOT YOUR ROLLERBLADES!

She felt a familiar feeling of dread. Why had she mentioned her desire to strap wheels to her feet and roll? It had just been a passing feeling, a fleeting desire with none of the practicalities considered.

Then again, so had her wild swimming. And while she'd taken the rest of the day to warm up, she'd been so thrilled once it was done that she'd actually ticked that experience off her bucket list.

Rollerblades though, she thought as she texted back, agreeing to meet Sabine close to the fish sculpture. Although she wanted new experiences, a broken hip wasn't actually on her wish-list.

Before she knew it, she was sitting on a bench close to the beach, the fish sculpture at her back, her shopping bag at her feet. She looked at the Promenade de la Plage, with its red tarmac walking and cycle path stretching wide and flat to the distance in each direction. Back home, the streets were uneven, paved, bumpy and far from flat. If she ever wanted to try rollerblading, this would be the place.

As she was thinking this, a small hand tapped her shoulder. 'Madame!' a familiar voice said. 'Your transport awaits!' And Sabine appeared at her side, brandishing the blades.

'Oh. Hi,' she said. She opened her mouth to express her uncertainty then remembered that so far, whenever she'd expressed any sort of doubt, Sabine's powers of persuasion had overruled her. She looked at Sabine's eyes and the mischief buried in them and realised she was just as unlikely to win this time. 'Thanks,' she said, taking the skates and starting to remove her shoes.

In the end, other than a slight graze on her hand, she survived unscathed. At first, she was almost walking in the blades, instinctively lifting her feet, much to Sabine's amusement. But then she was, very slowly and gradually, pushing herself forward, allowing the wheels to glide on the smooth tarmac, wobbling and looking rather ridiculous with her arms spread wide, but with an enormous smile stretching across her face.

'I'm doing it! I'm really doing it!' she said to Sabine who was walking at her side, snapping pictures with her phone.

Several youngsters on blades shot past her, as did a skateboarder, a cyclist and a woman on a mobility scooter. But she didn't care. She'd actually forced herself out of her comfort zone and it felt absolutely amazing.

Amazing that was until she wobbled into one of the palm trees set in neat stone rectangles along the path and, after teetering for a moment, her arms waving, landed heavily on her bottom.

Sabine raced to her side. 'You are OK?' she said.

Nina nodded, laughing and grimacing. 'Yes,' she said. 'But perhaps it's time to hobble home.'

* * *

'You look good,' Sabine said, appraising her the next evening before she set off. 'Smart, but relaxed too.' She gave Nina a thumbs up.

Nina looked down again at her outfit. The navy jeans she'd sourced in the boutiques of Cagnes-sur-Mer, with a black and white top with a simple neckline. Black ankle boots with the tiniest of heels. The ensemble had cost her dearly – it was pricey choosing clothes, and difficult to find the right size too. In the UK, she was a 10. Here, that meant a 38. Try as she might, she couldn't help but hate that her clothing number had gone up 28 points – even though she knew sizes were equivalent.

'Thank you,' she said. 'And they're not too...'

'No,' Sabine said, rolling her eyes and grinning. 'They are not too tight, madame! You look great and Pierre will perhaps be inspired to take you somewhere better next time.' She paused. 'But of course, Le Petit Grill, it is OK,' she added hastily. 'You will have fun, I think.'

'I hope so,' Nina smiled. She and Pierre had texted on and off since their last date, but things were still very new. She still felt a bubble of nerves inside her, panicked about what they might talk about, hoped that she hadn't read things wrong last time. Then she remembered the kiss – the sinking feeling she'd felt as she pushed herself against him. There was something there – she wasn't imagining it. This was real.

This time, she arrived first and was shown to a table by a waiter in jeans and a white T-shirt. His name badge read *Fabien* and he looked to be about eighteen years old. Other than an elderly couple picking over some sort of chicken dish, she was the only customer in the place at seven o'clock. So perhaps Pierre had chosen well, she thought, taking in the wide expanse of empty tables, imagining the peace and quiet they could enjoy together.

Half an hour later and a glass of wine down, he still hadn't arrived. She was checking her phone every few minutes, but there was no message, no missed call. She didn't yet want to call him – she wanted to retain some dignity, after all. But she began to wonder whether he'd turn up at all. Perhaps he wasn't as enthusiastic about reconnecting with her as he'd seemed. Perhaps he'd had second thoughts. After all, she didn't really know this man. Not really. A childhood version of him, someone she'd spent seven days with and a few months writing to. A stranger really. Someone she'd projected all her needs and feelings onto, but for what reason?

By the time he walked through the door ten minutes later, she'd drunk half the bottle and emptied a table basket of slightly dried bread. He saw her, his face split in a grin, flooding her with relief, and he raced over to the table. 'I am so sorry, my love,' he said, kissing her. 'We had a meeting at work and I couldn't leave, and I ran all the way as soon as I could.'

At once, everything she had been feeling changed. His enthusiasm, his apology made any doubts melt away. And something about his proximity to her felt so insanely 'right' that she suddenly she felt that did believe in fate and things that were meant to be, after all.

He slipped into the seat opposite and clicked his fingers for the waiter. She'd always hated people who did that, but it was different here, she supposed – perhaps it was just the French way. The waiter appeared and took Pierre's order of a beer and some bread for the table.

'I am sorry that they sat you here with this empty basket,' he said in a low voice when the waiter had gone. 'They should have at least given you some bread.'

'Never mind,' she said, wondering how she was going to manage to eat anything else after consuming what must have been half a French stick.

This time, their conversation was less interrogative. They filled in the blanks in each other's history, had the basic backstory, and were able to talk more generally. The things they liked, how they'd spent their day, what they thought of the restaurant. There were silences, too, but comfortable ones, where she'd sit and watch people pass by on the street through the restaurant window and imagine how she and Pierre must look. Perhaps like a couple who had been together since age seventeen, she mused.

Pierre made her laugh with some of his jokes, told her about a person at work who had produced a meticulously crafted birthday cake with an enormous spelling mistake. Asked her about life in England and whether she ever saw herself living elsewhere.

Just as she was trying to answer without saying, *Depends if you ask me to marry you and I move here and we have a couple of kids or puppies or both and a white picket fence or whatever the French equivalent of that is,* a woman stopped outside the window, just in front of their table. She seemed to be staring in, and at first Nina wondered whether she was looking at her own reflection, checking her hair, not realising there were people right on the other side of the glass. Nina looked down at her food and waited for the awkward moment to pass.

Pierre glanced up too. But rather than laugh or look away or say something to Nina, he rose suddenly to his feet and raced out of the restaurant towards the woman. Nina saw the woman turn and look at the approaching Pierre with a scowl on her face. He took her by the arm and led her a little along the road, although Nina could still make them out in bright light spilling from the small boutiques along this out-of-the-way backroad.

As she watched, feeling sick, she saw that they were arguing. Pierre no longer looked relaxed and affable, but seemed almost to grow in stature, towering over the woman, who looked up at him defiantly, waving her arms as she spoke. There was no mistaking her body language. This was a woman who was incredibly angry.

Who could she be? Did Pierre have a girlfriend? A wife? A sister? Who would get angry at seeing him in a restaurant with Nina, other than someone who felt they had a claim on him romantically? She watched as the woman turned to go and Pierre grabbed her by the arm quite forcefully. She span and slapped him in the face, then continued on her way, soon lost around the corner of the street.

Nina quickly turned her gaze to the plate of chicken she was working her way through, not wanting Pierre to know that she'd been watching the whole time. She felt her face burn. She'd make her excuses and leave, she decided. She didn't want to get mixed up in whatever this was. If Pierre had someone and hadn't told her, then he definitely wasn't the person she'd thought he was.

He arrived at the table seconds later, panting slightly, his face red. 'I am sorry,' he said, sliding into his chair, his body slumping slightly. He looked pained and somehow defeated. 'I wish that had not happened.'

'Who is she?' Nina said, trying to keep her voice light. Give him a chance to come up with an explanation, she thought. Don't get up and walk out and leave him in your past again. He deserves that much at least.

'Ah, she is a devil,' he said, his brow furrowing. 'She was my girlfriend two, perhaps three, years ago. And we broke up. But she still loves me, and now she has started to watch me sometimes. She cannot accept that we were not right for each other. And now she has seen me with you and she is jealous.'

'Oh,' said Nina, feeling simultaneously sorry for Pierre, a little suspicious and a tiny bit hopeful. Was it OK to hope that your date (boyfriend?) was being harassed? She wondered. It probably depended on the circumstances. 'What did you tell her?' she asked, thinking of Pierre's body-language, the way he'd pulled the woman by the arm.

He sighed and took a big gulp from his water glass. 'I told her that she must accept it is over. That we had a good time together, but she needs to forget about me now. I said that I have a new girlfriend and that we are very serious about each other.' He looked at her, his eyes intense. 'Because I think, and I hope it is not too much, that what we have, it might be serious, no?'

Her heart flooded. 'Yes,' she said. 'I feel that too!'

'I think,' he said, reaching for her hand, 'Nina, I think that I am in love with you already. Perhaps I never stopped loving you. Maybe this is why I can never stay with my girlfriends. Because perhaps I knew that one day you would come.'

She wrapped her fingers around his – they felt cold. Their eyes met – his earnest and honest and full of hope.

'Pierre,' she said. 'You're right. It is quick. But I think I'm starting to feel the same way.'

37

THEN

Dear Pierre,

Thank you for your letter. I am also sad that we didn't get to spend more time together. We have a long break this summer after our exams and maybe I'll talk to my parents to see if I can come to France. I am old enough to travel by myself after all! Or maybe you can come to England?

I loved meeting you too. And I was so glad when you came with the letter. I thought we might never see each other again.

Hope to hear back!

Nina x

38

NOW

The phone startled Nina awake.

'Hello?' she said sleepily into her phone the next morning, blinking in the soft not yet daylight.

'Don't tell me you're still in bed?' a voice said.

She sat up instantly. 'Bess!' she said, overjoyed to hear her friend's voice. 'Is everything alright?'

'Does something have to be wrong for me to ring you?'

'It does at...' she consulted her watch. '8.30 a.m., especially when I didn't get to bed until past midnight!' she joked.

'Oh, poor Cinderella,' Bess joked. 'I hope your carriage didn't turn into a pumpkin?'

'Very funny,' she said, grinning. 'It's lovely to hear your voice, actually.'

'So I'm told,' Bess joked. 'Oh, I just thought I'd better see how things are really going. Your WhatsApp messages have dried up a bit and I wanted to see how the date went. How it's all going, really.'

'Really, really good, I think,' she said, pummelling one of her pillows and setting it against the headboard so she could sit up comfortably.

'Hang on, he's not there, is he?'

'No. We're not quite... in that place yet.'

'Ooh, yet? So things are getting serious?'

'Come on Bess, it's been two dates.'

'Two dates and a lifetime of longing,' her friend pointed out.

'Very true. Well,' she smiled, remembering how Pierre had kissed her softly last night. He hadn't tried to come in – which was probably a good thing. She wasn't sure if she'd have felt comfortable with Sabine sleeping in the next room. He'd been a true gentleman throughout the evening, just as he had on their first date. And he'd already asked her if she could meet him again. 'You know what, Bess, I really think we've got something. I know it's early days, but you're right, it's as if I've known him for years. As if I've been with him for all the years in between. We've picked up where we left off, kind of...'

'Wow, so you're planning to elope?'

'Haha, very funny. No, no wedding plans as yet. But you know what I mean. All the feelings – they're still there. They must have been dormant for all those years and suddenly it's like they'd never stopped.'

'A bit like chickenpox?'

'What?'

'Well, you know. It lies dormant and then strikes again – shingles!'

'Are you comparing my rekindled love to shingles?' she laughed.

'Well, not in every respect...'

'You're an idiot.'

'I know. And seriously, that's really great,' Bess said.

There was a silence.

'But?' Nina said.

'But nothing.'

Nina had known Bess a long time. She recognised something in her friend's voice. 'You can say, you know,' she said. 'I'm not going to take offense or anything.'

'Alright, well, this is only because I love you and of course I'm worried about you as well as really pleased...' Bess began.

'OK?'

'It's just... be careful, you know? No rash decisions...'

'Rash? Is this the shingles joke again?'

'Not quite. It's just... Look, things are moving fast and like you said, Pierre's someone from the past, and it might feel as if you can just... well, fast-forward to happy ever after.'

'There's nothing wrong with that!' Nina said.

'I know. I know and I'm really pleased and want it to work out,' Bess said. 'It's just I wouldn't be a friend if I didn't say... well, take your time. You're going through a lot – the divorce, the house sale. Now you're in a foreign country. And Pierre sounds amazing, but there has been a bit of water under the bridge. You've still got a lot to learn about each other.'

'I know,' Nina said. An image popped into her mind – Pierre grabbing that woman's arm. Something in his stance, the set of his face had surprised her. She'd never seen his features morph into something other than pleasant and easy-going. But then, he was only human, she thought. He had every right to be angry with a woman who was making his life hell.

'Are you OK? You've gone quiet.'

'I'm fine,' Nina said. 'And you're right. I will take my time, I promise. I'm not planning to marry him for at least a couple of weeks.' She opened her mouth to tell Bess about the woman at the restaurant, the unease she'd felt. But then stopped herself. You had to have been there, she thought. Bess might misinterpret the situation. It was better left alone.

'Very sensible of you.'

They both laughed, the warmth in their conversation restored.

'And what's all this with Sal? I've barely heard from her.'

'I'm not surprised. She's all googly-eyed over Jean-Luc. What is it with these French men?'

'They have their little ways!' Nina joked. 'But... well, keep an eye on her, won't you?'

'That,' said Bess, 'seems to be my role in our friendship at the moment. Watching you two have fun and being the voice of caution and reason. It's not the most scintillating of roles, if I'm honest. Full-time party pooper.'

'Aw, that's not you at all,' said Nina. 'More like full-time brilliant friend.'

'Oh, stop it!' Bess protested, laughing.

'With a little party pooping thrown in there.' Nina added, grinning.

She was still smiling a little when she made her way downstairs an hour later after showering and dressing in her black, linen trousers and a light sweater. It had been nice to hear Bess's voice. It felt like you were in touch with people when you spoke to them online, she realised, but only really get that proper closeness from hearing or seeing someone. She resolved to pick up the phone more often. She already called her mum once a fortnight, and had once used to ring Rory at lunchtime every day. But she'd got out of the habit of calling her other friends. That would definitely have to change.

Downstairs, she opened her laptop and switched on the coffee maker, added a spoon of rich ground grains and watched minutes later as the dark liquid bubbled into her cup. She breathed deeply

– she loved the aroma of coffee almost more than the taste sometimes.

Sabine still wasn't up, so she kept her volume down as she scrolled her social media – nothing new. Her email inbox was showing twenty new messages, and she almost didn't look. It would, no doubt, be a bunch of spam and probably another email from Jemima. But then, she thought, clicking on the icon, she probably ought to take a quick look.

The first email in her inbox was her solicitor, Nick, informing her that the house was likely to exchange just after she was due back to the UK. Seeing the date and realising it was so close brought her back to reality. It seemed suddenly awfully soon.

Then, of course, there was another email from Jemima.

Dear Nina,

I haven't heard back on my other email and hope that my request didn't cause offense. Take it as a compliment – your absence has certainly made me aware of all you do for the company.

If you are unable to come back sooner, I look forward to seeing you on 5 November.

Either way, your response would be appreciated.

Best wishes,

Jemima

Every time she opened an email from Jemima, it was as if she was spirited back to her desk in St Albans. And each time, she felt pressure to make a decision about her future. She closed the laptop, deciding to get to it later.

There was a knock on the kitchen window and she jumped slightly, then smiled when she saw Antoine – his hair slightly wet, presumably from his morning shower – waving at her. She felt a prickle of embarrassment, remembering his declaration to her the other day, and hoped he wouldn't ask about Pierre. Fixing on a smile, she got up and opened the door.

'You know there's a doorbell at the front, right?' she said.

'Yes, but I also know that my sister, even though she told me to come at this time, is probably still asleep – and believe me I have learned the hard way not to wake her if this is the case,' he said, grinning. There was movement behind him and Nina realised that there was a young boy with dark hair standing behind Antoine, almost shyly.

'Ah,' Antoine said, following her eye. 'This is Theo, my son.'

'Bonjour,' Theo said, not making eye contact.

'Bonjour, Theo.' She smiled. He looked at her then and his own features relaxed a little. When Sabine mentioned that Antoine had a teenage son, Nina had imagined a scowling, hands-in-pockets stereotype. Theo, in reality, looked younger than she'd pictured. Barely into his teens. Yes, he was awkward but he seemed shy rather than surly.

'So Sabine is awake?' Antoine asked.

'No,' Nina said, laughing. 'You were right to be cautious. She's still sound asleep.'

He laughed and looked at Theo. 'I am sorry,' he said. 'I told you that your aunt is often very lazy.' Antoine turned back towards Sabine. 'He loves his aunt and wanted to see her before she leaves.'

'Oh, do you want me to wake her?'

'Oh, no! She will not be very agreeable. Theo is here all day so we will call back later. Could you tell her we have been by?'

'Of course – no work today?'

'No, I have Theo – his teachers, they take action, a strike, today. And I promised to help Sabine with the van. She says she does not need my help, but she does not know much about engines, so I prefer to check for myself,' he said.

'That's kind of you. Would you like a coffee, now you're here?' said Nina, indicating the pot that still contained at least enough for a cup. 'I've made too much anyway.'

'Thank you, that would be nice,' he said, 'if I'm not interrupting your work?' He nodded at her open laptop.

'Hardly,' she said, pouring rich, black coffee into one of Jean-Luc's porcelain mugs. 'Just my boss, reminding me that I am due back soon.' She rolled her eyes. 'Not sure she's too happy that I took such a long holiday.' She turned to Theo. 'Can I get you a drink?' she asked.

'Orange juice?' he asked timidly, and she filled him a glass. He sat at the table and pulled out his phone, scrolling rapidly.

'Theo, do not be rude,' Antoine said. 'We do not use our phone with company.'

Nina looked at the boy. 'Oh, it's OK with me, if it's OK with you,' she said. 'I'm on my laptop anyway.'

'OK,' Antoine smiled. 'See, Theo. I told you that Madame Nina is very kind.'

'Thanks Nina,' Theo said, a delighted grin on his face. He soon disappeared into his online world once more.

Antoine shook his head, taking the mug from her and blowing steam from the top. He took a sip. 'Thank you,' he said. 'And I am sorry that you have such a terrible boss.'

'Oh, she's not that bad,' Nina said. Why was she suddenly defending Jemima?

'But she contacted you when you're on holiday. I think this is a very bad thing.'

Nina nodded. 'Yeah, you're right. It's kind of put a dampener on my day. I hadn't wanted to think about all that yet.'

'You do not like your job?'

'No, it's more... well, I haven't decided whether I really am going back,' she said. She found herself telling him about her original plan, her dilemma. The fact that the two weeks between now and when she returned seemed far too short a period to come to any proper conclusion.

Antoine smiled, put his coffee down and reached to rub her arm. 'You are a very kind person,' he said. 'I can see this. Many people would not worry about other people. They would just think of what they must do for themselves.'

'I know. But maybe they're right! Maybe I should be doing that too.'

'Perhaps,' he said gently. 'But we are all different; we have to listen to our hearts. Perhaps for you, the security is important? Perhaps you love your work too much to leave?'

She shook her head. 'It's definitely not those things, not really,' she said. 'I just feel kind of obligated.'

'To your boss?'

Nina nodded. 'It's stupid, but I don't want to let anyone down,' she said, half smiling.

Antoine looked at her, his intelligent eyes seemingly seeing right into her. 'But you *will* let someone down,' he said. 'I think maybe you will let yourself down if you try to please others. And perhaps it is time to please Nina. To think about what she wants. This is not a selfish thing. It is necessary.'

Nina looked at him, understanding breaking through her stress. 'You're right,' she said. 'I should do that. Why can't I do that?' she shook her head. 'I'm such an idiot.'

'No, you are kind. And I think you are a little afraid.'

'Afraid?'

'It is not a bad thing to be afraid sometimes. We are all afraid,' he said, shrugging. 'Life can be scary sometimes.'

He was right. She had been operating, making decisions from a place of fear. Of wanting acceptance and security. Of wanting things to stay the same, to keep the fear of the unknown at bay.

But she hadn't succeeded anyway, she realised. She hadn't changed, but things around her had. Then she'd decided, in a mad moment, to come to France, to change how she reacted to life. Yet here she was, slipping back into her own pattern of self-preserving behaviour.

'Are you OK?' Antoine said, softly. 'I have not upset you?'

She shook her head. 'No,' she said, 'I'm just thinking.'

He nodded. 'Well, that is good. You have a lot to think about, I think.' He laughed at his own, repetitive wording. 'And I,' he said, draining a coffee, 'have some supplies to pick up for my lazy sister.'

'Of course,' she said.

They looked at one another for a moment, then Antoine shook himself slightly as if coming out of a daydream. 'Right, I must go,' he said. 'See you later.'

'See you,' she said. 'And thank you.'

'Thank me for what?' he said, turning to look at her again.

'Helping me to see more clearly.'

39

A light rain began to fall the next day. The kind of rain that seems so inconsequential, you wonder when stepping out whether you need a coat at all. It determinedly saturated everything it could, relentlessly sending tiny drops until puddles filled, guttering overflowed, windscreen wipers could barely keep up. It pattered onto windows and covered waterproof coats with tiny balls of water that gathered and formed runnels down the waterproof surface.

Until today, although the weather had been up and down, Nina had been able to deny to herself that November was coming and with it, her planned return to work, the exchange of contracts on the house, the plane ride home from Cagnes-sur-Mer and Pierre and Antoine and Sabine. A month away from her usual life had seemed unimaginable at first, but now the time had passed and reality was beginning to make itself known.

And Sabine was leaving.

When she'd first seen the rain, Nina wondered whether Sabine might delay her departure. And she'd felt a surge of hope that surprised her. It had been nice having someone in the house with her – she'd lived alone since Rory moved out six months ago – and Sabine had become a close friend in a short period of time. When you live with someone, there can't be shyness and subterfuge – they get to know the 'real' you pretty quickly and with that comes either intimate friendship or mutual loathing. Luckily for them both, they'd become firm friends. Nina would miss her.

Tonight, she had a date with Pierre, at yet another restaurant – she'd debated inviting him back to Jean-Luc's for a meal instead, but had worried it might sound too much like a guaranteed path to sex. Not that sex was completely off the cards – she just wanted to keep hers a little closer to her chest. She was looking forward to the date, although she hoped he'd have chosen a better restaurant this time and there would be no deranged ex-girlfriends peering through the window. But in between now and then, her new friend would be leaving – something she'd begun to dread. She wasn't sure whether she wanted time to pass quickly or slowly – and as a result, it seemed to speed up and slow down throughout the morning. It was seven o'clock, then nine, then ten past nine, then eleven.

Antoine had arrived with a bag of provisions at around 10.30 a.m. and Sabine had finally emerged from her room with her remaining bags to greet him. 'What do I need with more cans of haricots verts?' she asked him, raising an eyebrow. But she'd been pleased, nonetheless. 'He likes to look after me,' she said quietly to Nina. 'It is nice, huh? But he forgets I am almost as old as he is.'

Nina had smiled and agreed it was very sweet. As a child, having no siblings had never bothered her – she'd seen her friends' brothers burst into their rooms, their sisters steal their clothing, the mess and teasing and arguing and the sharing of things that came with having a larger family. But now, older, she saw that there was another side to having a sibling. Someone who would be there for you in the unconditional way that only family can be – someone who knows all your secrets and accepts and loves you anyway. Or at least, if you are lucky.

'What he really needs,' Sabine had said, 'is a wife to look after, or at least a girlfriend. I think he has a lot of love to give,' and she'd looked at Nina so pointedly, she'd had to look away.

It had taken them no time to consume a coffee and some tiny pastries Antoine had bought and by half eleven, Sabine was in the driver's seat, the engine chugged into life and her foot on the accelerator. Nina had a horrible feeling she might cry, so tried to choke down the tears by reminding herself of happy things – like Pierre and the fact she was on holiday and the financial freedom her little slice of equity could buy her. It had worked, just.

'Be careful,' Antoine had said as they'd stood in the rain to wave her off. He'd left his coat inside and had pulled the hood on his sweater up to cover his hair. It was already soaked through and he was shivering slightly. 'This is not good weather on the roads.'

For someone who rode some sort of deathtrap of a bike, this was a bit rich, Nina thought. He'd wobbled across town somehow despite the weather this morning which was about as safe as ice skating across a half-frozen lake in winter. Still, it was nice that he cared.

'Yes, do go carefully,' she found herself saying.

Sabine laughed. 'You are my parents, now? Yes?' she said. 'Yes, Mum and Dad, I will be careful, I promise.'

Nina laughed.

'But truly, I will,' Sabine said, a more serious look coming over her face as she looked at her drenched brother. 'In any case, I am only driving seventy kilometres tonight to the first campsite. I will take it easy – there is no rush.'

Antoine nodded. 'Good,' he said, with a small smile.

Goodbyes over, Sabine put her foot on the accelerator and the VW roared, sending a cloud of grey smoke from its exhaust pipe, which Antoine looked at worriedly, before bumping off the kerb and starting to trundle down the road, gaining speed. Sabine's arm remained out of the window waving until she turned the corner and was gone.

They waited a moment or two until they could no longer hear the sound of her van, then looked at each other. 'Coffee?' Nina asked, looking at the state of Antoine's jumper. 'I can pop that in the dryer if you like.'

He looked at it as if for the first time. 'Oh. Yes. Perhaps that would be a good idea, if you are not too busy?'

'Nothing to do at all,' she replied. 'Especially in this weather.'

Inside, he peeled off the offending sweater, his T-shirt lifting up a little to reveal his belly button. It was strangely intimate to see the little flash of flesh and she found herself looking away. Which was ridiculous – if it had been hotter, she may well have bumped into him on the beach with his whole torso on display. It was just the unexpected glimpse that made her feel a little strange, especially now they were alone.

'So,' he said as they sipped coffee and shivered as the warm liquid put paid to the damp cold they'd brought in from outside. 'You are looking forward to having some time alone?'

Nina smiled. 'Well, maybe,' she said. 'But I think I'm going to miss Sabine a lot.'

Antoine nodded. 'Yes, me also. It would be nice to have a sister and brother who stay in one place,' he said.

'But Jean-Luc is here most of the time?'

He shrugged. 'Yes. Then when he is here, we work together. Sometimes, we are too much for each other! Sabine, she connects us somehow. We both like to look after her, maybe,' he smiled. 'But she can never stay still.'

Nina smiled. 'I've noticed!' she said. 'I envy her really.'

'But you are here,' he said. 'So, it is the same. You are both free spirits.'

She almost laughed at his misreading of who she was. Yes, she'd come to France for a month, but doing a house swap – bricks, mortar and all – and having her job held open for her was about as far from being a free spirit as it got. Still, she liked him seeing her that way.

'I am sorry,' he said suddenly. 'For what I said to you.'

She felt her cheeks get hot. 'It's OK,' she said. 'It was nice.'

He nodded. 'I feel a little embarrassed about what I said. That Pierre might have changed,' he said. 'I am glad that you have found some happiness there. Well, almost glad,' he shrugged.

'Thank you.'

'And things, they are good?'

'Yes,' she said. 'I think so.'

'You only think?'

She blushed. 'I mean they are,' she said, her mind flashing back to the strange encounter with the woman at the restaurant.

'Then I am happy for you,' he said, smiling.

'Thank you.' She looked at him, feeling the need to say something else; to express something that welled in her chest when thinking about what he'd said to her. But it wasn't something she could put into words. Unless that word was: nngggghhhhaargh!

'And you have told your boss to break herself?' he said, changing the subject.

'To… to break herself?' she said, not quite sure what he meant.

He flushed. 'Ah it does not translate perhaps. I mean to go away, perhaps would be more polite?'

'Ah,' she said grinning. 'No, not yet. I can't seem to bring myself to.'

'Well, perhaps it is nice to have the stability of this job – and save your adventure for the holidays. Sometimes, I want to be like Sabine, but when it comes to it, I cannot sleep in a van.'

She laughed as he vehemently shook his head. 'I understand!' she said. 'Although it's not that for me. I've always wanted to travel… at least I've always felt a bit of an urge to know what it's like. I just… I suppose I've found myself at a crossroads before – when I was younger – and I've always taken the safe route.'

Antoine nodded. 'But there is nothing wrong with this,' he said. 'You do what is right at the time. And it does not mean you have to always make the same choices.'

That was exactly it, she thought. She had followed her head, let her logic and tendency to play it safe dictate her life so far. And it hadn't been a disaster – nothing to be ashamed of. But now that life had spat her out, everything was in flux. And maybe it was time to let her heart dictate her next steps.

'Thank you, Antoine,' she said. 'You've really made me think.'

He smiled. 'I am glad to be of service.' He glanced at the clock. '*Mince*! Now I must go. I am late for this afternoon's work.' He got up and put the cup on the draining board. 'Thank you for the coffee – and good luck tonight with your boyfriend.'

'Thanks,' she smiled. She'd almost laughed at the word 'boyfriend.' Pierre was definitely no longer a boy. But then it seemed somehow apt. Because she was in love with the younger man he had been – the one she still saw glimpses of through his more polished, mature veneer. She wondered whether Pierre felt the same. Whether he saw the old Nina still there somewhere under the woman she'd become.

He probably did, she decided. After all, she wasn't that different. A few more wrinkles, a couple of extra kilos, but essentially still Nina, in spite of it all. And maybe if she followed her heart, let her emotions or chance or fate dictate rather than trying to make everything safe and predictable, she could recapture a little of the girl she had been. The one who had hopes and dreams and hadn't yet been worn down by the dullness of daily life.

Closing her eyes, she tried to imagine a life here with Pierre. What it might look like. Or what might happen if she returned to England and came across to visit as often as she could. Or perhaps what might happen if Pierre came to St Albans? None of it quite felt right. But then, it was early days.

Everything could still all work out the way it was meant to.

40

THEN

Dear Nina,

Your letter gave me so much joy! Now that I know you feel the same way, I feel sure that we are meant to be together. You must talk to your parents and come in the summer. We can spend the holidays together. I am sure my mother won't mind you staying at my house – she is always wanting me to improve my English, and I know she will love to meet you.

I am working now for my exams, like you. But when they are finished, nothing will stand in our way!

I hope you can write back and say that you will definitely come.

Love, Pierre xx

41

NOW

This restaurant – a Chinese this time – was, if possible, even more hidden away and cramped than the others had been. Nina walked past it four times before she noticed the sign, tucked down a narrow alleyway next to someone's front door and a tiny antiques shop. She pushed on the door and it opened to a stairway which, once climbed – rather cautiously as it still felt as if it might be someone's house – opened up into a more recognisable restaurant space. She wondered whether Pierre had chosen the venue as it was safe from passers-by peering through the window – unless his stalker had a drone, they were probably going to be OK.

At first, she thought he wasn't there. She scanned the restaurant while waiting for someone to come and seat her, and could see only a family in the corner – two small children, one in a high-chair and presumably their mum and dad – and an older, middle-aged man sitting alone with a red neck and dark hair. Then, with a jolt of recognition, she realised the man was Pierre. On some level, she had still been searching for the younger, slimmer-shouldered version of him instead of the Pierre he had become.

He looked around and she smiled and started to walk over to him.

Tonight, she was wearing the navy jeans again – she'd worn them on their previous date, but enough time had elapsed for her to bring them back for a second viewing. She was looking forward to the date, less so to the prospect of another meal out. Perhaps she should suggest a different type of date next time – a stroll on the beach if the weather was OK, or a trip to the cinema. Perhaps he might invite her over to his place – he'd never even told her where he lived. Maybe she'd find the courage to invite him to hers – or Jean-Luc's, she reminded herself. Preferably before she needed to shop for an entire new wardrobe for nights out. She'd put on the necklace Pierre himself had given her, all those years before – the first time she'd given it an outing since her teens, when for a while she'd worn it day and night… It would be fun to see if he noticed.

As she slipped into her chair, a waiter rushed over. 'Have a seat, madame,' he said as if giving her permission to do what she was already doing. She wondered if he was put out that she'd taken the initiative to go to a table without being instructed, and smiled at him to hopefully diffuse any ill-feeling.

After he'd taken their drinks order and told them they could go and help themselves from the buffet when they wished, she turned to Pierre. 'It's nice to see you again,' she said.

'Yes,' he said, 'you too.' His hands were hidden under the table and he seemed to be rubbing them together, or struggling with them in some way.

'Are you OK?' she said.

'Yes,' he said, suddenly relaxing. 'It is just my watch; it was a little tight.'

'Oh. OK,' she smiled.

There was a clink of metal on floor and he bent down

hurriedly, almost banging his head. 'I am sorry,' he said, emerging. 'I dropped some money.' He seemed a little unsettled this evening, not the smiling, relaxed guy she'd been dating recently. Maybe, like her, he was sick of restaurant food. Perhaps he'd had a tough day at work. She needed to remind herself that, unlike her, he was not on holiday. Perhaps meeting her all the time was becoming tiring for him?

'You seem a bit stressed,' she told him. 'Was work OK?'

'Yes,' he said. 'I am sorry. I am a little preoccupied.'

'With the woman?'

His eyes widened. 'What woman? What do you mean?'

He really must be scared of this woman, Nina thought. It was a bit crass of her to have just dropped her into the conversation.

'Don't worry,' she said, trying to diffuse the situation. She reached across the table for his hand. 'I meant your stalker. Sorry. You're probably trying not to think about her.'

His furrowed brow smoothed. 'Oh yes,' he said. 'Her. Yes, she is a difficulty. But I suppose not really a stalker normally. She saw us and it made her mad, I think. But no, I am not worried about her.'

'Good,' she smiled.

He leaned forward, smiling. 'In fact, I can only think of you,' he said. 'And I wonder – there is a beautiful hotel near here. Perhaps we can go there after this... Perhaps to spend some time together?' He looked at her meaningfully and her heart skipped a beat.

She'd been wondering when he'd ask to come back, or ask her back to his. But this was far more romantic – the idea of spending their first proper night together in a beautiful, neutral setting was simply perfect.

'Perhaps,' she said, coyly, and trying to repress the urge to simply shout, *YES! What took you so long!?*

When they'd filled their plates, they sat opposite each other again. Pierre was still quiet and Nina tried desperately to think of ways to fill the silence. Their other meals had been concentrated on filling the blanks – talking about their past twenty years and what they'd been up to, or talking about Cagnes-sur-Mer, with Nina asking Pierre about various places and him suggesting she visit this sculpture or that museum or try a walk along the front.

They'd talked very little, she realised, about their shared past, though. She seized on a memory. 'Hey,' she said, smiling. 'Do you remember the disco?'

He looked up. 'A disco?' he said.

'Yes. Oh, not a recent one. I mean the one back when we were at school. How you...'

'Oh yes,' he smiled. 'We danced the night away.'

'No,' she said. 'You know, when you grabbed my hand and we...' It had been one of the most thrilling nights of her teenage life. To have this boy who she'd fancied and talked to but who she'd assumed she didn't have a chance with, grab her hand and take her from the dance floor to a quiet spot at the side of the building and kiss her so lovingly, had made her melt.

He looked at her. 'We...' he said, encouragingly.

'You don't remember?' she said, surprised. 'When we ran off and well, you know...'

'Ah yes,' he said, his features breaking into a smile. 'When we kissed for the first time.'

'No!' she said, a little sharply. 'We didn't. It was more than that... it...'

'Ah sorry,' he said. 'I think it was my expression. Of course I mean when we made love. I remember it very well.'

'OK,' she said, feeling a little hurt that the moment that had meant so much to her had seemingly meant so little to him. But then that was a man thing, maybe. Perhaps he'd romanticised other moments and dreamed about those.

'What's your best memory from that week?' she asked him, biting into a spring roll.

'Ah, there are so many,' he smiled. 'It is impossible to choose.'

A sudden, horrible thought gripped her. 'What about when we went to the zoo,' she said slowly. 'You know, when you were allowed to hold the baby monkey?'

'Ah yes, that monkey. He was a rascal!' he said, grinning. 'But what an experience, huh?'

Something inside her stomach dropped. The spring roll tasted like sawdust in her mouth.

'Pierre,' she said. 'There was no zoo.'

'I don't understand.'

'There was no zoo trip, no monkey. I made it up.'

He flushed. 'Why would you do this?'

'Pierre, do you really remember *any* of this?'

He shrugged. 'My memory is not good. Perhaps I need to go to the doctor...' He lifted a forkful of rice to his mouth and chewed on it thoughtfully.

'But why would you say...' she said. 'I mean, why didn't you tell me you...'

'Ah, Nina,' he said. 'It was so long ago. And I suppose there have been many, many women since for me. And perhaps I forgot this or that. But when a beautiful woman comes up to me and I feel such a spark for her, you can forgive me for being a little... well, for imagining things to make her happy.'

'You don't remember me very well?' she asked, trying to keep her voice steady.

His head dropped, his face turned towards his plate like a young boy being told off for not finishing his vegetables.

'Pierre...' she said, feeling nauseous. 'Do you remember me *at all*?'

He looked at her and his face looked different, resigned.

'A little, perhaps,' he said. 'I remember kissing girls who were here on French exchange. They came to our school each year. And I do remember writing to someone called Nina. But the memories, in my head. They are muddled. It is hard for me to know who is who.'

'But you – I mean, you asked me to elope with you!' she said. 'And you don't remember?'

'Ah Nina, I was a child. I would perhaps have said anything to a beautiful girl to make her want to be with me. But this is all in the past!' he said, reaching for her hand. 'It does not matter, because we have the whole future in front of us.'

Was she being ridiculous? she wondered. She'd harboured this dream of Pierre being a lost love – the one who got away. But if he hadn't had similar feelings for her, hadn't been sincere, then this relationship she'd seen as a connecting of souls was, to him, just a casual date or two.

She looked at his hand on hers. At his earnest eyes fixed on her face. Then, feeling a prickle run over her skin, back at the hand. Then, quietly, she said. 'Pierre, what is this?' She pointed to the red indentation on his fourth finger.

He whipped his hand back. 'It is a little eczema,' he said, rubbing it. 'It always bothers me.'

She thought of his strange behaviour when she'd arrived, the clink of money on the floor. The waiter on their first date with a ring. And suddenly she knew. 'Pierre, are you married?' she asked.

He blushed. 'What?' he said, in a voice that sounded more like a squeak.

'Are you married?' she said. 'You are, aren't you?'

Oh my God, was the woman who'd been outside the restaurant his *wife*? She wondered suddenly.

Something changed in Pierre's face. 'Well, maybe a little,' he said.

'You can't be,' she said, 'a *little bit* married. You either are or you aren't.'

He flushed. 'Well, perhaps I am not happy in this marriage.'

'But you wear a ring. You take it off when it suits you, right?' she said. 'And sometimes you forget until the last moment.'

'Well, yes, but...'

'Pierre,' she said, slowly. 'What am I to you?'

'Nina, what do you mean? We have this connection. From long ago. We...'

'A connection you don't even remember. And what is this – the dates we've been on or whatever – to you? A bit of fun at my expense?'

'No!' he said, reaching his hand out again then thinking better of it. 'No, this is real. Something special, something...' he trailed off.

'Who was the woman?' she said, into the silence.

'The woman?'

'That woman at the window. Was she your wife?' Nina said, feeling sick.

'No of course not! She is nobody,' he said.

'Pierre?'

'A girlfriend, perhaps.'

'You have another girlfriend? And a wife?' she said. A buzzing noise started in her head and she thought for a minute she might pass out.

Something changed in him then. The game was up. He dropped his fork and looked at her, his face sulky, like a teen caught out in a lie. 'So, what is it to you?' he said. 'We are just having fun!'

'I... but...'

'We met by chance, we had some dinner. Perhaps we would have made love a few times. But then you are leaving soon. It is a holiday romance. A bit of fun, eh?' he said. 'What is it to you if I play into your romantic idea – that we find each other after twenty years. That we still love each other? You think maybe we were going to get married and have children together?' He laughed, then, looking at her, his face dropped.

She looked at the tablecloth, big tears pooling in her eyes.

'My God!' he said, shaking his head. 'You really do think this! But we do not know each other, Nina. What can really come of this? It was just a bit of fun, a bit of...'

Every dream and fantasy she'd been harbouring about this man, this meeting, crumbled. She'd made this happen, hadn't she? And how could she be mad at him when she'd also based this relationship, or fling or whatever, on a lie? He didn't know she'd come specifically to find him. He was just having a bit of fun with a stupid, divorced woman on holiday. And clearly, she wasn't the first.

She stood up abruptly, flung a couple of €20 notes on the table and stumbled out of the restaurant. Pierre did not try to follow her.

In the street, it was dark and cold. Her jacket remained on the back of her restaurant chair, she realised. But she wasn't going to go back and get it. She pulled her phone from her bag and made to dial Bess's number. But what was the point of calling her friend – who would probably be at work in any case – to cry down the phone when there was nothing she could do to help?

She started to call Sabine but remembered with a wash of sadness that her friend would now be miles away. She should just call a taxi, she thought. She should just get back to Jean-Luc's and pack her bags and get the hell out of France, back to a life that, while a little dull, was at least safe.

But her Uber app wouldn't connect, and she hadn't the energy to google a new taxi firm. She stood, bereft, half an hour's walk from home, and of course the skies decided to open – as if to confirm, if there was any doubt, that she was at rock bottom.

She took a few steps, thinking she would walk. But her slight heels – she cursed her choice of footwear – and her thin, tight jeans and top were no match for the weather.

So she called the only local person she knew and prayed he wouldn't mind the intrusion.

42

Nina had never been so glad to hear the buzz of an underpowered electric bike in her life. And there he was, suddenly, rounding the corner, the light illuminating a little of the road in front of him. He stopped, propped himself up against the kerb, and removed his helmet, his hair springing up in its wake. Antoine.

He looked at her, shivering, concerned, before removing his jacket and offering it to her. Underneath, he was wearing what appeared to be a pyjama top and, as her eyes moved down, she realised that in fact he was completely dressed for bed – the jacket had obviously been flung over the ensemble in haste when she'd called.

'Take it,' he said. 'You are shivering.'

'I couldn't. You'll freeze.'

'But I insist.'

He looked at her, raised his eyebrows and continued to hold his arm out until she relented. Slipping the warm jacket over her shoulders made her shiver with relief. But she felt terrible, both because of what had happened and because she was racked with a terrible guilt at having dragged Antoine out of bed – albeit only at 10 p.m. – to ride the freezing cold streets on his bike, in his PJs.

'I'm so sorry,' she said, finding to her horror that her voice was thick with tears. She hadn't even realised she'd been crying. 'I shouldn't have called you. I was just going to ask you for the number of a taxi firm!'

'That is ridiculous,' he said. 'I am glad you called me.' He shuddered slightly as the cold pierced his striped top. Nina wondered how it would feel for him on the bike. The rain had thankfully petered out, but with the wind chill factor taken into account, he might well lose a body part or two. 'I am happy to help you. To take you home.'

Nina looked dubiously at the bike. Remembering her last white-knuckle experience on the thing, she wasn't sure whether this was a genuine rescue or more of an 'out of the frying pan into the fire' moment. Perhaps she could ask Antoine to walk back with her instead? But she looked at his steady gaze and couldn't bring herself to insult his mode of transport. He was here. In his pyjamas. The least she could do was risk her life on the roads in return.

'Get on,' he said, nodding to the empty part of his seat. 'You can wear the helmet, of course.'

'Are you sure?' she said.

'Yes,' he said. 'I cannot have you being hurt.'

'But what about you...'

'Quickly, before I lose all sensation in my hands,' he said, with a hint of a smile. 'And if we crash, it is my fault, because I should have bought another helmet for this thing by now.'

Despite her misgivings, the rain and the cold forced her to acquiesce. 'Sorry,' she said again – although she wasn't sure what for this time – and obediently lifted her leg and slid onto the chilly seat, slipping her arms around his waist as instructed.

The ride home seemed to take forever – she was aware that he must be suffering, taking the cold air straight to his chest – and the colder she felt, the colder she knew he must feel. It made for an uncomfortable ride. At the same time, there was such relief to know that she was moving further and further away from Pierre, from her mistakes and from the version of herself that thought that horrible man held any of the keys to her future.

They arrived at Jean-Luc's at last, and once Nina's jaw had thawed enough to talk, she thanked Antoine again. 'You really saved me,' she said.

'It is nothing,' he said, slipping on his helmet again.

'Oh, no,' she said. 'Don't go. Come in and warm up.'

'You are sure?'

'Yes, you must,' she said, rushing up the front path with Antoine in her wake. 'You'll catch your death.'

Inside, the air was warm and the room, slightly lit by the light of a lamp she'd left on in the corner, felt welcoming and safe. She quickly raced up to find a jumper and returned with another – her largest – for Antoine. He squeezed into it gratefully, not seemingly bothered to be wearing a giant picture of a cute kitten. She noticed his hands and the part of his chest she could see above the pyjama neckline were red.

'Shall I make you a drink?' she said. 'Something hot.'

'Yes, but then I must go,' he said. 'And it looks like you need to rest.'

'What I need,' she said, able to half-joke, now she was warm and safe and rescued and had had time to think everything through, 'is a stiff drink and a good talking to. I must have been mad to track Pierre down, to think I could recreate something from two decades ago.' She smiled, but could feel tears just below the surface, threatening to spill.

'But what happened?' he said. 'I thought things were very good.'

As she stirred their hot chocolates, she told him, watching his face furrow as she explained what Pierre had done.

'Well, he is a pig,' he told her at last.

She laughed, still on the verge of tears, but with something like happiness in the mix too. 'Yes,' she said. 'But you know, I suppose I was a bit of an idiot.'

'Pah, why?' he said. 'There is nothing wrong with hoping. With wanting a happy ending for yourself.' His phone beeped and he looked at the screen, then smiled. 'It is Sabine,' he said. 'She will be here soon.'

'Sabine?' she said, aghast. 'Oh no! she isn't coming back because of... Oh, tell her not to. It's not so bad. I just...'

He shook his head. 'You think that I can influence Sabine, then you don't know her very well,' he said. 'I called her earlier and when she heard you were in trouble, she said she would come. She said she was only fifty kilometres away and it is not far.' He shrugged. 'When you have known her as long as I have, you learn not to try to change her mind.' He smiled. 'Anyway, I think it will be good. I think you need a friend.'

She nodded. 'Well, it's so nice of her,' she said. 'And you're right. It will be good to talk. But when it comes to what I need...' She sighed deeply and put her chocolate down on a small side table. 'Antoine, I need to get back to reality, I think. I need to get back to work, back to my normal life. And I need to start seeing this for what it was.'

'What do you mean?'

She turned to him. 'I suppose it might have been a bit of a midlife crisis,' she said. 'Turning forty, getting my divorce through. The house selling. I think I might have gone a little mad. Racing off to France to find a lost love. What an idiot!'

He shook his head, his hand suddenly on her arm. 'No,' he said firmly.

'No?'

'No. You are not an idiot. Pierre is the idiot. You will not be the first he has taken in, or the last, I think. You say you were mad to race here, but perhaps the real madness would be to race again. Perhaps the idea of Pierre was wrong, but that doesn't mean the whole idea was wrong.'

'The idea?'

'To have an adventure,' he said. He set his own drink down then looked at the floor for a moment, before taking a deep breath. 'To take a chance on life... maybe on love.'

She snorted. 'Sorry,' she said. 'I suppose you're right. I just wish the chances I chose worked out sometimes.' Maybe she was chronically unlucky. Maybe that was why she never took a risk, because she'd end up like this – feeling foolish and more alone than ever.

'Nina,' he said. 'Sometimes, I think that maybe you are here for a reason, only perhaps that reason wasn't clear. Maybe... *we* were meant to meet. You and me.' He looked at her hopefully.

'Us?' she said.

'Yes. I wish I had time to get to know you more. Or that things were different. Maybe in time, they can be?'

She met his gaze, taking in his earnest eyes, his kind face. The pyjama bottoms on his legs and what they meant – that he'd rushed to her without a thought.

'Thank you,' she said. 'And I do know what you mean. I will never be sad to have met you, or Sabine. And...' She wanted to say that if she hadn't come with one mission – to find Pierre – things might have been different. But after his admission, it would sound too contrived. 'But it's time,' she said. 'I think you know when it's time.'

He nodded. 'I understand.' Then got to his feet. 'I should go,' he said. 'And you will be OK?'

'I will,' she said. Already, the whole Pierre situation felt a little like a bad dream. And she realised that although she'd thought she'd begun to fall for him again, her feelings had been superficial, not the deep feelings she'd imagined. He would soon be back in the past, exactly where he belonged.

She had to say goodbye to the seventeen-year-old Nina, to the hopes and dreams of someone long ago. Many people had regrets about their past, and at least she knew now that she hadn't made a mistake in ghosting Pierre all those years ago. If she hadn't, well, maybe they would have married, but she was pretty sure he'd be sitting in a restaurant now with someone else, spinning his lies and false promises, while she sat at home, oblivious. If anything, it was a lucky escape.

Once Antoine had gone, she stepped in the shower, feeling the warm water wash the cold from her skin, along with thoughts of Pierre and her dreams and her seventeen-year-old self. When she stepped out, wrapped in a towel, she felt better. No longer teary, but still kind of flat. But maybe that was what being older was. She couldn't expect life to be exciting in her fifth decade. In fact, in having this adventure, she'd done more than most, and at least now had a good anecdote to add to her collection.

Her phone rang and she picked it up, smiling. 'Hi Sabine.'

'Are you OK?' her friend said, the growl of an engine in the background.

'Yes. Honestly. I'm sorry Antoine involved you. I think he was worried.'

'It is nothing. I was not far.'

'Still.' She wanted to tell Sabine she needn't bother coming. But she'd probably already been driving for more than an hour. It was too late – it would make things worse.

'It was a bit of a horrible evening but your brother stepped up.'

'OK, well you can tell me everything in just a moment,' Sabine said. There was a click then Nina could hear the growl of the VW engine in the background as it drew up outside the house.

'Thank you for coming.'

'Pah, it is nothing. We are friends, yes?'

'Yes,' said Nina smiling. 'We really are.'

43

THEN

Dear Pierre,

I asked my parents about coming to France, but they say it is too expensive this year. And even though I'm an 'adult' now, they don't like the idea of me travelling on my own or going to stay with a boy they have never met. THEY ARE SO UNREASONABLE! I feel like running away – they don't understand how important it is.

I am so sorry, Pierre. I really wanted to come.

Love, Nina xxx

44

NOW

BESS

So you're coming home in four days' time?

NINA

Yes. Only a few days early and I've kind of had enough now.

BESS

Back to work?

NINA

Unfortunately! Not till the 5th though. Will just have a bit of a break before getting back into it all.

SAL

Have you told Jean-Luc? He's still got a week left in your house and I'd hate him to…

NINA

Yes, don't worry. I'm going to move in with Mum and Dad for a bit. We're selling up after all, there doesn't seem to be much point settling back.

SAL

Well, your mum will be pleased.

NINA

Apparently, she already has a list. Hopefully no gutters need cleaning though.

SAL

Haha. That was hilarious what happened on your birthday!

NINA

Nothing like a near-death experience to keep you smiling.

SAL

Lol.

BESS

Sorry about the whole Pierre thing. What an arsehole! We can put the world to rights over a vino when you're back.

NINA

Deal, although I don't think I'm going to be making any surprise journeys anytime soon. This one was a disaster!

BESS

Was it, though?

NINA

Did you not read my message earlier? Pierre is a complete waste of space.

SAL

But some things did work out.

NINA

Like?

SAL

Well, you had a month off work. That's pretty cool! And you said you made some friends? And played pétanque? It sounds good.

BESS

Plus you sent over a handsome French guy for Sal. You know Jean-Luc's going to hang around for a bit. He's going to manage his work remotely to see more of her.

NINA

Wow, that's amazing!

SAL

What, that someone would find me attractive?

NINA

Haha, you know. That's not what I meant. I'm seriously happy for you.

SAL

Thank you.

BESS

See, so maybe things have worked out a bit – just not in the way you hoped.

Nina closed her laptop, smiling. After sitting up late into the night with Sabine – who was even more enraged than Nina had imagined she'd be – she felt she'd laid the worst of her hurt to rest. Her trip had ended badly, but at least her journey hadn't been wasted. She'd made friends, good ones. Plus, the house swap had had an impact on Sal. Nina hadn't found *her* happiness. But it was happiness, nonetheless.

Was it fate? Or was it chance?

She'd visited a road untravelled and found that after all, she'd taken the right track all those years ago.

She thought again of all the risks she'd avoided in the past. She wondered what would have happened if she'd taken the TV job all those years ago. Would she have begun to rise up the ranks? Would she be some sort of daytime TV show star by now? Or would the contract have fizzled out after six months, leaving her with no option but to apply for something more ordinary and predictable?

She'd never know. Sometimes, she wished she could pick up all the threads – find all the places in which her life had forked and see where the other road could lead. But nobody could do that, she thought. The best you could do was hope that the choices you made would lead you to where you wanted to go.

She took a notebook from her bedside drawer and wrote pros on one side and 'cons' on the other.

COMING TO FRANCE

Pros:
Put the 'ghost' of Pierre to rest
Meeting Sabine
Meeting Antoine
Got a month's break!
Got to revisit Cagnes-sur-Mer
Sal found love!

Cons:
*Pierre turned out to be an a*hole*
The terrifying electric bike rides
Put on 6 lb
Jemima will probably never forgive me

Perhaps her lists weren't so terrible after all, she mused. Putting it all on paper, she could see that overall, the holiday hadn't been a disaster at all. In fact, taking the risk had in many, many ways, paid off.

But enough for now. For now, she was done.

She pulled her laptop onto her lap and opened up an email.

Dear Jemima,

Just to confirm I'll be back in the office on 5 November as agreed. Bright and early!

Thanks again for the opportunity.

Best wishes,

Nina

Her hand hovered over 'send' but at the last moment, she saved it to drafts. There was no need to rush into these things, after all.

She dragged out her suitcase and began to fold clean clothes into it. She had a few days, but she'd do it properly so that she could unpack at her parents' without having to abuse their washing machine from the outset. She had the impression that Mum was quite pleased she was staying, but it didn't shake off the additional shame she felt at moving back in with her folks at forty – like a caricature of a promising daughter gone off the rails.

Still, it was what it was.

She opened some of her drawers and began sorting through products she could pack now and others she'd need to use until the last minute. And her hand touched paper. Pierre's letters. She drew them out, looking again at the photo of them both from all those years ago. Her smiling. Pierre grinning along too. She picked up her pen and drew a moustache on Pierre, then a beret. Then sunglasses. Then, gaining momentum, she began to scribble out his face entirely.

A few minutes later, she was in the kitchen, the photo and a pile of paper by her side, scrabbling in the drawer for the matches she'd seen a few days earlier. Her hands grabbed the packet and then she was out in the garden gathering what she could – leaves, small sticks, anything that looked potentially combustible. After four attempts, she managed to get a tiny flame glowing; it gained strength when it began to lick at a particularly dry collection of sticks she'd stacked on top and finally, she had a tiny bonfire.

'Goodbye Pierre,' she said, taking the first of his letters. Crouching down, she fed the corner of it to the flames and watched as the fire made its way across the cursive writing, until she was forced to drop the whole thing. Despite the tiny size of the flames, the smoke the aged paper made was impressive and spiralled skywards.

She watched, satisfied then picked up the next.

There were ten letters in all, plus the photo. And she wanted to do this slowly. To erase Pierre from her life with purpose and pleasure. But only five letters in, she heard a commotion outside. A man's voice, raised. Then Sabine, shouting from her window, saying something she couldn't make out. Nina debated what she should do – she oughtn't really to leave the fire, and surely Sabine would call her if there was any real problem. Still, it was unsettling.

Not as unsettling, however, as the sight of several *pompiers* arriving in the garden seconds later, their faces stony. 'Madame,' one of them said. 'No!'

What were they? Some sort of letter-preserving society? It wasn't as if these missives from the past had any value. She straightened up, confused.

Sabine rushed in front of the men, wearing a dressing gown, her hair in disarray. 'No!' she said. 'Nina. It is illegal!'

'Illegal?'

'Yes, to burn waste in the garden. It is illegal!'

'But these are letters. I was… it was symbolic.'

'I do not think,' Sabine said, nodding half-comically over her shoulder at the angry-faced men in her wake, 'that these gentlemen will appreciate the symbolism.'

'Ah,' she said. 'Sorry.' Nina waved at the men, as Sabine began to fill a bucket of water from the garden tap. She poured it over the tiny fire and watched it fizzle out.

'Madame, I will have to give you a fine,' one of the men said. 'It is forbidden to have a fire in the garden here.'

'But...' Nina began.

'Marcel, is that you?' Sabine said, looking closely at the man.

He coloured. 'Yes, it's me.'

'Ah Marcel, but we are friends!' said Sabine. 'I think we can forget about this one for now. It was a tiny fire and I think probably only the neighbour saw it.'

'But... it is not the point...'

'This is Marcel,' said Sabine brightly to Nina as if the whole 'going to get fined' situation wasn't happening. 'I used to play with his older sister when we were kids. I've actually got quite a few photos from Marcel's past – I'll have to *show you them.*' She smiled, but her eyes were suddenly on Marcel.

There was a silence as various emotions seemed to wash like a tide over Marcel's face.

'In fact,' he said at last. 'Perhaps you are right. Perhaps we can overlook this for now.'

'Or perhaps I won't be able to find these photos,' Sabine mused as if he hadn't spoken, giving Nina an enormous wink.

Whatever Sabine had hinted at seemed to have done the trick. The *pompiers* retreated, leaving them with a smouldering heap of half-burnt, soggy papers.

'What did you mean, the photos?' Nina asked, once they were alone.

'Ah, I know his sister from way back,' Sabine said. 'When we hung out together, sometimes Marcel was there. We maybe smoked a little weed, maybe had a drink. Maybe he was a little underage? He is a teacher now and volunteers for the pompiers. It would not be good for his reputation if this got out.'

'Ohhh,' said Nina. 'And you have photos of him?'

'No,' Sabine grinned. 'But then he does not need to know this!'

Nina laughed. 'That's awful. But also... well, thanks.'

They were silent for a moment. Then Nina felt a bubbling inside her and let out a snort of laughter. Catching her mood, Sabine laughed too – a deep, throaty laugh that had her bent double. Soon they were in fits of giggles. 'We are terrible for each other!' Sabine said. 'You have your illegal fires, and I threaten a *pompier*!' She shook her head. 'But what were you doing? Why were you burning these things? It is terrible for the environment.'

'Oh I know,' she said sadly. 'But they were Pierre's letters. I felt... it felt like a good thing to do.'

Sabine nodded. 'I understand,' she said. 'You want to burn him, but you cannot. So you do the next thing.'

Nina laughed. 'Something like that. You know. Just closing the door on that chapter of my life. Those hopes... It felt like a great way of letting go.'

'I understand,' Sabine said, looking thoughtful.

Nina looked at the letters sadly. 'Never did get that closure,' she said.

'Ah, but that is still possible.'

'But I obviously can't burn them now.'

'Ah,' said Sabine, picking up the soggy, papery mass. 'But there is a much more appropriate thing to do with letters from a man like Pierre. We go to the toilet. And we *flush*!'

Five minutes later, they were standing together in the bathroom in fits of hysterics. 'This is what we think of your proposal of marriage, Pierre!' Sabine cried, dropping a shredded letter and pulling the little handle on the side of the toilet. They watched it roar out of sight.

'And this is for being a cheat,' said Nina, tearing and dropping the thin airmail sheets into the loo. She flushed with a flourish, and Sabine was right – it did feel entirely appropriate.

45

She sat on her suitcase and finally managed to force the zip around the side. 'Yes!' she cried. It had been quite a feat – hopefully, the weight wouldn't have changed too much since her outward journey. She hadn't really bought very much while she was here. Barely a souvenir in sight.

But she had her photos – selfies taken at dinner with Antoine and Sabine, pictures of the beach and the beachfront walk. The restaurants she'd visited with Pierre (she'd deleted the one picture they'd taken together), Sabine's VW, Jean-Luc's house. There were a lot of memories in there to sift through later.

In some ways, it felt a little defeatist to be going home. To be resuming her life in England after throwing caution to the wind for a few weeks. Worse, she was now going to go to live with her parents. Yes, she loved them. Yes, she'd be happy to be spending some time with them. But on paper, it did nothing for the self-esteem.

Before she'd set off again, Sabine had invited her to come on her road trip to Vienna. 'It is just seven, eight weeks,' she said. 'You can fly back home after for Christmas. And it will be an adventure.'

Nina had seriously considered it for a few minutes, but then remembered the house sale was due to complete, and Jemima was expecting her back at her desk. Even Mum had probably made some preparations – perhaps filling the fridge with some of Nina's childhood favourites as she had in the past. She couldn't let everyone down; and besides, she'd had enough adventuring for a bit. Predictability was under-rated.

When she'd told Bess on the phone, her friend had surprised her by saying, 'Why don't you try it? You said you were going to take risks, remember? Find out where fate leads you.'

'Maybe I will, just not yet,' she'd said. 'Plus you know, if fate does exist, I guess it'll happen whether I like it or not. Right? Maybe I'll just wait for a sign...'

She'd tried writing a list afterwards, to see exactly what she was giving up. But it, too, had been inconclusive.

Pros:
Get to see the world!
Vienna Christmas markets
Have fun with Sabine
Take a risk for once

Cons:
Have to quit job properly this time
Need to be there for house sale
Mum and Dad might feel let down
Not sure if I could sleep in a campervan!

So she was here, packed and ready to go. To say goodbye to Cagnes-sur-Mer for now. And nobody looked likely to stop her.

'It's back to reality, I guess,' she said to herself, looking at her ticket and her passport before opening the front door. She'd spent the morning cleaning, and her taxi was due outside in ten minutes' time. Antoine had popped in on the way to work to say a quick goodbye, but she was leaving as she'd arrived – alone. And it was OK.

It was colder than she'd imagined it would be when she stepped out of the centrally heated house and into the autumn air and once she'd rolled her suitcase to the end of the drive, she slipped her hands in her pockets. Inside one, she discovered a crumpled tissue, but in the other, her fingers touched something small and metallic. Drawing her hand out, she realised it was Pierre's necklace – the one she'd brought with her as a talisman. Much good it had done. She smiled at the little silver heart with its tiny, spiky arrow one more time before dropping it over the bars of a nearby drain. 'Bye Pierre,' she said, wondering whether the necklace and soggy letters would somehow meet again in the sewers of southern France.

She didn't notice that the necklace didn't quite make it between the grill, but hung on, secured by the little heart that had caught on a tiny flaw in the metal drain cover.

The taxi turned up, reversing in front of her, and a woman got out, took Nina's bag and slid it into the boot. 'Airport?' the driver asked, to double-check, and Nina nodded, finding suddenly that her eyes were full of tears.

'Please,' she managed to respond.

And they were off. Nina tried to remember the journey she'd had getting here – when she'd felt a world of possibilities in front of her. It had been just over three weeks ago, yet it seemed like an absolute age. She wondered what her former self would have thought about how it all turned out. It was a miracle that she'd found Pierre, had spent time with him – even if that time only revealed he was a bit of a bastard. At least she'd closed the door on that chapter.

She thought about Sabine and Antoine, and the friendship they had created in such a short time. She'd already added them both to her social media and was determined to keep in touch – maybe even visit them again one day. How something had stirred within her when Antoine had revealed his feelings.

She thought about Sal. Without Nina opening her heart to the idea of love and fate, Sal wouldn't have met Jean-Luc.

She thought then about work. About walking back into that office again. Finding it practically empty. Driving to and from her parents' place to get there. The equity sitting in her bank.

Was she crazy? She wondered. She'd had a chance to travel – another thing she thought she'd missed the boat on – but again, she had decided to pass it up. What might have happened if she'd said yes to Sabine and taken a longer vacation? Would it really have been so disastrous? And Antoine – he really was a genuinely nice person – should she have explored it all more?

But there was no use speculating. She was here. She'd chosen her fork in the road and now she'd see it through.

The taxi bumped as they went around the corner and Nina felt herself rise up slightly in her seat. Perhaps it was a pot-hole. But the bumping sensation continued and minutes later, the taxi driver pulled to the side of the road. 'One minute, madame,' she said. Outside, she inspected the car, crouching down at its side. And Nina heard her cursing.

'Everything alright?' she said, winding the window down just in time to see her driver kick the rear tyre.

'No,' she said, her eyebrows knitted together. 'We have a flat tyre.'

'Oh no!' Nina said. 'Shall I help you change it?'

'Thank you madame, but no. It is worse. I think we have hit the kerb, and something is bent.'

Nina climbed out of the car to have a look. The driver was right – the wheel arch had somehow dipped into a high bit of kerb, and it looked as if changing the tyre would be impossible.

Nina had never missed a plane in her life, but she still had two hours to get to the airport before the gates closed, she reminded herself. 'Can you call someone?' she said. 'Breakdown cover, perhaps?'

'Yes, I will call the garage,' said the woman. 'I am sorry.'

'Not your fault,' Nina said, although in truth, she was a little annoyed. The tyre must have been damaged or breached or worn down to burst so easily – the driver must have had some idea it was on its way out.

As the woman spoke on the phone, Nina made her way around the back of the car, opening up her ticket on her mobile just to check for the hundredth time that her plane was indeed still hours from take-off. Tucking it back into her bag afterwards, something caught her eye and she gasped.

Glittering against the rubber of the severed tyre was a tiny pendant – a love heart, with a spiky arrow. She bent down and pulled it from the tyre. The arrow was small, but solid and had somehow pushed into the tyre. Just a quarter of an inch or so. But that was all it had taken.

The puncture was her fault.

She slipped the necklace in her pocket and, feeling guilty, went to speak to the driver. 'It is OK,' the woman told her. 'Someone is coming from the town to help us.'

'That's great,' Nina said. She wasn't sure how to explain that it was her fault. But it seemed wrong to say nothing. 'I think it might have been my fault,' she said, but the woman looked so confused, she didn't carry on. She'd tip, she thought. Give an enormous wad of cash – whatever the mechanic charged – or pop in an extra zero when she keyed in her debit card. Something.

In the meantime, she needed to get out of the cold air. She slipped back into her seat and began to browse online. Then through her photos. The one of Antoine and Sabine at dinner, another of them laughing over a glass of wine. Each time, she noticed as if for the first that Antoine's eyes were looking at her with a warm intensity. There was something mesmerising about it – to be looked at that way.

She quickly flicked to another photo. This time of Sabine, leaning out of her campervan and waving. Smiling. She looked so free, so happy. So young. But she was only three years her junior. It was the way she carried herself, her essence that made her seem young. The fact she was not weighed down by anything.

Sabine didn't have the same obligations as Nina.

But obligations to whom? To Jemima, who didn't really care about her beyond her effectiveness at work? To her parents, who would probably prefer she was off having a great time than moping in the spare bedroom? She'd let these things feel insurmountable, yet they weren't really obligations at all.

On a sudden whim, she texted Sabine.

Definitely going to book to fly to Vienna and meet you! Get a taste of travelling.

Sabine sent back, almost instantly.

It would be wonderful. Although not strictly travelling. More a holiday!

She'd added a laughing emoji. But something about her words struck Nina. Because she was right.

OK, well next time I'm also going to come with you. Properly.

Then she added,

If that's OK.

(She was throwing caution to the wind, after all, but she was still British.) She sent a picture of the deflated tyre as a follow up.

Might not even make my plane at this rate.

Before she could speculate further, a small truck pulled up and a man unfolded himself from the front seat. He was dressed in blue mechanics' overalls and carried a wrench in his hand, as if to prove he was indeed the real deal. He began speaking to the driver, and Nina turned her attention back to the phone.

Until there was a knock at the window. A smiling face met hers as she turned. Antoine.

Of all the flat tyres in all the towns in all of France, he'd been called out to this one.

46

THEN

Dear Nina,

I am sorry that your parents feel this way.

But we are seventeen now. It is old enough to make our own decisions. Perhaps if you come, we will get married – and then it will be our life, not theirs. We could be together forever.

Please find a way to come – I don't know what I will do if you can't be with me.

Love, Pierre xxx

47

NOW

'Antoine!' Nina said, rolling down the window.

He smiled. 'It is quite a coincidence, yes? But I am afraid I have some bad news for your driver. The car, it will need to be towed. I will send out for the truck.'

'But why are you here in the first place?' she asked.

'Ah, my garage works for the breakdown company,' he said. 'Sometimes, if we are close, we get the calls to come and help.'

'Wow,' she said. Checking her watch, she realised how much time had passed while she'd been lost in thought – too preoccupied to think of calling another taxi to take her onwards. 'Oh no, my plane!' she said.

'It is fine,' Antoine said. 'I can take you. If we are quick, it will be OK.' He opened the door and she stepped out into the fresh afternoon air. It was pleasant, without the nip of cold or touch of damp there had been before. She saw his work truck parked on a corner, and the road stretching out both ways – one route back to Cagnes-sur-Mer, the other to the airport.

'At least you didn't bring your bike,' she joked, nodding at the truck.

He laughed. 'Ah but it would be a little difficult to carry my tools.'

'Or my suitcase.'

'Yes, although it would perhaps be faster when we get to the city, when we are amongst the traffic.'

She wasn't 100 per cent sure if he was joking. The bike must have a top speed of 40 kmph. But she didn't say anything in case she offended him. Just smiled and made a small noise that could be a laugh but could equally be read as agreement. 'How far are we from the airport?' she asked, checking her watch again.

'Perhaps thirty minutes. It is not far. Just along this way,' he said, lifting his hand towards the road as if presenting it to her.

They could make it.

She looked down the road, imagining sitting next to Antoine in the truck, making her way to her plane. He was right, if they got on the road now, she could carry on with her plan. She could fly home and resume her ordinary life. Whatever that meant.

Maybe they wouldn't quite make it. Perhaps if she missed it, she could call it fate. A sign.

She touched the necklace in her pocket. Maybe she'd already had a sign. Maybe – if signs really existed – the universe was saying, '*Seriously? You need more of a sign than this that you shouldn't be going? I literally punctured a tyre with Pierre's necklace. What else can I do for you? There are eight billion people on this planet. Give me a break!*'

She looked down the road from which Antoine had come. It was leafy, green, flanked by fields. Fifteen minutes at his side and she'd be back in Cagnes-sur-Mer, where Jean-Luc's house would likely still be available to her, at least for a little while longer.

The other way would take her to the plane, back to her life. She could see along it the tyre marks and wear of thousands of cars, all travelling the same way. Despite her assurances to her friends, she wasn't sure when she'd be able to come back to France. Life would resume, she'd sit at her desk and the years would slip by in the same, good-enough, rhythm.

She thought about how she'd always let herself get lifted up by the flow of life – doing the things people expected. How she'd let those roads slip away. With Pierre, perhaps, she'd had a lucky escape. But she'd never know about those other roads.

'Are you OK?' Antoine said, returning to her side. 'We do need to go, and the taxi driver will be fine.'

'You know,' she said, feeling her face get hot, 'it was my fault.'

'What was your fault?'

'The puncture.' Antoine looked at her strangely and she pulled the necklace, with its sharp little arrow. 'This was embedded in the tyre.'

He took it from her. 'It is yours?'

'Yes. Pierre gave it to me... well, years ago. And I thought it was time.'

'So you put it under the car?' he asked, confused.

She laughed. 'No, I threw it away, but somehow it must have ended up in the road. The driver reversed over it, I think. And now she's got a huge bill for her car probably, and can't work to boot.'

He looked at the necklace, doubtfully. 'Her tyre must have been already quite fragile for this to have made a difference.'

'Maybe,' she said, taking it back and looking at it again. But somehow, she knew that what had happened was due to the necklace. That against all odds, it had stuck in the tyre at a catastrophic angle, the tyre had deflated quickly and then the axel had bumped the kerb.

'Perhaps,' Antoine said, looking at her with a grin, 'we should send an invoice to Pierre?'

She laughed. 'That would be very difficult to pin on him, although I do sort of blame him for all this.'

Antoine smiled at her. 'I tell you what,' he said. 'I will make sure the garage confirms what the cause of the problem was. And if it is… I will tell you. But I would not worry about the driver. She works for a big company. It is not her car; they will provide another. And she is paid, no matter.'

This was a relief. 'Thank goodness,' she said. 'I felt very guilty.'

'So, we should go,' Antoine said, gesturing to his ride.

She nodded, picking up her suitcase and carrying it to the truck where she climbed in beside Antoine. As she did so, a tow-truck arrived to take the taxi to the nearest garage. The taxi driver smiled and exchanged kisses with its driver; perhaps she knew him.

'They're friends?' she said to Antoine.

He shrugged. 'Perhaps. I think the taxi company – they are not the best. Perhaps has had to call out a tow truck many times.'

Nina laughed and Antoine turned the key and put the car into gear. As they pulled off in the airport direction, Nina's phone rang. It was Sabine.

'Hello, you are alright?' her friend asked.

'Oh, yes. The tyre – yes, Antoine arrived, actually. He's giving me a lift. And the taxi's being towed.'

'And you will make your plane,' she said.

'I think so,' Nina said, feeling something heavy drop inside her chest. 'Yes.'

There was a silence. 'Because I am not so far away yet,' Sabine said.

'What do you mean?'

Another silence. 'Look, I know you have plans. But really it is not too late to come with me. Antoine can bring you to me. We can go to Vienna together!' said Sabine excitedly.

'Oh, I don't know,' Nina began.

'But why not? You want to do it; you can do it. What are you waiting for? And plus, it is not so much fun on the road alone. We can have more fun together, I think,' Sabine said.

'It sounds amazing. It's just... I'm not sure it's the right time,' Nina said, carefully.

'Pah! The right time. The right time is only the time we make it right,' said Sabine. 'What have you got to lose right now? Your job that you hate? You are afraid, I understand. But I think, perhaps, this is the right time. It's just that you don't see it. You will see it later, perhaps. But maybe then the moment will have passed.'

'Oh,' said Nina. Was she right – was this another chance that she might one day regret turning down? It was rare at her age (and she hated thinking this way) for someone to be properly free. Divorced, untethered, in a job that she disliked. Her parents didn't need her to be around in the way they might in a few years' time – so long as they stayed away from wobbly ladders.

'I'm sorry,' Sabine said. 'It is up to you. Maybe in your heart, you don't want to come, to travel. Many people say that they would like this, but really it is not the life for them. And many people think that I am crazy to live like this. And it is OK. It's just I feel you have spent a long time forgetting to think about what you want. For you. Not for anyone else.'

Nina was silent. 'Maybe you're right,' she said. 'I'm just not sure.'

'OK, well you know where I am,' Sabine said, although in actual fact, Nina didn't, exactly. 'And you know, the offer is there.'

'Thank you. Maybe next time,' she said.

Sabine laughed. 'OK, and I will still see you in Vienna, I hope?'

'Definitely.' She would book the tickets when she got back, she decided. They'd have a great time at the markets, and perhaps she'd book another month's leave next year some time and go travelling for real – find out what it was like to go where the wind took you.

When she ended the call, she gave a quick sigh and saw Antoine glancing at her. 'You are OK? You look worried,' he said. 'Don't worry. I can get you there, I am sure of it.'

Had she made the right decision? Her fingers itched for her notepad and pen. But then she realised, this was not the time to mull over the pros and cons of something. This was something that couldn't be measured by pluses and minuses. On paper, the scales would no doubt tip towards St Albans, Jemima, her friends, her parents, her obligations.

But maybe this time, she had to think with her heart.

48

As they drove closer and closer to their destination, Nina tried to look out of the window and take in the beautiful scenery, rather than think of the gurgling going on within her stomach. It was bound to feel odd, she told herself. She was just nervous. And being nervous didn't mean you'd made a horrendous mistake – just that you felt a little unsure. It was a natural feeling whenever any of life's natural stressors occurred. It didn't mean a thing.

Antoine looked over at her, taking his eyes from the road for a moment, then looked back without saying anything. Were her feelings written all over her face, she wondered? And if they were, perhaps Antoine would be able to explain to her just how she was feeling, as she actually had no idea.

Despite the afternoon's promising start, it had begun to rain heavily as they drove, and the windscreen wipers of the truck were swiping across the glass at a hundred miles an hour. Rain was beginning to gather at the edges of the road and flow into drains. Antoine slowed a little – peering forward through the splattered screen – and put his lights on. 'It is truly autumn,' he told her.

'Looks like it,' she said.

She felt a little shy sitting next to him, knowing how he felt about her, and unsure how she felt about him. She definitely felt something – there was a spark, an ease between them – but after the experience with Pierre, she no longer felt certain of herself; wasn't ready to trust her own feelings for a while.

Despite the rain, the journey passed quite quickly and soon the houses they passed became bigger and more densely packed, the road widened and they were in the town itself. People were scurrying about in the rain, the disorganised with scarves or bags over their heads, those who'd checked the forecast strolling more slowly with umbrellas.

She checked her watch. Even if they turned around now, she'd never make the plane. The choice had definitely been taken out of her hands.

They passed a sign which read *Cagnes-sur-Mer*. She was home. She was the opposite of home. There was no longer a decision to make. She was free – whether she liked it or not.

And then she saw him. Striding in the direction of his office block with a large, black umbrella, wearing well-fitted, charcoal trousers and a black jumper. Pierre. He looked up at the passing traffic, and for a moment, she thought he might have seen her.

She sank slightly in her seat.

'What's the matter?' Antoine glanced at her, then back at the road as realisation crossed his face. 'That is Pierre?' he asked.

'Yes.'

'With the umbrella?'

'Yes.'

'And you don't want him to see you?'

'No. I'm too embarrassed. Too... I don't know. I just don't want to see him after everything.'

'After he hurt you?'

'Well, yes,' she said. 'After he hurt me.'

'He is a bad man,' Antoine said, almost to himself. 'A pig.'

Pierre reached the sliding door of an office block and, under the concrete portico, took down his brolly and began to flap it, sending droplets from the fabric as he dried it off. She was watching him, feeling a mixture of sadness and anger, when Antoine suddenly said. 'Hold on,' and she was flung sideways as the truck veered wildly to the right.

By the time she realised what he was doing, it was too late to stop him, even if she'd wanted to. Antoine had driven hard into a large puddle on the side of the road, sending up a torrent of water which soaked Pierre – and one other passer-by – from head to toe. Pierre looked up, his eyes wide, his hair dripping. His trousers clung to his legs and the umbrella dropped, uselessly at his side.

'Antoine!' she said, putting her hand over her mouth. 'You... you...'

He was grinning. 'Ah, it is a bad thing,' he said. 'I know. To do this. But then he is a bad man, no. And he treated you dirty. So maybe it is time he cleans up his act.'

'But...' she said, turning in the seat to see Pierre, still staring after the truck. 'You...' and then she felt it, the delicious, bubbly feeling of laughter rising inside her.

Antoine heard her make a noise and glanced at her. Then, seeing her laugh, began to laugh too. It was a hysterical, awful, wonderful type of laughter and within it, she felt all the stress, all the pros and cons lists, all the ups and downs of her journey, all her agony over her decisions melt away. She was completely lost in a moment of wonderful, terrible joy.

When she'd recovered, she put a hand on Antoine's arm. 'Thank you,' she said. 'I mean, it was awful thing to do. But – *oh my God* – it felt *so* good to see him covered like that!'

'*Avec plaisir*, madame,' he said, with a wink.

* * *

Back at Jean-Luc's, having retrieved the key from Antoine once again, she wrote a quick email to Jemima, advising her that she would no longer be working for Hamish and Co. with immediate effect. She thought of sending an email to Jean-Luc, but then what would she tell him? She wasn't going to be staying in his home another night. This was just a pit stop.

Another email had arrived in the time it had taken to drive halfway to the airport and back – with the added delay of a flat tyre. From the solicitor. It confirmed that exchange had gone through and completion of the property was now fixed for two weeks' time. She'd spoken to her parents and her dad had promised that he'd talk to his friend's removal firm to arrange the storage and collection of the rest of her things.

An email response had arrived almost instantly from Jemima, but she decided to ignore it for now; she knew how susceptible she was and didn't trust herself not to apologise and get on the next plane home immediately.

Instead, she picked up the phone and called Sabine.

* * *

BESS

You're what?

NINA

Yep.

SAL

Wow, that's amazing. Go you!

BESS

Are you sure you haven't been drinking or something? *winking emoji*

NINA

No, but maybe I should start! I know, it's a bit much isn't it. But I thought, it's kind of now or never.

BESS

Honey, I think you've proved it's never now or never. It's now or later. I think you're doing the right thing for what it's worth.

SAL

Oh God, definitely.

BESS

Don't listen to her, though. She's too loved up to think clearly.

NINA

Haha – I won't. I'm listening to my gut from now on.

BESS

Ooh, what is it saying?

NINA

Gurgle, at the moment. I'm starving!

SAL

Well, we want constant updates. And PICTURES please!

BESS

And what about the gorgeous Antoine?

NINA

Well, it does feel as if maybe something's there. But there's no rush. I'll be back at Cagnes-sur-Mer before Christmas so...

BESS

If it's meant to be, it'll be.

NINA

Exactly.

* * *

The rain had thankfully stopped by the time she had finished packing and she stood in the mild air, waiting for her lift to arrive.

Sabine's original plan had been to reach Geneva on the first day, then spend a few days exploring. But in fact, she'd only made it as far as Andorra – just an hour and a half down the coast. 'It was so beautiful,' she explained. 'I thought I would stay for one or maybe two nights. It will be easy for you to catch up with me.'

She'd offered to come back to collect Nina, but Nina hadn't had the heart to let her drive back yet again at her behest, to cut her travels even shorter. 'I'll take a bus, or a train or something,' she'd told her friend. 'How hard can it be?'

Then Antoine had offered her a lift. 'I have the afternoon now,' he'd said. 'There is not much point to be the boss if you cannot take some time. And we can spend some of the evening in Andorra with Sabine – it will be lovely, I think.'

She'd smiled and agreed.

Now, standing on the edge of the pavement, she heard a tiny, tinny noise in the distance. It sounded very much like... but of course, it couldn't be. She strained a little, hoping that the sound would increase as the vehicle neared her, turn into the low growl of the truck she'd assumed he'd be using. Because nobody would think they should travel 100 km on a small electric bike, would they?

Her answer came moments later when Antoine rounded the

corner on his tiny bike. He pulled up alongside her, his eyes widening at the sight of her suitcase at her feet.

'Um, I don't think that's going to fit on the back of your bike,' she said with a grimace.

Antoine threw back his head and laughed. 'I love my bike, but even I do not want to sit on it for 100 km!' he said. 'I'm on the way to collect my van; it's parked around the corner. I was going to take you with me, but I think I will come back with the van – you do not travel light, I see!'

'Oh, phew!' she said, laughing too.

'But I have brought a helmet for you, just in case,' he said, his eyes twinkling with mischief. 'I hope eventually you might come to love the bike too. And I'm bringing her to Andorra, so perhaps we can ride a little there?'

'Well, maybe,' she said.

He disappeared again and a few moments later returned in his van, pulling close to her on the kerb and jumping out. He took her suitcase to the back, and as he opened the doors. she saw the bike, with his black helmet on one handlebar and a white, neat helmet on the other. Especially for her.

She smiled. 'Thanks,' she said and he met her look.

'If you like it, it's not too late to ride all the way?' he suggested, with a grin.

'I think we'll stick to the van.'

Once they were in the van, Antoine stuck to a scenic route. There was little traffic, and the weather behaved itself so although she felt a little jittery and excited, she'd taken in the views, tried to relax.

The two-hour journey passed quickly; they'd break out in conversation from time to time, but sometimes just sit in silence, taking in the view, lost in their own thoughts. It was nice to feel so comfortable.

Then, almost before she knew it, they were in Andorra, close to the coast. There was a light breeze, but it felt fresh rather than perishingly cold. The view was peppered with sailing boats and flanked by apartment buildings – everything looked new and well cared for. The cars that passed were shiny and there was an air of luxury – even in the sea that stretched before them. As if it was a better sea than the one that they were used to, made for people with more expensive tastes.

Antoine pulled the van into a space and they got out, feeling the warm breeze touch their skin. Wordlessly, they made their way to a small bench which looked down as the land fell away to the water.

She should be on a plane. Or perhaps even landed by now, lugging her suitcase to the train, then taxi, then up the front steps of her parents' place. Perhaps in another universe, another Nina was doing just that.

But she was in Andorra.

Andorra, Cagnes-sur-Mer, Vienna, Italy, France, Austria – all these places had existed throughout her life. At any point since adulthood, she could have elected to come here, but somehow it had taken her forty years to take the plunge.

She thought of all the other places out there. How they, too, were always there, waiting for visitors. Whether she decided to go there was entirely up to her. Until now, she'd played it safe. And she still felt the call of home, a longing deep inside for the comfort of the familiar. But she'd tasted something new too – something like freedom and a sense of her own power. Realised that where she went was up to her, not Rory, not Jemima, not her anxiety. Just her – the person she was deep inside, who she'd always been.

'It's beautiful, isn't it?' she said to Antoine.

'Yes,' he said, but his eyes were fixed on her face. 'Beautiful.'

She raised her face to his – this kind, thoughtful, handsome man. Who had been there through the whole adventure, but who, with all her plans and romantic ideals from the past, she simply hadn't seen. 'I'm sorry,' she said.

'For what?'

'Because I was so wrapped up in my past, I was blind to my present. To the good things. The new things.' She waited, not sure if she dared to say it. 'To you.'

He smiled. 'I think you were not blind,' he said. 'I think sometimes things take time to become clear. And it is OK. Because we have time. We have all the time we need.' And he leaned forward and pressed his lips gently to hers.

She leaned into him, feeling the familiarity of him, the sense of knowing this near-stranger more deeply than was possible. But mingled with this, the fizz and excitement of something unexplored and brand new. For the first time, she felt grateful that Pierre had cleared the way and allowed her to see more clearly.

Then, as if to remind them that although they were sitting in rather luxurious surroundings, the truth of their station in life was a little humbler, they heard the unmistakable sound of the ancient VW engine. Sabine rounded a corner, driving the dented, blue van that was somehow to be home to both her and Nina over the next few months and honked her horn loudly and unnecessarily. A woman, dressed immaculately in a raincoat, looked at the van with distaste. But Nina felt her lips stretch into a wide smile.

The van might look a wreck, but it represented freedom and the joy of roads untravelled.

49

THEN

Dear Pierre,

I've tried to write this many times. I've spoken to my parents but they just won't let me come over. They say that this is just a teenage crush. I'd love to marry you – it would be so wonderful to be together all the time! I'll find a way to get to you somehow. Wait for me?

Nina

50

NOW

'What are you doing?' Sabine said later as they sat in the van and sipped coffee from a flask. Antoine had stayed for a few hours; they'd eaten and then bid their goodbyes. He'd hugged them both and lightly kissed Nina, who'd felt a shiver of pleasure when his arms wrapped around her back. Perhaps Antoine, too, had been waiting for her all her life. She would see him again just before Christmas, she reminded herself. The idea of Christmas felt both imminent and a hundred years away at once. Sabine, on seeing them embrace, had raised an eyebrow and smiled widely but had said nothing.

'Just checking my emails,' Nina said, looking up from her phone.

Sabine rolled her eyes. 'We are going to have to break that habit,' she said.

'But you have a phone.'

'Yes, but I am not its slave. It is a tool for me.'

Nina felt herself blush. 'I know,' she said. 'I just wanted to check...'

'Let me guess... you are worried about your boss?'

Was she really so transparent? 'Sorry,' she said, clicking on an email that Jemima had sent, with an urgent red exclamation mark against it.

Nina,

I am very disappointed to discover that you are not intending to return to Hamish and Co. and I must say quite put out that you decided to let me know this on such late notice. I am afraid you have put the company in quite a difficult position!

While, as you state, there is nothing in your contract that prevents you from giving such a short notice period, I would appeal to your sense of responsibility and insist that you show a little more loyalty to a firm that has kept you in work for fifteen years!

I await your response.

J

At first, Nina felt her heart flip over and the familiar guilt flood her chest. Jemima was right – she had behaved completely unprofessionally. But then, it was Jemima who seemed to prefer to keep notice periods short for employees – it gave her more flexibility to hire and fire as she saw fit. Perhaps this situation would make her value her employees a little more. The company had employed Nina for fifteen years, but it had been fifteen years, in many ways, of being taken for granted.

Taking a deep breath, Nina deleted the email, then passed her phone to Sabine. 'Take it,' she said. 'I'll check it once a day, but if anyone other than my mum or Bess calls, it's going straight to voicemail.'

Sabine slid the phone into a small compartment below the steering wheel. 'That's my girl' she said, with a smile.

'Actually, hang on,' Nina said, holding her hand out.

'Ah,' Sabine said, with mock annoyance. 'What is it now? You wish me to drive you to the airport, to go and work for this horrible woman again?'

'No, just sending a message to my friends.'

* * *

Sabine had chosen a little campsite a half hour's drive away from Andorra for the night, and they'd parked up in the near-empty field, with just four other inhabitants, two in vans and two braver individuals in tents. 'We will drive much further tomorrow,' she'd said. 'But I think this will be enough for today.'

She showed Nina how the benches folded out to create two relatively comfortable beds, how the linen was kept in tiny compartments underneath. A table stretched along the centre and they sat on their beds eating bread and charcuterie and cheese and knocking back a couple of glasses of wine each. Sabine had left the back door of the van open and although it was a little chilly, they were able to look out beyond the field and see the night sky peppered with stars.

'Do you ever wonder,' Nina said, 'about the universe?'

'Wonder what, exactly?'

'Well, you know. Whether fate exists? Whether we all have a guiding star? Whether there's some bigger purpose?'

Sabine shrugged, biting down on an olive. 'Sometimes,' she said. 'When the night is clear and I am alone and it makes me feel very small. But most of the time, I know that I already have the best guide of all.'

'Your GPS?' Nina said, joking.

'Ha. Well, yes, it is very handy. But I mean in here,' she patted her chest. 'I listen to my heart and it tells me what is right.'

Nina nodded. 'I suppose we're all looking for meaning sometimes, aren't we?' she said. 'And adventure. And wondering if we're doing the right thing, or whether we should make different choices.'

'A little,' Sabine said. 'Sometimes. How could we not?'

Nina imagined she was one of the stars shining above them in the dark sky, looking down at her – a tiny, insignificant human perched inside a camper van. She thought of her current situation – unemployed (but not, thankfully, without means), unattached (but with perhaps a rather tempting option awaiting her), unsure of where exactly she would be tomorrow (but excited too). It seemed terrifying on the one hand, but wonderful on the other.

She looked at her new friend.

'Well,' she said, raising her glass. 'Here's to freedom.'

'And to taking chances.'

'To taking our time.'

'And getting it right.'

'To endings.'

'And brand new beginnings.'

'And more than anything, to following our hearts.'

ACKNOWLEDGEMENTS

As usual, there are lots of people to thank. My editor, Isobel Akenhead, who helped to make this book sparkle, and all of the team at Boldwood Books, who work so hard for me and all the other authors.

Thanks to Ger Nichols, my agent, who has become a great friend over the years. She's a fabulous cheerleader and always has my back.

To the brilliant D20 authors, and the Savvy Authors online and all the authors who've championed, blurbed, read or supported my work. Including: Veronica Henry, Beth Morrey, Isabelle Broom, Sophie Cousens, Natalie Jenner, Nicola Gill and so many others.

I'm part of a great online community of readers and writers – my favourite groups include 'The Bookload,' Anita Faulkner's 'Chick Lit and Prosecco', 'Global Authors', 'The Fiction Café Book Club', and there are many others out there. Social media isn't always the friendliest place, but the book community is fabulous!

Thanks to everyone who has read, rated, reviewed, shared or shouted out about my work, readers who have read every book, and those who've picked up one of my books for the first time. It means the world.

ABOUT THE AUTHOR

Gillian Harvey is a freelance writer and bestselling author who lives in France. She writes escapist fiction set in France, including bestsellers A Year at the French Farmhouse and A Month in Provence.

Sign up to Gillian Harvey's mailing list for news, competitions and updates on future books.

Visit Gillian's website: https://www.gillianharvey.com/

Follow Gillian on social media:

- facebook.com/gharveyauthor
- x.com/GillPlusFive
- instagram.com/gillplusfive
- bookbub.com/profile/gillian-harvey
- tiktok.com/@gillianharveyauthor

ALSO BY GILLIAN HARVEY

A Year at the French Farmhouse

One French Summer

A Month in Provence

The French Chateau Escape

The Bordeaux Book Club

The Riviera House Swap

Printed in Great Britain
by Amazon

42841255R00178